T0275420

SHERLOCK HOLMES

Gods of War

SHERLOCK HOLMES

Gods of War

JAMES LOVEGROVE

TITAN BOOKS

Sherlock Holmes: Gods of War
Print edition ISBN: 9781781165430
E-book edition ISBN: 9781781165447

Published by Titan Books
A division of Titan Publishing Group Ltd
144 Southwark Street, London SE1 0UP

First edition: June 2014
10 9 8 7 6 5 4 3

A CIP catalogue record for this title is available from the British Library.

Printed and bound in the USA.

What did you think of this book?
We love to hear from our readers. Please email us at:
readerfeedback@titanemail.com, or write to us at the above address.

To receive advance information, news, competitions, and exclusive offers online, please sign up for the Titan newsletter on our website.
www.titanbooks.com

SHERLOCK HOLMES

Gods of War

FOREWORD

Sherlock Holmes retired from his practice as a consulting detective in 1903, decamping from London to a village in Sussex near the cliffs at Eastbourne. His intention was to lead a quiet life, keeping bees and composing monographs on whatever eclectic subjects took his fancy.

For the most part he was successful in realising this goal. Until his death, his days were tranquil and largely untroubled by the complex and sometimes perilous intrigues in which he – and I – had habitually been embroiled.

Occasionally, however, Holmes was obliged to abandon his beehives and his serenity and throw himself into the fray once more. Two such instances I have recorded under the titles "The Adventure of the Lion's Mane" and "His Last Bow". Here, in the pages that follow, is another.

I intend to consign this manuscript to a tin dispatch box in the vaults at Cox & Co. at Charing Cross, as I have so many others. The bank's current manager, a sharp, efficient Welshman by the name of Llewellyn, has taken to rolling his eyes every time I arrive in his office with yet one more sheaf of paper to entrust to his safekeeping. "Another of your Sherlock Holmes chronicles that nobody will get to read, Dr Watson," he sighs. "Such a shame to deprive your loyal readers of further entertainment."

Entertainment it may be to him, and to many, but the cases Holmes and I investigated were anything but entertaining to us. They were a serious and sometimes deadly business. Often we were lucky to escape with our lives, or indeed with our sanity intact.

In this particular instance, I refrain from tendering this account for publication in *The Strand* or elsewhere on the grounds that it touches on events still fresh in the public memory. It is only five years since the armistice ended the catastrophe in Europe, the so-called Great War. The cessation of hostilities may have brought peace to the continent, but the hearts and minds of the British public are still troubled. We have seen slaughter on an unprecedented scale, millions dead, an entire generation decimated, and the psychological wounds inflicted on all of us have yet to heal, in much the same way that physical wounds continue to blight the lives of countless veterans of the campaign.

This case, which I have dubbed *Gods Of War*, pertains directly to the conflict, as its title suggests. The events in these pages occurred in late 1913, when the storm clouds were already gathering above Europe and, as Holmes himself would put it a year later, an "east wind" was threatening, a "cold and bitter" one which would see a good many men "wither before its blast".

It is perhaps too soon to reopen the subject, and certainly it would not be politic at this time to reveal that there were some in England who, far from being appalled at the prospect of war, eagerly anticipated it.

John H. Watson, MD (retd.), 1923

CHAPTER ONE

The Case of the Purloined Pearls

"Ah, there you are, Watson. Come quickly. We must hurry."

Scarcely had I disembarked from the train at Eastbourne than Sherlock Holmes was accosting me with these words.

"What, no hello?" I said. "No handshake? No greeting whatsoever?"

"Yes, yes, remiss of me," said Holmes. He clasped my hand for the briefest span of time conceivable. "How are you, old fellow? Well, I hope. You look in good health."

"And how was my journey?"

"Are you wanting me to tell you or entreating me to enquire?"

"The latter, although I've no doubt, you being you, you could manage the former."

"Then how was it?"

"Very agreeable. The compartment was not too crowded, and there is that very scenic view from the Ouse Valley Viaduct just north of Haywards Heath when one can look out of both sides of the carriage and see for miles in either –"

"Good," said Holmes. "Good, good. That's quite enough pleasantries. Come! No time to waste."

We hustled across the station concourse, I lugging my leather portmanteau which held toiletries and changes of clothing sufficient for a week's sojourn in the country. It was notable that my friend had not subjected me to the customary list of deductions about my recent doings and circumstances based on close scrutiny of my appearance. This had long been his habit since he abandoned London for a rural idyll and he and I saw each other far less frequently than we once did. It would amuse him to assess, with his usual uncanny accuracy, in what ways my life had changed – both for better and for worse – during the intervals between my visits.

That he had refrained from the practice today told me that he was greatly preoccupied. But then I could also infer it from the brightness in his lively grey eyes and the agitation with which he moved. I knew Holmes better than any man, I daresay better even than his own brother, the late Mycroft, had. I knew his character and moods intimately.

"Holmes," I said as we emerged from the station building, "if I'm not mistaken, you are on a case."

"Watson, you read me like a book."

"I don't need to be Sherlock Holmes to understand Sherlock Holmes. You are behaving exactly as you did when you were resident at Baker Street and had just caught the scent of some intriguing and seemingly intractable problem which you felt deserving of your energies and attention. My only quibble is, I thought you were no longer in the consulting detective game. You have, have you not, forsworn the gloom of London for that soothing life of Nature you so often yearned for. Your own words, Holmes. 'That soothing life of Nature.' Yet here you are, quite evidently in the throes of an investigation."

"Not in the throes, my friend, not yet. We are, as of this moment, en route to the scene of the crime. I have not assimilated a single clue, nor formed a single theory. I am coming to the case as fresh as you are. We are both equally *tabula rasa* in this instance. All I know is that I received an urgent summons less than an hour ago. By sheer happenstance I was just leaving my house to come and meet you. I thought to myself, 'I shall pick up Watson on the way and together we shall peruse the evidence and identify the felon, just as in the old days.'"

"This is hardly what one would call retirement, old chap."

"Shall I tell you what retirement is, Watson? Retirement is a balm to the weary soul, a respite from quotidian cares and stresses, the contented evening after a hard day's toil – and also at times extremely tedious. I have found myself feeling particularly under stimulated and restless of late. The novelty of beekeeping has worn off. The allure of penning monographs has waned. Life has lost a little of its savour."

"You're bored, in other words."

My friend turned to me, amusement twitching the corners of his mouth. "Bored stiff, Watson. Bored almost to tears. And when a case presents itself, however trifling it may seem…"

"You jump at it."

"What can I say? Detection, like any addiction, is a hard habit to break."

We proceeded down Terminus Road, which connected the station directly to the seafront. Eastbourne's main commercial thoroughfare was bustling at this midmorning hour, full of housemaids fetching the daily groceries, matrons eyeing up the garments displayed in windows, and children spending their pocket money on sweets. All the shops had their awnings down against the surprisingly strong late-September sunshine. We had just endured a dismal summer, but as if in compensation for the weeks of unseasonal wind and rain the autumn of 1913 was glorious, bathing England in a mellow amber warmth.

An open-topped motor charabanc clattered raucously down the road, bearing a party of my fellow travellers from the train to their rooms at one of the town's many hotels. Since its inception in the mid-1800s Eastbourne had grown and flourished to become one of the country's most popular seaside resorts. Year round, visitors flocked from the capital and further afield to enjoy its health-giving sea air and the delights and diversions of its promenade, as well as to bathe in the refreshingly bracing waters of the Channel.

"Not far now," Holmes said with an "onward" gesture.

His strides were rapid and long, and I would have struggled to keep pace even if I weren't burdened by my luggage. I was two years' Holmes's senior and at that moment was feeling every day of it. His vitality seemed little diminished, for all that he was just shy of his sixtieth birthday. Mine, by contrast, was a shadow of its former self. The vigour of my youth seemed a long way away, a far distant memory. I had slowed and thickened as I inched towards senescence, whereas my friend retained most if not all of the nervy energy which had rendered him so lively and dynamic in the past.

We were waylaid outside a branch of W H Smith by a cloth-capped ragamuffin who was doling out handbills to passers-by.

"Final day, sirs," he said. "Last chance to see the marvels and miracles before we strike tent and move on."

Holmes peremptorily brushed the boy aside, uttering an airy "Not now. Busy. Shoo!"

I, stricken by a twinge of pity for the lad, though he appeared unbothered by Holmes's brusque rebuff, took one of the proffered handbills.

"You won't regret it, sir," the urchin said. "Matinee or evening, the show's a wonder. You'll never see the like. Never mind you won't believe your eyes – you won't believe any of your senses!"

The handbill advertised a travelling circus that was ensconced somewhere just outside town. I glanced at it long enough to glean that much information and no more, before promptly stuffing it into my coat pocket and hurrying to catch up with Holmes.

Presently Holmes halted outside a jeweller's shop, Barraclough's, which appeared to be closed despite this being a Saturday, surely the busiest day of the week for such an establishment. The blinds were drawn and the sign in the window invited customers to return during business hours.

Holmes rapped hard, and the door was unlocked and opened by a bewhiskered middle-aged gentleman whose choleric complexion and glassy stare spoke of anxiety verging on panic.

"You Holmes?" he barked. "Detective fellow?"

"I am he. You, I take it, are Gervaise Barraclough, proprietor of these premises."

"Yes. Enter. Quickly." Barraclough was in such a state of discombobulation that he did not query my presence, or for that matter acknowledge it. "I hope you're the genius everyone says you are."

"If I'm half as clever as I am imputed to be, not least by my esteemed biographer here," replied Holmes, "then I'm sure I shall be more than adequate to the task. What is it I can do for you, Mr Barraclough? The messenger you sent to me was short on specifics. All he would tell me was that there had been some catastrophe at your shop and that, with a promise of remuneration for my services, I was to come as quickly as possible. I have done so, and would be grateful if you could enlighten me."

"It's a disaster, sir, an absolute disaster," Barraclough wailed. "Robbery. My prize goods, the cream of my collection, gone. Gone!"

I looked round the shop. The shelves and cabinets were bare. Velvet-lined ring trays contained no wares. Display boxes showed indentations where bracelets and necklaces should have been.

"You do seem to have been completely cleaned out," I observed.

"This? No, no, you've got it wrong. This is how the shop

normally looks first thing of a morning. We remove all the jewellery overnight and stow it in the cellar. Otherwise thieves could smash the windows and pilfer as they pleased. The cellar has safes large enough to store all of our stock. They're Chatwoods, moreover, with intersected-steel coffers and unpickable, gunpowder-proof locks. Nobody should be able to steal from them."

"Yet somebody has."

"A thousand pounds' worth of stock has vanished. And that's a conservative estimate."

"My goodness," I said with a whistle.

"A sizeable sum," Holmes allowed.

"Including," Barraclough went on, "a dozen beautiful Tahitian black pearls which I took receipt of only last week, almost perfectly spherical and worth more than diamonds, along with a choker of domed cabochon emeralds, a truly exquisite piece which caught the eye of the Duchess of Devonshire, no less, on a recent stay in the town, and which Her Grace requested me to lay aside with a view to purchasing it on her next visit." He wrung his hands. "Oh, Mr Holmes, you must know how influential the Devonshires are in Eastbourne. Why, they more or less built this place from the ground up. Near enough every street name commemorates them or some piece of land they own. If I were to lose the duchess's patronage, if it were to become public knowledge that I had let the family down so grievously..."

His expression finished the sentence for him. He was contemplating the prospect of a sullied reputation, of abject ruin.

"There, there, Barraclough," my friend reassured him. "No need to fret. I shall recover these gems for you if it is at all in my power to do so. Now, show us these safes of yours. Let us see what we can see."

CHAPTER TWO

AN INSIDE AND OUTSIDE JOB

Down in the cellar we were introduced to Hubert Searle, Barraclough's senior shop assistant. He was a slightly built, pale man who peered at the world through tiny, brass-rimmed pince-nez spectacles. In his hands he held a bowler which he nervously turned and turned anticlockwise as though he wished he could somehow reverse time and undo what had been done.

"It wasn't my job to open up this morning," Searle told us. "On weekdays it is, but on Saturdays the duty falls to Tremlett, the new hire. Tremlett's supposed to be at the shop at eight o'clock sharp and have everything in place by nine. This morning, however, I arrived at five to nine and the place was still locked. Imagine my horror when I entered and found everything just as you see it, and the safes ransacked. Mr Barraclough lives in the Lower Meads, not five minutes' walk away, so I ran to alert him."

"And I hastened back with Searle," said Barraclough, "only to see for myself, to my utter dismay, what had happened."

"Naturally one of you went to this Tremlett fellow's home immediately," Holmes said.

"That I did," said Searle. "He lodges at a guesthouse in the Seaside area. His landlady let me in, but said she hadn't heard him come in last night. I checked his rooms. There was no sign that he had slept there."

"Interesting. Any idea where he might have been?"

"Well, I know for a fact that he went out drinking yesterday evening after work, for I was with him for a while. We have become friendly, he and I. We went to the Lamb Inn up in Old Town and supped a pint or two there, until some acquaintances of his joined us at our table and I made my excuses and left. The others were of the same age as him, and seemed bent on a night of roistering. I don't have the stamina for that sort of carry-on any more, being somewhat older and also the father of two infants, twin girls, who shatter my and Mrs Searle's sleep at all hours with their caterwauling. If only we could afford a wet-nurse, not to mention a nanny…"

"You believe Tremlett is still sleeping off the effects of drink somewhere? It would certainly account for why he hasn't reported for work."

"That would be one explanation," Searle said.

"Another being that he is behind the theft? He has absconded, taking a king's ransom in jewels with him?"

"That's not for me to speculate, Mr Holmes. My main and abiding concern is this."

Searle gestured at the safes. There were three of them, large ones standing in a row like cast-iron sentries, their bases fastened firmly to the floor with bolts. The doors stood ajar, and the interiors were barren save for a scattering of trinkets which even I, no expert when it comes to finery, could tell were of average quality and no great value. The gemstones were small and shone with little of the lustre of their larger brethren. The gold articles that I saw – tie clips, cufflinks, fob chains – were low-carat, many of them dull and reddish owing to the large proportion of copper in the alloy.

"If Tremlett is responsible," growled Barraclough, "I'll... I'll... I don't know what I'll do." He seemed to have some idea, though, judging by the way his hands clutched an imaginary neck. "I've shown that boy nothing but kindness. He had no qualifications for this trade, yet I took him on, I pay him tolerably well, I'm training him up, sharing with him my years of expertise – and this is how he rewards me."

"Let us not jump to any conclusions," said Holmes. "Tremlett may well be guilty of theft. He may equally be guilty of nothing more than a young man's propensity to drink heavily with no regard for the effects on his constitution or on his vocational commitments. Either way, we must examine facts – the evidence – before we start pointing the finger of blame."

So saying, Holmes knelt to study the safes. His knee joints creaked as they bent, and I was perversely pleased to hear this audible manifestation of physical frailty, however minor. He produced a magnifying glass, another sign that age was taking its toll, for his eyesight had once been the keenest of any man I knew. He inspected each safe painstakingly and thoroughly, going over every square inch of metalwork and mechanism.

"Half-inch body plates, machine-fitted," he murmured. "Porpoise-action clutch bolts. Fondu cement infill. Handsome constructions, these. Best peters in the land."

Then, straightening up with a soft, suppressed grunt, he said, "I can find no indication of forced entry. No scratch marks within the keyhole or on the lock plates suggestive of the use of a screwdriver or lockpicks. Nothing to point towards anything other than the appropriate keys being used to open the safes. Tremlett, I take it, has those?"

"As do I," said Barraclough, "and Searle too. We each keep our own set. It's a mark of how much I've come to trust the lad, that he has full access to both the premises and the safes. And to think that he has betrayed me."

"He's a good man, Mr Barraclough," said Searle, "but even the best of us can succumb to temptation. Especially when we're young and callow."

"Again, a rush to judgement before a full and fair survey of the data has been made," said Holmes with some asperity. "Thus far we have only supposition to go on with regard to Tremlett's involvement in the theft. I would like to think the young fellow is innocent until it can be proved beyond all reasonable doubt that he is not."

"But his absence…" Searle began.

"Is incriminating on the face of it, but far from conclusive. You haven't called the police yet?"

"No," said Barraclough. "I hoped by hiring you, Mr Holmes, I might obviate the need. When police are brought in, privacy is not always guaranteed. Members of the constabulary have an unfortunate tendency towards loose talk, most often when there's beer before them and journalists within earshot. You, sir, on the other hand, seem to me a man of discretion, at least if the published accounts of your exploits are to be believed."

"And they are," said I. "Every word."

"If possible," the jeweller continued, "I would like to keep this affair out of the press, at least until my stolen stock is back where it should be and the thief has been apprehended."

"This cellar is itself fully secure?" Holmes asked.

"Whatever do you mean?"

"I mean there is no method of ingress available other than that door and the staircase leading down here from the rear of the shop?"

"None. But have we not established that keys were used?

Why would the culprit require any other access? I thought this a straightforward enough case, at least as far as the how of it is concerned, if not so much the who."

"I am simply pursuing all possible avenues of enquiry," said my friend. "There may be more to the crime than meets the eye. My habit is always to examine the broader picture and look for further details, if only to eliminate them should they prove irrelevant. There is this small window, for instance."

He positioned himself below a tiny, narrow oblong window, set just beneath the cellar ceiling. Illumination crept in via a lightwell above.

"There is a back yard behind the shop, am I right?"

"A small one."

"And the lightwell is covered by a grating?"

"Indeed."

"Is the window ever opened?"

"Sometimes, for ventilation. The cellar is apt to get damp."

"Yes, I observed some rust on the safe corners. When was the window last used?"

"I don't recall. Searle?"

"I don't recall either," said Searle. "Certainly in spring, and more recently than that, I imagine. It was a terribly wet summer."

"You're not trying to tell us someone came in through that window, are you, Mr Holmes?" said Barraclough. "Preposterous! The thing's no wider than a handspan. I doubt even a child could wriggle through. And the lightwell is no less narrow and descends vertically. For anyone to contort himself like that, bend through ninety degrees in such close confines – it would be a physical impossibility."

"Besides," said Searle, "I thought this was an 'inside job'. Now you're of the opinion that it's common opportunistic burglary?"

"Not opportunistic, nor common," said Holmes. "This has the hallmarks of something that was planned, and with some precision. The window *has* been opened not long ago. One can tell by the disturbance of the cobwebs adhering to it."

He unlatched the little window and swung it inward. Standing on tiptoe and craning his neck, he peered up into the lightwell, which rose some three feet to ground level.

"The dust on the surfaces of the shaft has been disturbed too," he said. "As though by the passage of a body or some other object."

"But the window catch lies on the inside," said Barraclough. "The thief could not have opened it without smashing a pane, even supposing he managed to squeeze himself down into the lightwell in the first place, which I sincerely doubt."

"Not if he had an accomplice on your staff. It would be child's play to leave the latch undone at locking-up time, allowing the window to be pushed open from the outside. Who would notice a tiny discrepancy like that?"

"So whoever was down here contrived to leave the window openable for someone else to gain access later. That would mean... Was it you who was last out of the cellar yesterday evening, Searle, or was it Tremlett? I can't remember."

"It was Jeremy, I believe, sir. That is – Tremlett. We both shut the safes together, but I left the room before he did."

"Damn it. The evidence against the lad continues to mount," said Barraclough. "He is clearly in cahoots with another. What about those rowdies he met at the Lamb? Any of them strike you as shifty, Searle? The criminal type?"

"They were a mixed bunch certainly," said Searle. "Come to think of it, one or two of them did seem a little less than respectable."

I evinced surprise. "In a town like Eastbourne? Renowned for its gentility?"

"Indeed, sir. The fact is you get all sorts here. Rough-and-ready fishermen. Labourers, bricklayers, navvies – the town is expanding and there's a constant stream of work for them. It's possible that Tremlett has fallen in with a bad lot. One of them must have put him up to this, intimidated him, or blackmailed him with some indiscretion from his past."

"It is to your credit, Searle," said his employer, "that you continue to give the benefit of the doubt to that miscreant. I, for my part, wish to see Tremlett clapped in irons and left to rot in jail."

"As I said, I count him a friend. A kind of protégé, indeed, much as he is to you."

"Does that not make his abuse of your benevolence all the more galling?"

"I try to think well of all men."

"Then, my good fellow, you are more of a saint than I shall ever be."

"If I may," said Holmes, "I would like to go outside and inspect the grating. I have a strong suspicion I will find that it has been levered out from its setting, doubtless with a jemmy, and subsequently replaced. After that, Dr Watson and I will make a short detour to another part of town before returning with, if all goes well, your stolen jewels, Mr Barraclough, and also with the co-perpetrator of the robbery, who should be able to furnish us once and for all with confirmation or otherwise of Tremlett's involvement."

Barraclough brightened. "Really, Mr Holmes? Capital!"

"I would appreciate it if you and Mr Searle would do us the favour of staying put in the meantime."

"Of course. Hurry back."

CHAPTER THREE

SHADES IN THE FOREST OF THE MIND

The grating had indeed been jemmied out and then put back. Holmes ascertained this to his satisfaction by study of the moss which grew in the groove surrounding it.

"Note how easily I can uproot it," he said, plucking out a clump of furry green plant matter with his thumb and forefinger. "The villain took the precaution of stuffing the moss back into place after he had completed his work and lowered the grating, which was cunning of him. At a glance, one might not notice. However, well-established moss would not normally come free without some effort on my part. I would have to dig it out, whereas here it is as loosely anchored as ripe cotton in its boll."

"But that still does not explain how someone could slither down the lightwell and into the cellar, Holmes," I said. "I could barely fit my arm down there, without a hope of reaching the window. Unless some other method was used in the theft..."

"Such as?" Holmes gave me a sly, inquisitive look.

"Well, how about a fishing rod? Or some similar such device? Something that could be insinuated into the aperture and manipulated from out here. Something that could be telescoped outward until it extended to the safe doors."

"And how would this ingenious contraption of yours unlock the safes, Watson? How would it retrieve the jewels?"

"A hook on the end? A pincer? I don't know." I pondered further. "What about a monkey, then?"

"What ever put that thought in your head? Are you perhaps thinking of the orang-utan that committed those extraordinary murders in Paris some years back?"

"The Rue Morgue case? The one your esteemed Auguste Dupin solved? I had forgotten about that, but yes. Obviously we're talking about a far smaller primate in this instance, perhaps a marmoset or a capuchin monkey. One of those would have sufficient agility and intelligence, not to mention dexterity."

"Esteemed?" Trust Holmes to alight on that single remark, among all the other salient points I had raised. "I hardly *admired* Monsieur Dupin, Watson. He had a few professional qualities that I, in the early stages of my career, found inspirational and worth emulating, but his personality – oh dear! On the one occasion our paths crossed he came across as a shallow, pompous and vain little man, so full of himself he would hardly let anyone else get a word in edgewise. He was very old then, so I allowed him some latitude out of respect for his age. But still, a tiresome individual. He was forever scanning one's face, searching it for subliminal clues, for insights into one's innermost thought processes."

"You didn't care for someone subjecting you to the kind of scrutiny you routinely visit on others?"

"You may mock, Watson, but my methods are far subtler and neater than Dupin's ever were. The man was deplorably prone to supposition and flights of fancy. There was not nearly enough logic in his workings, his ratiocination based as much on intuition as on impartial observation. But we digress." He dismissed the subject of Dupin with a flap of the hand, as though swatting aside a fly. "A capuchin monkey, you say. Clearly this would be a creature so well-trained that it can open safes with a key *and* select Barraclough's finer wares while rejecting the inferior. I picture it with a jeweller's loupe screwed into one eye socket, holding gemstones up to the light to gauge their clarity and brilliance."

"Now you're the one who's mocking, Holmes. But my conjecture is not unsound. Without question it is more credible than your notion that a *man* was able to insert himself into the lightwell. Unless..."

"Unless?"

"Unless he was a small man. A midget. Even smaller than that Andaman islander, Tonga. The chap who nearly killed you with a poison dart during the Pondicherry Lodge affair. Accomplice to the ex-soldier who double-crossed my Mary's father..."

I broke off. I had called her "my Mary", but she had not in fact been mine for quite some time. For only a handful of years did I and Mary Watson, née Morstan, live together as man and wife before callous fate made me a widower, and though I had since remarried and been more than content with my current spouse for a little over a decade, yet, for all that, Mary remained my first and perhaps my only true love. There were times when I could not help but think of her as alive, still as amiably handsome as when she first entered our rooms at 221B Baker Street and presented to us the riddle of her father's disappearance. She now lay buried in Brompton Cemetery, along with the stillborn infant whose torturous arrival took the life from her, yet forever in my heart there is the sound of her sweet voice, the generous understanding with which she viewed my relationship with Holmes, the worry that she fought so hard to disguise every time I raced off to join my friend on yet another dangerous investigation...

Holmes nodded sombrely, knowing what a pang I felt

whenever the forests of my mind were revisited by the shade of Mary. "I grant you that a person of Tonga's stature might, just might, have pulled off such a feat. At the very least he would be able to get his body into the lightwell, and possibly even his head – but through the window too? The body is pliable but not the skull. The skull is of fixed solidity. It cannot be compressed into spaces smaller than itself, at least not without permanent and in all likelihood fatal injury. Then there is the matter of the right-angled turn at the foot of the shaft. No normal human being, whatever their dimensions, could pull off that manoeuvre. The mechanics of physiology do not allow it."

"But you maintain, all the same, that someone somehow managed to?"

"I do."

"Well then, who? How? What sort of man?"

"You hold the answer – the key to the answer, at any rate – in your pocket, Watson."

The only objects I had in my pockets were my wallet, my house key, a handkerchief, a train ticket stub and a small hip-flask of whisky – the last purely for medicinal purposes, it goes without saying.

"I don't follow you," I said.

"The handbill, Watson," said Holmes. "The one you so heedlessly thrust into your jacket on Terminus Road."

I took the piece of paper out, unfolded it, smoothed the creases and studied the wording. *MCMAHON'S TRAVELLING THREE-RING EXTRAVAGANZA*, it said in an ornately patterned font, alongside photogravure images of a striped Big Top and various acrobats and wild animals. *PLUS MENAGERIE AND FREAK SHOW.*

"A… circus performer?"

"Let us go," said Holmes briskly. "McMahon's has pitched camp to the east of town at Gilbert's Recreation Ground. At a fair lick we can be there in under half an hour."

Scarcely had we travelled a hundred paces, however, when Holmes slapped his forehead.

"Oh, how careless of me!" he ejaculated. "I've left my magnifying glass back at Barraclough's. Wait there, Watson. I shan't be a moment."

He hastened back down to the road to the jeweller's, returning some five minutes later.

"I'm getting forgetful in my dotage," he said, brandishing the magnifying glass at me. "The old grey matter is starting to wane."

"It comes to us all, my friend," I said with a rueful smile. "Even the mightiest of intellects."

CHAPTER FOUR

REPTILIO THE HUMAN COBRA

We arrived at a stretch of elegant park, complete with boating lake, putting course and bowling green. Beyond lay scrubland, and it was here that the circus was situated, within a stone's throw of the sea. The red-and-white Big Top dominated, its canvas snapping and its guy-ropes twanging in the persistent onshore breeze. People were drifting into the tent, the matinee performance due to begin in half an hour. Barrel organ music played jauntily and, more distantly, a lion roared. A burly strongman in a leopard-skin tunic strode past us carrying a two-hundred-pound barbell on his shoulder as though it weighed no more than an umbrella. A clown juggled a half-dozen balls, much to the delight of a small knot of children.

Holmes did not head for the Big Top but rather diverted past it to a longer, lower tent. Around the entrance a painted hoarding announced that this was *McMahon's World-Famous Freak Show – A Cavalcade of Oddities, Monstrosities, and Curiosities!* Holmes paid the sixpence entry fee for each of us, and as we stepped inside he murmured to me, "I don't suppose you happen to have brought your trusty service revolver along, have you?"

"Holmes, I haven't fired the thing in anger in nigh on ten years. My wife won't even allow it in the house."

"That's a no, then."

"Forgive me but I hardly could have predicted I would need a gun. This was meant to be a social visit, old friends catching up, not two superannuated sleuths rushing headlong into danger. There is, I take it, some risk attached to what we're doing?"

"Perhaps, perhaps not. I asked about your revolver more in hope than expectation. It never hurts to take precautions. On balance, however, I believe we are both up to the task of collaring the suspect should he refuse to come quietly. My *baritsu* skills have not entirely deserted me, in spite of a lack of practice, and I'm sure your military training is still embedded in your muscles, for all that it's been more than three decades since you were on campaign. The reflexes remember, even if the mind thinks it has forgotten."

Holmes's faith in my combat prowess, while I was sure it was hopelessly misplaced, was nonetheless heartening.

The freak show tent smelled of mud, trampled grass, and a strange, indefinable odour which I am going to call "fascinated revulsion". Holmes and I, along with a handful of other paying customers, strolled past a series of roped-off booths where the bizarrest specimens of humanity disported themselves for our benefit.

There was the Tattooed Man, every inch of his bare skin a network of designs and arabesque patterns. There was Giganta, a lady so fat that she appeared to have three chins and a similar number of folds of flesh over each ankle. And of course the obligatory bearded woman, whose luxurious facial hirsuteness would have been the envy of any pirate captain.

There was also an unfortunate afflicted with Von Recklinghausen disease, which had left him with warty growths all over his body, a twisted pelvis and a distended cranium. The swelling of his skull was such that a conical bony protrusion stuck out from the centre of his forehead, and this had earned him the sobriquet the Rhinoceros Man, no doubt in homage to Joseph Merrick, the Elephant Man, who had suffered from the same syndrome. Holmes and I had made Merrick's acquaintance during an adventure I have yet to write up but which I am thinking of bestowing with the title "The Deformed Angel", and I can honestly say I have rarely met a gentler, humbler, more delicately mannered creature than he, for all the grotesqueness of his outer self.

People peered and ogled at the freaks, buoyed up with a sense of "there but for the grace of God go I". Children, with the absence of self-restraint that is the mark of immaturity, gesticulated and jeered, although some of the adults present behaved little better. One or two of the women, and not a few of the men, looked visibly unwell.

For my part, I was overcome by curiosity, to such an extent that I couldn't tear my gaze from the array of weirdness and ugliness on display before me, even as I berated myself for my prurience. As a general practitioner it was my sworn duty to treat all the people in my care alike, no matter what repellent medical condition afflicted them, but here, outside my surgery, I found it hard to maintain a professional detachment. I wanted to stare like anyone else, much though I berated myself for it. Wasn't that what we had paid for – the liberty to regard fellow human beings as dispassionately as though they were museum exhibits? Sixpence was all it cost to leave our sympathy and our decorum at the door.

Holmes touched my elbow. "Ah. Here we are. Watch, Watson."

On a wooden podium stood a man. Most of him looked fairly normal, apart from his head, which was flattened on top and pointed in front, so much so that his eyes were set further apart than is customary. He was dressed solely in a loincloth, revealing a frame that was thin almost to emaciation. His sign described him as "Reptilio the Human Cobra". His looks alone seemed deserving of the name, for the profile of his head, with its low brow and forward tapering, reminded me distinctly of that of a snake.

At the centre of the podium was a wire birdcage. Reptilio opened the door, whose dimensions were perhaps seven inches by nine. He inserted one foot in the cage, then, crouching down, the whole of one leg. Before our very eyes he proceeded to introduce the rest of himself into the cage. He bent, twisted and doubled over in ways that the most limber of contortionists would have had difficulty emulating. He seemed able to dislocate his shoulders and hips at will, with no evident distress, and to flex his hinge joints such as the knee and elbow in completely the opposite direction than the good Lord in His wisdom intended. In less than a minute he was fully ensconced inside the cage, and a small tug of his fingers enabled him to close the little door, sealing himself in.

I have to admit I was more than a tad impressed, and more than a tad disconcerted, and I applauded, as did most of the others who formed an audience for the feat, even as I winced squeamishly.

When I perceived that Holmes was not clapping, but rather merely looking on with a wry fascination, that was when it dawned on me that before us lay the accomplice of whoever had masterminded the robbery at Barraclough's. Only a man as eerily, unnaturally lithe as Reptilio could have wormed down the lightwell and penetrated the cellar via the tiny window.

"Him," I whispered. "He's the one."

"Indubitably," said my companion. "Just yesterday the redoubtable Mrs Tuppen described to me a trip to this very circus where she had seen a man climb into a birdcage no larger than the one in which she keeps her own pet parrot." He mimicked his housekeeper's thin, querulous voice. "'Tweren't natural, Mr Holmes. Not right that a man should be able to fold himself like that, like crumpling up a piece of paper. Almost witchcraft, it was.'"

Reptilio undid the cage door and began to climb out. He

emerged head first, his peculiarly shaped skull just fitting through the aperture.

"We should rush him now," I said. "Grab him while he's still half in, half out and we have him at a disadvantage."

"Unwise." Holmes cast a meaningful glance towards a couple of circus employees – roustabouts is I believe what they're called – who were keeping an eye on things in the freak show tent. Both were big, beefy men with faces that spoke of former careers as bareknuckle pugilists or else a general, leisure-time fondness for fisticuffs. "I'd prefer not to earn the unwanted attention of those two. Anyway, I have a better idea."

We repaired outside and waited until the freak show closed briefly to allow the "exhibits" a rest. Soon enough the Tattooed Man, Giganta and the rest filed out of the tent, making for the wooden caravans that were parked haphazardly round the back of the Big Top. Holmes and I stole after them, at a distance. We saw Reptilio bid the others a casual farewell and climb the steps into his own caravan.

"Now to beard the serpent in its nest," said Holmes. "I will approach from the front, formally. You, Watson, are to stay here and stand guard. I fear the Human Cobra may prove as slippery as his namesake, so be prepared and on the alert."

Holmes knocked on the caravan door, and when Reptilio answered, looking surly and not a little suspicious, my friend launched into a monologue about being a talent scout for a rival circus, they were on the lookout for new acts, the terms of any contract would be highly favourable, et cetera. Reptilio was by no means persuaded at first, but such was Holmes's silver tongue that he soon began nodding his snakelike head, intrigued. He invited my friend inside, and I remained where I was, some dozen yards from the caravan. Behind me the orchestra in the Big Top struck up a rollicking march, accompanied by the tramp and trumpet of elephants and cheers from the crowd.

Further minutes passed, and I regret to say that my eyelids grew somewhat heavy and began to droop. I had reached the age where some kind of nap during the day was no longer an option, more a necessity, and the urge to take forty winks was pressing hard upon me now.

I had almost dozed off where I stood, when all at once I beheld an eerie sight which jolted me out of my somnolence. Reptilio was squeezing out through a tiny window in the side of his caravan: his head, then one arm, then the top half of a wriggling torso. Feeling a crawl of horripilation up the back of my neck, for a moment or so I was too stunned and aghast to move.

Then a sound of splintering wood issued from within, followed by a sharp, urgent cry in a voice which I recognised as Holmes's. This roused me from my paralysis, and I dashed over and seized Reptilio firmly by the available wrist.

"Watson!" Holmes called out. "He is trying to get away! Do you have him?"

"I do," I called back. "Do you?"

"By the heels, literally. But the man's deuced hard to keep hold of."

I knew this myself, for I was having difficulty maintaining my grasp on his arm. Reptilio writhed and squirmed like an eel, cursing me and Holmes all the while in terrifically colourful terms. He demanded we release him, on pain of damnation to hell, which made me all the more determined not to comply, and doubtless Holmes too.

Eventually Holmes found a means of securing Reptilio's legs, and the man was trapped, suspended part-way through the window. The commotion drew people's notice. One of the roustabouts from the freak show tent came up and challenged me. I stated that I was in the process of making a citizen's arrest and that Reptilio was wanted in connection with the commission of a burglary. The roustabout expressed scepticism and was on the verge of manhandling me very forcefully when Holmes emerged from the caravan bearing a heavy burlap sack. From it he produced several pieces of jewellery and a loose handful of iridescent black pearls, each the size of a child's toy marble, of the kind Barraclough had described.

"Is this," he said to the roustabout, "the usual property of a circus artiste? Are you all in the habit of concealing hundreds of pounds' worth of gemstones in your caravans?"

The roustabout had to allow that they were not.

"Perhaps, then, you'd be so good as to fetch your employer, Mr McMahon, if he is available."

The roustabout glanced at Reptilio, poking from the caravan window like some huge misshapen tongue from a pursed mouth, and said, "Yes. I think I'll do that."

In no time the circus proprietor was on the scene, an affable, ruddy-cheeked fellow in tweed, and once Holmes had shown him the jewellery, McMahon was in no doubt as to Reptilio's guilt.

"Up to your old nonsense again, eh?" he said to Reptilio, contempt in his voice. "I gave you fair warning last time, after that business with the banker's strongbox in Dorchester. It was only you could have done it, what with there being no way in save the chimney. I didn't speak up then, when I ought to have, and I regret it. Now what have you done? Robbed a jeweller? People like you do little for the reputation of circus folk. You bring shame on us."

Reptilio blustered, but soon the bluff and bravado turned to spite. "You don't pay us nearly enough, McMahon," he snarled. "What kind of life is this anyway? Being paraded in front of all those goggling eyes, those slack jaws, those poking fingers, day after day, night after night. I deserve more than this. I deserve a better life."

It was tantamount to an admission of guilt. The game was up. Reptilio the Human Cobra had been caught with his ill-gotten gains. Now all that remained was for him to surrender up the identity of his partner in crime.

CHAPTER FIVE

THE PRISONERS

As we returned to Barraclough's, Holmes enlightened me as to what had transpired inside Reptilio's caravan. His talent-scout imposture might have got him through the door, but Reptilio quickly smelled a rat when Holmes was unable to furnish him with proof of his bona fides. Reptilio, sensing trouble, dived into his small dressing-room-cum-washroom with a view to making an escape. He bolted the door behind him and retrieved the stolen jewellery from its place of concealment. Holmes broke down the door, which was little more than a piece of plywood, and seized Reptilio from behind, even as I was struggling with the fellow's front portion outside. Ultimately Holmes lashed his legs to a coat hook with the man's own longjohns.

It wasn't until we got back to Barraclough's that I learned of the skulduggery my friend had got up to when he had gone back to fetch his mislaid magnifying glass. The proprietor and Searle were still in the cellar, having been imprisoned there by Holmes! Holmes had asked Barraclough to hand him the keys on some pretext of wishing to inspect them. Then he had darted out of the cellar and locked its sturdy door behind him. By this means he had sealed both men in securely, for the cellar door could be opened only from the outside.

Barraclough and Searle were extremely irked by Holmes's behaviour. I could sympathise. He had practised a deception upon me as much as them. He had not in fact forgotten his magnifying glass at all. That was merely a pretext.

"What is the meaning of this?" Barraclough thundered as Holmes unlocked the door. "Three hours we have been stuck down here. Three whole hours! We've cried out for help 'til we were hoarse, to no avail. You had better have a very good explanation, you scoundrel, else you'll be hearing from my lawyers. To detain a man against his will – unconscionable!"

"Forgive me, Mr Barraclough. Your sequestration was quite necessary. I had to ensure that neither of you was able to leave the premises before I returned."

"But in God's name, why? You surely don't suspect me of robbing my own shop. The idea of it! What could I possibly hope to gain?"

"You are well insured, I imagine."

"Indeed I am, but… Ah." Barraclough's demeanour hardened, fire becoming frost. "I see. So that is what you are accusing me of. You have fallen in my estimation, Mr Holmes. You really think that I would stoop so low? Me, a prosperous businessman with a thriving trade? My lawyers will definitely want to have words with you."

"As a matter of fact, sir," said Holmes, "it isn't you I needed to imprison. It is your subdued and rather sheepish-looking colleague over there, who would surely otherwise have absconded the moment he was sure I had gone."

Searle was skulking in a corner of the cellar with a very wretched air indeed, like a dog that has been caught with the lunchtime joint of ham in its jaws. He was trapped and he knew it. He couldn't get past us up the stairs, not without a struggle, and he was no fighter. Certainly, despite being half our age, he would be no match for the two of us. All he could do was pace the floor and fume impotently.

Barraclough, the penny dropping, rounded on him. "Searle? It was you? Not Tremlett? *You* stole from me? From *me*?"

Holmes quickly elucidated. Reptilio, now in the custody of the police, had named Searle as his co-conspirator. The whole plan, he had told us, was Searle's doing. "Gent came to me, asking if I wanted to earn a great deal of money," the Human Cobra had said. "He'd got these duplicates made of the safe keys. It seemed like a bit of a bludge – in and out in quarter of an hour – with the proceeds split seventy-thirty. Not sure why I should get the lesser cut, being as I was doing all the hard work, but still it weren't a sum to be sneezed at."

"But why?" said Barraclough to his employee. "Granted, the salary I pay you isn't stupendous, but it's a living wage. Why did you want more?"

"Searle, would you care to respond to that?" Holmes asked.

Searle offered nothing but a truculent silence, so Holmes answered on his behalf.

"Remember how he complained about not being able to pay for a wet-nurse? This is a man with aspirations, dreams of a lifestyle that he can't, as things stand, afford. Children can be terrifically demanding, a drain on one's resources in more ways than one. Searle has been finding fatherhood hard. Is that not so, Mr Searle?"

Again no response, so Holmes continued, "It has stretched him thin, both financially and personally. Perhaps, after all those sleepless nights, he became desperate."

"He could have gone to his bank manager for assistance," said Barraclough. "Or even asked me. I would have given you a loan,

Searle, to tide you over. I might also have considered a small raise."

"Why should he need one," said Holmes, "when a single theft, if pulled off successfully, would set him up handsomely for life? Why abase himself when, in one fell swoop, he could get the better of you?"

Searle's baleful glare confirmed it. "I've had enough of people lording it over me, Barraclough. You. Your snooty clients. Everyone looks down on me. I want more, and there's no reason why I shouldn't have it. A loan? A small raise? Spare me your charity!"

"But this means Tremlett, wherever he may be, is innocent," said Barraclough.

"As a newborn babe," said Holmes. "Searle did everything he could to cast the burden of suspicion on to him, all the while feigning disbelief that Tremlett could ever have done something so heinous. A devious, unscrupulous fellow, aren't you, Searle? It occurred to me from the outset that you might be the villain of the piece, but I could not reasonably conclude that without compelling, incontrovertible evidence. That is why I took the precaution of corralling you here, along with the unfortunate Mr Barraclough. Here, by the way, is part of the loot." Holmes handed the burlap sack to Barraclough. "I imagine that when the police search Searle's house, which they are on their way to do even as we speak, they will find the remainder – the lion's share."

Barraclough took the sack without even bothering to look inside. He lowered his head. "Mr Holmes, I wronged you earlier. I insulted you. I apologise. You have done sterling work. Please accept my deepest, sincerest gratitude."

"As long as it comes with a cheque attached, that is all I need," said Sherlock Holmes.

CHAPTER SIX

TRUTH AGAINST MYTH

There isn't much else to tell about the incident. Young Jeremy Tremlett was discovered that same afternoon, passed out behind the cricket pavilion of Eastbourne College. He did not recall much about the previous night's events, but had a vague memory of his companions abandoning him to continue their revels after he complained of feeling unwell. He wandered feverishly for a while, then fell into a swoon which lasted the rest of the night and most of the subsequent day. It was later established in court that Searle had slipped a sleeping draught into Tremlett's beer. Tremlett was intended to be Searle's dupe, unable to remember with any clarity what he had got up to on the night of the robbery and therefore incapable of attesting to his own innocence.

The bulk of the jewels were indeed found at Searle's house, as Holmes predicted, and restored to Barraclough for his safekeeping.

Although Searle could simply have stolen the jewels himself using his shop keys, this would have entailed too great a risk. He might have been caught red-handed. At the very least he would have been one of the prime suspects for the felony. His stroke of

genius – though it was no match for Holmes's own prodigious
intellect – was engaging Reptilio as his accomplice. It allowed
him to have a cast-iron alibi: he was at home all night. He could
account for his whereabouts when the robbery occurred, whereas
the drug-befuddled Tremlett could not.

Searle's professed fondness for the junior employee had, it
seemed, been an imposture all along. When Barraclough had
taken on an extra pair of hands at the shop, Searle had realised
that here was just the thing, the perfect scapegoat for a scheme
he was already in the process of hatching. Befriending Tremlett
meant that he could get close enough to administer the fateful
sleeping draught when it was required. The arrival of McMahon's
Circus in town and a swiftly-reached pact of collusion with the
supple Reptilio gave Searle the final impetus he needed to set the
wheels of his act of larceny in motion.

"A mildly diverting affair," Holmes said that evening as he
and I enjoyed a quiet supper in the snug of his local public house,
the Tiger Inn, which sat diagonally across the village green from
his cottage. He ate milk-poached haddock, I a helping of pigeon
pie. It was good, solid fare, hardly Escoffier but hearty and filling.
Holmes complained that the cook had "gone a bit heavy on the
pepper" but he seemed to have no trouble clearing his plate.

"Proof, too," I said, "that trust is a commodity which should
not be bestowed lightly."

"Alas yes. Barraclough unwittingly nurtured a viper in his
bosom, while all too readily condemning the one person whose
probity was not actually in question. The moral should be: judge
not by the outward display."

"Does that not contradict your own practices, Holmes? You
regularly draw conclusions based on appearances alone."

"You do me a disservice, my dear fellow. It is one thing to
make reasoned deductions according to how someone speaks,

dresses or comports himself, the tiny but telling details of his person. Observable facts reveal inner truths. It is quite another thing, however, to let oneself be swayed purely by a man's actions, the image he chooses to present to the world. We show to others ourselves as we would *wish* to be seen. The trained, expert eye penetrates beneath the obvious to the subsurface. When presented with a crime scene, the question I invariably ask myself is not 'What am I looking at?' but 'What am I being allowed to see?' The same goes when assessing a man's character and circumstances. Often that which is not present is as informative as that which is. Where Hubert Searle is concerned, his inability to speak ill of Tremlett was a red flag to me. No one is naturally that benign and charitable. Hence I began to harbour doubts about him."

"How dashed cynical you are, Holmes."

My friend smiled briefly. "Over the years I have come to expect the worst from everyone. It is, shall we say, an unavoidable consequence of the line of work I used to be engaged in. So many murderers, so many blackmailers, so many fraudsters – it jaundices irredeemably one's perception of humanity. I moved to the coast in the hope that I might encounter less duplicity and dishonesty than in the city."

"Yet here you still find crime," I said, "or rather crime finds you."

"Nowhere is perfect," Holmes admitted. "Have I not expressed to you before my opinion that the lowest and vilest alleys of London do not present a more dreadful record of sin than does the smiling and beautiful countryside?" He lowered his voice so that the other patrons of the pub might not overhear. "My one great bugbear with the stout yeomanry by whom I find myself surrounded these days, however, is not that they're as regrettably prone to delinquency as their urban equivalents. It's their terrible propensity towards superstition. There was my Mrs Tuppen, all but claiming that Reptilio's extraordinary contortionist abilities were the stuff of witchcraft, when they are all too easily explicable in medical terms."

"Marfan syndrome," I said. I had come up with the diagnosis earlier in the day and was glad of an opportunity to share it at last with Holmes.

"Yes, I would have said so too. He had the characteristic symptom of the disorder, the hypermobility of the connective tissues, allowing an unusually large range of motion of the joints."

"It would also account for the abnormal shape of his head. All babies' heads are elongated by their passage through the birth canal but regain their natural roundness subsequently as the bones harden, except for Marfan syndrome sufferers who are often left with permanently disfigured craniums. The capacity to subluxate joints voluntarily and without undue discomfort is a secondary by-product of the condition. In many ways Reptilio's birdcage act was the ideal one for a man in his state – the career he was born for."

"If only he had been able to accept that and not yearn for more. The same goes for Searle. They were a matched pair in that respect. But to return to the topic of superstition," Holmes continued. "The area is riddled with it. You know that not far from here, on Windover Hill near the village of Wilmington, there is the outline of an enormous figure of a man carved out into the hillside chalk."

"The famous Long Man. I spied him from the train when passing between Lewes and Eastbourne."

"None other. He holds some sort of rod in either hand fully his own height. Local legend has it that he was a giant who fell out with another giant, his best friend. They fought at length, laying waste to their surroundings in the process. Eventually the other giant won, killing the first giant and striding away. Locals, lacking the wherewithal to bury so vast a corpse, instead drew a line around it in commemoration. The rods are the quarterstaffs with which he battled his foe."

"A harmless enough legend."

"Yet many here still believe it to be true. A Neolithic chalk figure drawn for who knows what purpose by Stone Age men – perhaps to worship some primitive deity – gives rise to a fairy story about giants, which then becomes entrenched as an article of faith. Even in our modern, supposedly enlightened age you will hear many a person speak of the 'Wilmington Giant' as though such a being genuinely existed!"

"But isn't the tale more entertaining than a more pedestrian explanation?"

"To the naive, infantile mind maybe," replied my friend. "As something to amuse children with, it has its place. But when adults who ought to know better cite as gospel this sort of fanciful fiction, I do find it…" He groped for a suitable adjective, settling on: "Tedious. Truth and myth must never be confused, Watson. Why, just the other day as I was in my garden tending to my pruning, I had a blacksmith come up and lean on the wall and engage me in idle conversation. Soon he was telling me that, as a small boy, he had seen a 'witch hound' over at Harewick Bottom near Jevington, not five miles from here. He regaled me with the story of this ghostly black dog for several minutes, not once doubting that I would credit every word of it. He told me of the thrill of terror he had felt as the thing darted across his path, its eyes aglow in the twilight. 'An omen of doom,' he said, and the very next day – who would have thought it? – his father, whose forge he would go on to inherit, died unexpectedly, keeling over while beating a ploughshare into shape."

Holmes looked bleakly gleeful as he recounted this.

"A reasonable assumption would be that the father suffered a sudden heart attack as he exerted himself strenuously at his anvil," he said. "Yet to this gullible rustic buffoon the only probable, the *likelier* explanation, was the malign influence of a sinister, unearthly creature. Absurd. At the very best he had stumbled across some stray dog, whose retinas had happened to catch and reflect the rays of the setting sun in an eerie fashion, and the death of his father was merely a tragic coincidence. Eh, Watson? Wouldn't you agree?"

I did not answer, instead helping myself to a long, deep sip of my ale, for this talk of eldritch hounds had stirred up a memory I did not care for.

Holmes interpreted my silence correctly. "Oh, my dear chap, surely you are not casting your mind back to Dartmoor and Baskerville Hall?"

"I regret that I am," I said. "Can't help it."

"But the black dog in that instance was real, as real as you or I or this table we are sitting at, a beast born of this world, not some demonic spirit or creature of legend. You know this as well as I do. We both saw its corpse, felled by our bullets. Nothing could have been more corporeal and tangible than that animal."

"Yet the horror lingers – the horror of what it might have been, what it purported to be. That is something I can never forget, however well I recall that Stapleton's diabolical monster dog was, all said and done, just a dog. There must be some reason why the supernatural exerts such a powerful hold over the human mind, Holmes, and why we are so predisposed to believe in it. Is there not the merest chance that there really are forces at work in the world which cannot be accounted for by any empirical means? Is it not possible that one day you and I might encounter phenomena which no amount of rationalisation will explain or debunk?"

"Are there more things in heaven and earth than are dreamt of in our philosophy?" Holmes regarded me levelly across the table. "I cannot in all honesty answer that question. So far I have met nothing, however otherworldly it might appear, that has not revealed itself under the glare of scrutiny to have a perfectly mundane origin. A hellhound is an ordinary dog coated in phosphorus paint. A vampire is a Peruvian mother sucking poison from a wound in her baby's neck. A mysterious, sinister 'speckled band' is an Indian swamp adder. Yet, that said, past form is no guarantee of future performance."

"You mean you keep an open mind?"

"I mean that I wait for something to come along that will defy explanation and prove conclusively that the world we live in is stranger than we can know. It would be refreshing if, for once, I met with some chimera or phantom which would entirely and indisputably overturn my conviction that the supernatural does not exist. I would be willing to discard a lifetime's scepticism on the subject, just to have that one brush with the genuinely, irrefutably paranormal."

"Can it be? Is the hard-headed Sherlock Holmes getting sentimental in his old age?"

"I am not growing any younger. Neither are you. We are both at that stage where we have many fewer years ahead of us than we do behind. The chill breath of mortality is on our necks. It would be nice to be given a firm hint that the priests and mages are right, that something lies beyond the veil, that death is not mere oblivion."

I had never heard Holmes speak in such terms before. There was no twinkle in his eye to suggest this was all some abstruse intellectual jape, perhaps at my expense. He was wholly in earnest.

"I do wonder," I said, "if we are to be reunited with our loved ones in some afterlife. It would not be a disagreeable prospect."

"I concur. Your Mary, my Mycroft..."

He pouched his lips wistfully. Holmes's brother had passed on some seven years earlier, having been taken ill mid-dinner at the Diogenes Club. A ruptured stomach ulcer had led to gastrointestinal bleeding, perforation of the duodenal wall, and ultimately acute peritonitis from which, despite the best efforts of surgeons, he failed to recover. The funeral had been a muted, understated affair, for all that those attending included some of the mightiest and most influential people in the land. Such was Mycroft Holmes's great bulk that a special casket had had to be built, its proportions sufficient to contain him, its wood reinforced with metal braces. The pallbearers had numbered eight rather than the traditional six, and still they had struggled under their burden. At any less sombre occasion it would have been a comical sight.

"You know that I am as old now as he was when he died?"

"Yet, if I may say so, your health is considerably better than his was. Your brother was a man of huge appetites, with a choleric disposition. Your asceticism promises greater longevity than he could ever have hoped for. I should not be surprised to see you live well into your nineties, with your faculties intact."

"Still, it feels like I have reached a milestone. I knew it likely that I would outlast Mycroft, but from here on each year seems a step into the unknown. He was always ahead of me, being so much my senior. Now I am venturing into territory he himself never got to chart. I am, for the first time in our siblinghood, the trailblazer."

"You always were. Your path in life has taken you to places Mycroft could never have dreamed of going."

"You're kind, Watson, but as you know from having an older brother yourself, the younger brother never truly feels that he has done anything first. Everything he achieves seems like second best – a hand-me-down."

I nodded in recognition. Even though my own brother, long deceased, had been something of a ne'er-do-well, the shadow he had cast over me while we were growing up had been a long one. He had been a boisterous soul and, for all his faults, I had never ceased to admire him. Clearly Holmes felt the same way about Mycroft, despite the friction and sometimes downright antagonism that typified their relationship.

"Anyway," said he, "enough of this maudlin talk. Let us settle the bill and make the short journey homeward. A nightcap before bed is in order. Perhaps a snifter of Armagnac? And tomorrow we shall start afresh, and I shall make every effort to ensure that your week in Sussex is as pleasant and interesting as it can possibly be."

Interesting it undoubtedly proved, although only if one can stretch the definition of the word to mean "hair-raising" and "life-threatening". As for pleasant? Even a veteran author such as I cannot manipulate the English language to make that an apt descriptor.

CHAPTER SEVEN

A GRAHAME-WHITE TYPE VII

The next morning I was up well before Holmes. The dawn chorus awoke me as though it were the most deafening alarm clock. In London I was capable of sleeping through any amount of racket. The cries of street vendors, the clatter of passing cabs, the whirring rumble of a tram – these were a veritable background lullaby. Yet here in the silence of the countryside, all it took was a few birds singing in the treetops to rouse me from my slumbers like a gunshot.

I stoked the kitchen stove, put on the kettle, took it off just before it started to whistle, and made myself tea. Then I went out for a stroll, to inhale plenty of lungfuls of revivifying, brine-tinged sea air.

The village where Holmes lived, East Dean, lay less than a mile from the coast. If I listened carefully I could hear the susurration of surf breaking on shingles. Along a bramble-fringed lane I was passed by a dray loaded with freshly filled milk churns, pulled by a strapping Shire horse. I saluted the driver, who touched the brim of his felt hat in return. Both his and the horse's breath steamed.

There was, for the first time that year, something of a bite to the air, an intimation of autumn proper. The weather was on the turn, our Indian summer nearing its end.

Returning to the cottage, I stood before it and took a moment to appreciate its plainness and modesty. Built in the traditional Sussex style – brick and knapped flint – it sat four-square on the village green and was, from the front elevation at least, as symmetrically proportioned as a doll's house, with neat windowboxes and a narrow strip of front garden hemmed in by a low wall and a waist-high iron gate. A two-storey extension ran off perpendicular at the rear, clad in wooden slats, and the rest of the L-shaped plot was taken up with the kitchen garden, which covered perhaps an eighth of an acre and was well dug and maintained. The growing season was mostly over, but Holmes's runner beans were flourishing and his raspberry canes groaned under the weight of ripe fruit. His half-dozen hives stood in a row by one wall, each circled by a few drowsy bees warming themselves up in the thin sunlight before they commenced the day's labours.

Holmes, with the savings portfolio he had accumulated over the years, could well have afforded somewhere grander, and it spoke well of the man that he had no wish to flaunt his wealth and was content to live out the remainder of his days in relative obscurity. Yet, given that he had on more than one occasion refused the honour of a knighthood, it was not surprising either. Holmes lived for himself, not for the admiration or recognition of others. He was the most insular, self-contained man imaginable, and I counted myself lucky that he allowed me across the drawbridge into his life, not least since I was so much his intellectual inferior.

Back inside the house, I wandered round the cosy sitting room enumerating the items I recognised from our Baker Street days. Here was the Moroccan slipper in which Holmes still kept his black shag, though it was somewhat more threadbare these days and sat not by the fireplace but atop a stack of yellowing back issues of *The Times* within easy reach of his favourite armchair. Here was the jack-knife with which he used to stick unanswered correspondence to the mantelpiece, much to Mrs Hudson's despair; it had taken up residence on a writing desk where it now fulfilled the function of letter opener. Here were the copious and wildly diverse textbooks which had served as Holmes's personal reference library, still as dog-eared as I remembered but looking a trifle dustier and less oft-consulted than of old. Here was his beloved violin, although when I stroked a finger across its strings they let out a plangent, discordant arpeggio that suggested they had not been tuned, and the instrument had not been played, in some while.

Dotting the room were several familiar pieces of furniture which likewise evoked a prick of nostalgia. Holmes had purchased these from Mrs Hudson for a more than fair price, electing to take with him things he was accustomed to, shabby and worn though they were, so that he would not have to kit out his new home completely from scratch.

It was like looking at my own past in a warped mirror, everything rearranged, disordered, recognisable but still strange. A bookcase had been added to the room since last I had come to stay. It occupied an alcove by the hearth, filling the space from floor to ceiling, and every volume in it appeared brand new, the leather binding freshly tooled and the gold intaglio lettering immaculate. Examining the spines, I failed to find a single title or author I knew. Most were foreign, so amongst these the very British name of Samuel Chatwood stood out. I had heard the surname mentioned recently but couldn't at that moment recall precisely when or by whom.

I was just about to reach for the book when I discerned a queer sound coming from outdoors. It was a low drone, soft but insistent, with a distinct vibrato to it.

"Holmes?" I called up the stairs to his bedroom. "Holmes, do you hear that?"

Answer came there none, so I stepped out of the back door to see for myself what was making the noise. It occurred to me that it might be the bees. Perhaps something had disturbed them and the drone denoted the onset of an angry swarm. Having no great desire to be stung, I lingered in the doorway, poised to flee back inside should the situation warrant it. The bees, however, were still languidly circling the hives, looking in no way minatory or aggressive.

The noise revealed itself to be emanating from higher in the air and to be manmade rather than natural. For, as I stood there peering out, an aircraft came soaring over the rooftops of the terrace of artisans' cottages adjacent to the pub.

It was a biplane with an upper wing twice the span of the lower and an undercarriage that consisted of paired wheels attached to ski-like struts. The front end where the pilot sat was a wooden oblong with a rounded nose, not dissimilar in proportions to a coffin. The rear was a wedge-shaped construction of spars and braces leading to a broad flat tailfin with ailerons set vertically above and below at the centre. A large engine positioned behind the cockpit drove the thing along, its propeller a gleaming whirr.

The plane shot almost directly overhead at an altitude of no more than thirty feet. I ducked reflexively and covered my ears against the machine's puttering din. As it carried on by, I straightened up, feeling not a little foolish.

Eager to see more of this rarity, I dashed through the house and out of the front door onto the green. There, I watched the biplane wend its way southward along the shallow valley that led to the coast.

Just at the point where it would have been above the cliffs, the plane, now no larger in my eyesight than a fly, made a sharp left turn and began following a course running parallel to the shore. Within a minute it was lost from view, the racket of its engine reduced to a faint, almost inaudible hum.

This grew again in volume, and shortly the biplane reappeared, heading in the opposite direction, due west, still in line with the shore. As it passed from sight a second time, I became aware of Holmes standing beside me. He had thrown a dressing gown over his pyjamas and his feet were sheathed in carpet slippers.

"A wonder of the modern age, eh?" he said with just a touch of irony. "Progress in motion."

"Alarming contraption," I said. "The thing looks hopelessly spindly and fragile, as though it might collapse at any moment. One strong puff of wind, that's it, done."

"Oh, I don't know. It seems sturdy enough to me. The frame is mostly made of ash wood, strong but flexible, and the skeletal design lends it considerable rigidity. In Europe they prefer a monocoque structure for their aircraft, an outer shell which provides both shape and support, but that plane's a British one, a Grahame-White Type VII, and uses tension-compression – far more stable and reliable."

"You seem to know an awful lot about aeroplanes all of a sudden. Is this some new hobby of yours?"

"Hardly. I know something about this particular plane because I've seen it several times before and, out of curiosity, undertaken some research on it. It belongs to a local bigwig, somebody-or-other Mallinson, his Christian name escapes me for the moment. He lives a few miles that-a-way" – Holmes gestured to the north-west – "near Alfriston. Flying is one of his passions. He works up in London most of the week, but at weekends, when the weather's clear, he's often aloft and buzzing around in the skies. Self-made man. Worth a fortune."

The biplane returned for yet another sweep along the coastline.

"Though it isn't his usual habit," Holmes remarked, "to track back and forth like this." He shaded his eyes with both hands and squinted. "Normally he darts around hither and yon at random, sporting in the air. This looks more as though he has a specific aim – as though he's searching for something. Hmmm."

We watched the aircraft glide in and out of our eyeline several more times, heading first one way then the other. There definitely appeared to be a purpose to its journeyings, a pattern, though I could not fathom what it might be; nor could Holmes.

"Well," I said at last, "you'll never catch me in one of those, that's for sure. I read the papers. Aeroplanes are forever plummeting out of the sky. That Frenchman – what's his name? – Blériot – he barely made it across the Channel, didn't he? It wasn't a landing at Dover so much as a controlled crash. And he's supposed to be one of the experts, a pioneer. No, I'm perfectly content to keep both feet on the ground, thank you very much."

"Watson, Watson." Holmes clapped me on the back good-humouredly. "Your stubborn resistance to change is one of your most appealing features and a true constant in life. You're a rock, a granite monument, able to weather the storms of time, and I wouldn't have you any other way. Now, how about some breakfast? There are kippers in the larder and some of Mrs Tuppen's excellent kedgeree. Then perhaps a walk to Birling Gap and along the beach to Beachy Head lighthouse. What do you say?"

It seemed a capital idea, and I gladly re-entered the cottage, enlivened by the prospect of food.

Holmes followed, but not before casting a last glance in the direction of the biplane. His brow was ever so slightly furrowed, his lips pensive, and had I been thinking less about my stomach I might have recognised the signs. Something had intrigued him. What it might be, even he himself did not know then, but his mind was a crystal-set with a highly sensitive antenna, attuned to the anomalous. A mystery was hailing him on some special secret frequency, and he was starting to adjust his inner cat's whisker, the better to hear its summons.

CHAPTER EIGHT

THE BODY ON THE SHORE

Walking-boots on, we set off down to Birling Gap. Here the undulating run of cliffs known as the Seven Sisters made their deepest dip and access to the beach could be gained by means of a set of rickety steps.

The tide was out, exposing a rugged sweep of rock pools shaggy with kelp and bladderwrack and riven with tidal runnels. Ever since his encounter with a lion's mane jellyfish some years earlier, Holmes had become something of a keen amateur naturalist, especially where littoral fauna were concerned, and he took delight in showing me the dark red, cherry-like globes of sea anemones and in rousting a large greenish crab out of hiding.

As we toiled on along the beach, sometimes losing our footing on the treacherous pebbles, we reminisced, as old men will. We discussed Inspector Lestrade, now settled in comfortable pensioned retirement in Weston-super-Mare.

"You know he still writes to me," I said. "Almost every time a new story of mine is published I'll get a letter from him, either drawing me up on a point of police procedure or objecting to my characterisation of him, or both."

"Ha!" Holmes exclaimed. "If you ask me, you are unusually generous towards Lestrade. He was always infinitely more dull-witted than you portray."

"He keeps threatening to pen his own memoirs – 'to set the record straight."

"That would be a work of fiction I would be most fascinated to read."

Wiggins, the former leader of the Baker Street Irregulars, had turned his prospects around entirely and was now a police officer himself.

"It is the most wonderful *volte face* I have known," Holmes said. "From street urchin to uniformed upholder of the law. Perhaps consorting with us had a beneficial influence on him. He is prospering within the force, too. I have it on good authority that he has applied to become detective constable, and I am in no doubt he will make an excellent one."

"You wrote him a letter of recommendation, did you not?"

"Only to help him get a foot in the door at Scotland Yard. Wiggins's subsequent advancement is entirely his own doing. He was born with a lively, incisive mind, and it is no small pleasure to me that he has overcome the disadvantages of his background and upbringing and put that mind to good use. An Inspector Wiggins, as he will certainly one day become, will be worth a dozen plodding Lestrades."

Another old acquaintance of ours had recently been in communication with Holmes.

"Fred Tilling?" I said. "The engineer fellow?"

"None other. I contacted him to pick his brains about a few small practical matters, tapping his wealth of expertise. He was only too happy to help."

"Does he still sally forth in his other guise? I can't say I've read any reports of his alter ego's activities in the newspapers lately."

"I believe *anno domini* is creeping up on him as well as us."

"He can't be more than forty-five."

"Too old for a double life, especially one as demanding as his. Time gets to us all, Watson, some sooner than others."

"Well, what was it you consulted him about?"

"Perhaps you've noticed…"

Holmes's voice trailed off, and I would not have the answer to my enquiry for another five days.

We had just passed the lighthouse, which stood atop a concrete plinth a hundred yards offshore, resplendent in striped red-and-white livery. It was a relatively new structure, built to replace the older clifftop lighthouse called Belle Tout, whose beacon could not always be seen from out to sea. Rounding a promontory, we spied a small knot of people ahead. They were gathered beside an object on the beach which I could not make out but which looked for all the world like a heap of damp laundry. Seagulls strutted and squawked nearby in indignation, as though thwarted of some prize.

"What's this?" Holmes mused, and quickened his pace.

As we drew closer it became apparent that a gruesome discovery had been made. Just above the tide-line lay a sodden, mud-stained body, sprawled on its front. From its stillness and the skin pallor there was no disputing that the individual was quite dead.

The crowd around it were a meanly dressed lot with gnarled, weatherbeaten complexions and the lean, rangy frames of those who earned a crust through hard physical labour. Holmes quietly informed me that they were fisher folk.

"There's a community of them that lives along there." He pointed out a cluster of dark, spindly shacks which sat hard against the base of the cliffs some quarter of a mile further on. Skiffs and ketches were drawn up next to them just above the foreshore. Between, nets were strung out on poles to dry, resembling giant ragged spider webs. "Winnicks, they're known as, and they are proud people and wary of outsiders. However, I have had some dealings with them. I shall make the overtures. You follow my lead. Hello!"

At his cry of salutation, the fisher folk turned. Gimlet eyes studied us. Mouths were tightly set.

"My name is Sherlock Holmes. Perhaps you remember me. There was that business two years ago when a holidaying family's baby went missing and one of your number was falsely accused of the abduction. I had some hand in bringing the true culprit to justice."

"Aye, uz remembers you well, Mr Holmes," said the eldest among them, a grizzled old salt with a clay pipe and a moth-eaten peaked cap. "You be no cupboard lover but a true bread-and-cheese friend. Uz be pleased to see you, sure-lye."

They shook hands, and the old man, in his broad Sussex accent, continued: "Young Jenny Fitch, what never stole that babby, still speaks gurt highly of the upstanding gentleman what got her out of moil, for if you hadn't catched the brabagious wretch what truly scaddled the child, Jenny'd be turning crummy in jail even now. Not as uz sees the maid much these days, on account of she's gone and wed some Chop-back over in Hastings."

Chop-backs, I gathered, were a rival fishing community just along the coast. From the way the old man spat the name, there was no love lost between them and Winnicks.

"May I introduce my long-time colleague and comrade Dr John Watson," said Holmes. "Watson, this is Tom Enwright."

The calloused hand that gripped mine was as dry and tough as boot leather.

"Any friend of Mr Holmes be a friend of mine," Enwright said.

"So what have we here?" said Holmes, glancing at the body.

"Some poor sock-lamb what has drownded, and it be an

ernful dissight and all. Dunnamany get washed up on the shore roundabouts every year in total, but it ain't a few. That there's Beachy Head." He pointed to the steep, towering cliff that rose at our backs. "There be mort what does for themselves off there."

I frowned. "Mort?"

"It means a large quantity," said Holmes. "Come on, Watson, it's not that difficult a dialect to fathom."

"Yes," Enwright went on, "lovers what has got into pettigues with the object of their affections, them what feels pick upon or pithered by life, some runagates as want to escape justice and chooses a long leap over the hangman's noose. Thissun, she be the ninth this year uz has happened upon along our stretch of beach. Common a sight as midges, they be to uz."

"She?" I said. "But this is plainly the body of a man."

"The third-person singular pronoun is always feminine," Holmes explained.

"That be right," said Enwright. "Like the saying goes, she be always a she, except a tomcat, and she be a he."

"How long is it since you found the body?" Holmes asked.

"Not gone a half-an-hour. Uz sails in with the tide, all beasted but chipper after a hard morning's dezzick at sea, boco white-herring and dab in our baskets, and no sooner has uz hung up the seines to dry than one of these here ken of mine sets up the hue-and-cry. Was it you, cousin Davey? Sharpest eyes of any of uz, Davey has. So along uz hurries, end-on, for to see if there's still soul in the body, but she be like this, just as you see, sirs, dead as a hollard."

I refrained from asking what a hollard was, but presumed that it was something from which the life had wholly departed. Holmes filled me in later: it was the Sussex word for a fallen, rotten tree branch.

Holmes knelt to give the body his full attention, scanning it from head to toe. The Winnicks stood back at a discreet distance. Every now and then one of them shooed away a gull that strayed too close. The birds wished to be free to scavenge from the cadaver and retreated only with much wing-flapping and haughty head-tossing.

Holmes beckoned to me. "Watson, perhaps you could lend me the benefit of your medical opinion."

I squatted beside him. "I shall try."

"Does this person look as though he drowned?"

"From appearances alone, it's hard to tell. His skin is roughened and pimpled, suggestive of immersion in water for some significant period. I think we can take it as read that he has been in the sea at least since the last high tide."

"Anything else?"

"It would be for a coroner to determine whether the lungs contain water. That is the surest indicator of death by drowning. However, another less common indicator is a fine white froth in the airways which sometimes emerges around the mouth and nostrils." I bent lower, trying to get a clear view of the dead man's face, which was half buried in the shingles. "It is often present, but its absence does not automatically rule out drowning. The same goes for haemorrhaging from the ears, of which I can also see no sign."

"On balance, you would declare that he died through inhalation of water?"

"It is the likeliest cause, surely. Asphyxiation due to suffocation by a liquid. The alternatives are hypothermia or vagal inhibition – the sudden stopping of the heart due to shock from being plunged into exceedingly cold water – but the temperature of the Channel is mild at this time of year. I doubt very much our victim here froze to death."

"He is not dressed for bathing, which rules out a swimming accident. Those are day clothes."

"Perhaps he fell overboard – from a ferry, for instance."

"Possible, possible." Holmes peered up at the beetling white brow of Beachy Head. To my mind the crag had taken on a forbidding aspect, as a locus of despair and death. "Or perhaps he threw himself off the cliffs as Mr Enwright surmises. Had he done so during high tide, the sea could have claimed his body immediately, washing him out away from shore and depositing him back when the tide turned. What else about him do you observe, Watson? Apply my methods of forensic analysis, if you will."

"He is young, in his late teens or early twenties, and well dressed. His suit appears tailored, bespoke, rather than off the peg. The one cufflink I can see appears to be solid gold. His shoes are of good quality. He is moneyed."

"Very good. I concur."

"If we could get a better look at his face…"

"I am loath to disturb the body just yet," Holmes said. "One should attempt to preserve the integrity of a crime scene for as long as possible."

"This is a crime scene?" I said. "But so far everything points to either suicide or mishap. If his death was an accident, that is a tragedy but nothing more. Do you suspect foul play, Holmes?"

My friend did not answer but instead resumed his scrutiny of the body. I could not help but wonder if he was actively trying to find some evidence that this was anything other than death by misadventure. The bucolic life had its attractions for him, but was he missing the excitement of being on a case? Had yesterday's incident at Barraclough's whetted his appetite for detection? If that jewellery theft had been the hors d'oeuvres, could this drowned man be the entrée?

He leaned forward over the back of the body's neck, so close his nose almost touched it. The salt water had preserved the corpse to some extent, so that it had not begun to rot as swiftly as it would have if exposed to the open air, but still, I myself would have been unwilling to place that particular sensory organ in quite such proximity to it.

"Interesting," my friend said softly to himself.

"What is it, Holmes?"

Then a loud, gruff shout resounded along the beach.

"Hey! You there! Get away from that corpse!"

CHAPTER NINE

INSPECTOR GEORGE TASKER

A brace of police constables were making their way towards us, led by a short, ginger-haired man in a trenchcoat who was waving an arm irritably.

"Did you not hear me?" he yelled. "I said get away from it. This instant! In the name of the law."

"Ah, the gendarmes," Holmes said, straightening up and taking a step back, as bidden. "Now the fun begins."

"Who do you think you are?" the trenchcoated man demanded as he covered the last few yards between us and him in a series of rapid, panting strides. "You've no right to be nosing around the body like that. This is police business."

"I beg your pardon, Mr..."

"*Inspector* George Tasker," said the plainclothes policeman, laying emphasis on his official title. "And you are?"

"Sherlock Holmes, and this is my friend –"

"Oh yes." Tasker raised a wry eyebrow. "I've heard about you, Mr Holmes. The amateur sleuth. The prying busybody."

My companion remained outwardly unperturbed, but

beneath the calm surface I could tell he was bristling. Who knows which term offended him more, *amateur* or *busybody*?

"You were a lion in your day," Tasker went on. "We're well aware of the reputation you had. Plenty of my boys read about your exploits in the pages of the *Strand*. What do those stories have in common?"

"A near one-hundred-per-cent success rate in solving crimes?" I offered.

Ignoring me, Tasker barrelled on. "They took place many years ago, and in London, not here. Down here, in this new century, I think you'll find things are a bit different. I know how Scotland Yard granted you plenty of latitude, sir. You had free rein to do as you pleased. Those conditions do not apply in Eastbourne. This is my turf, and I will not have the likes of you trampling all over the place, interfering and getting under foot. Are we clear?"

Holmes withstood the tirade with every show of meek acquiescence. Offering Tasker the most courteous of smiles, he said, "Of course, inspector. Implicitly. I have done nothing here beyond cast an eye over the body of this poor wretch. I have not touched it. I have not tampered with it in any way. I have no desire to obstruct you in the pursuit of your duties. I'm sorry if you may have acquired an otherwise impression. I am merely a concerned citizen, not to mention an ardent supporter of His Majesty's constabulary."

"Yes, well." Tasker was a little mollified. "It was my day off yesterday, and when I came into the station this morning, all anyone could talk about was the great Mr Sherlock Holmes nabbing a couple of jewel thieves the day before. I do not care to hear such things. I will not have members of the public taking the law into their own hands. Policing is a serious business, best carried out by those with the appropriate training. It is a vocation, not a pastime. If it weren't, why else would I be out on a Sunday morning when I should be at church?"

"Now see here!" I began intemperately. I had had enough of Tasker's condescending attitude. "How dare you talk that way. The damned impertinence. Sherlock Holmes has done more for this country, for the Crown, for the Empire, than a mealy-mouthed functionary like you ever will. Why, while you were still in short trousers, this man…"

Holmes forestalled me with a hand on my arm. "No, Watson, it's all right. The inspector is quite correct. I lack his training and his professional experience. I am content to concede gracefully. This corpse falls squarely under his jurisdiction. Let him deal with the matter."

Inspector Tasker glared at me for a good long while, clearly weighing up whether or not to discipline me for my outburst. I have no doubt that he could have arrested me for insulting an officer of the law or on some other such charge, and that he was tempted. In the end, he decided against it.

"I would caution you not to speak to me like that again, sir," he warned with an upraised finger, "or we'll have you off to Lewes Assizes quicker than you can say Jack Robinson. A gent of your advanced years has no wish to spend a night or two on a pallet mattress in a damp cell. It will do little for your constitution. Now then, Pumphrey, Ayers!" The two policemen with him stiffened to attention. "Get these gawpers out of here, will you? Clear the area, and let's have no further 'concerned citizens' sticking their beaks in where they don't belong."

Constables Pumphrey and Ayers began directing Holmes, myself and the various Winnicks away from the corpse with brusque ushering gestures and orders to "move along" and "go back to your homes". Tom Enwright grumbled that he was "not a man to be druv" but complied nonetheless. Holmes, for his part, set his foot on a large, limpet-covered rock and began fussing with a bootlace which had apparently come loose. Constable Pumphrey invited him to hurry up, but my friend said it was no easy matter tying a lace at his age, when arthritis was playing merry havoc with his finger joints.

By this subterfuge he contrived for both of us to be within earshot when the following exchange took place between Inspector Tasker and Constable Ayers.

"Is it him, sir?" Ayers asked.

Tasker grasped the body by the shoulder and heaved it over onto its back. His face assumed a grim cast. "By God, I'm afraid it is."

"You can be sure? Even with all the bloating?"

"Yes. Patrick Mallinson, in the swollen flesh. I'd recognise him anywhere."

"So the father wasn't mistaken."

"I wish, for his sake, he had been. And for mine, since I'm the one who'll have to break the news to him and confirm that his worst fears are well founded."

Constable Pumphrey could not endure any more of Holmes's prevarication and instructed him to leave whether or not the lace was tied, threatening to help him along with the toe of his own boot.

"Mallinson," I said *sotto voce* as Holmes and I followed the Winnicks along the beach. "As in our weekend aviator."

"Indeed. The late Patrick we can safely assume was his son. I think we can also safely assume that the father spied the body from his aeroplane and despatched the police to this spot to check on his behalf."

"So Mallinson senior *was* searching in the plane. His son went missing and he had a shrewd idea what might have become of him."

"Enter Inspector Tasker and his cohorts. You know, whatever one thinks of Lestrade, and of Gregson and Athelney Jones and Bradstreet and Hopkins and all the other Scotland Yard men we were obliged to associate with over the years – they may not have been of the brightest but they were never knowingly a hindrance. Tasker, on the other hand, is an obtuse, puffed-up little martinet, the classic big fish in a small pond. I fear he shall prove problematic if we are to attempt to clear up this mystery."

"Clear up…?" I said. "You mean something has given you to believe that the drowned man – Patrick Mallinson – died in suspicious circumstances?"

"Had I had longer to inspect the remains, I might have been able to establish one way or the other with a degree of certainty. The father being prompted to search for him is a telling detail. As is the matter of the angle of his neck. Did you notice? His head was bent sharply forwards, so sharply that it was unnatural, and I discerned an indentation at the base of the skull where the axis, the second cervical vertebra, lies. It appeared to have been shattered."

"So his neck was broken," I said. "But would that not be consistent with a fall from a great height – a height such as Beachy Head?"

"It might, but for the lack of cuts, abrasions and other forms of external damage, which there would be had he plunged straight onto rocks."

"If the tide was all the way in, could not the sea have spared him from superficial injury, while not cushioning his bones from the trauma of impact?"

"Very possibly so. But then there is the question of the mud."

"The mud?"

CHAPTER TEN

THE MANIFOLD PROPERTIES OF MUD

In lieu of answering my question, Holmes abruptly accelerated, at the same time calling out Tom Enwright's name.

The venerable old fisherman halted, permitting my friend to catch up with him.

"What be heggling you, Mr Holmes?"

"Tell me, my good man, did you happen to get a thorough look at the mud on the body?"

"I'd reckon as so."

"Was it smeery, would you say, or stoach?"

"Hmm, now there be a thing, Mr Holmes," said Enwright. "It weren't neither. It were more sleech or gawm."

"Definitely closer to slub than stug, then?"

"Oh aye, for certain." Enwright scratched his head beneath his cap. "Queer, that, now you come to mention it."

"Thank you, Mr Enwright."

"Most welcome, sir." The Winnick resettled his cap and walked on toward the shacks.

"Care to explain what that was all about?" I asked. "It sounded as though you had slipped into pure gibberish. Stoach? Slub? Is that even the King's English?"

"You know how the Eskimo has fifty words for snow."

"Yes."

"Well, likewise the Sussex fisherman has numerous words for the various types of mud he encounters in his daily course. That stolen-baby case Enwright referred to earlier? My solving it hinged on the fact that the kidnapper's shoes bore clods of the right kind of mud, whereas those of Jenny Fitch, the Winnick girl who was alleged to have taken the infant from its pram, were covered in the wrong kind of mud."

"I don't follow. Mud is mud, surely."

"On the contrary. Have I not demonstrated to you time and time again that everything, no matter how homogenous it seems, is unique, and in its uniqueness, enlightening? To take an example dear to my heart, no lump of tobacco ash is like another. Each tells its own individual story. Thus it is with mud too. The sediment on a river bed is of an entirely dissimilar consistency and composition to the silt at the bottom of the sea. And, for Winnicks and their fishing brethren, there are even finer distinctions, such as between, say, shoreline mud and deep-sea mud. Still with me?"

"It's as clear as mud to me, old chap."

"Pawky as ever, Watson. The woman who stole the baby – a young creature driven half mad after a succession of stillbirths and miscarriages, overcome by her desperation to have a baby of her own, any baby – had trodden through mud at the exact spot on the beach where the abduction occurred. Jenny Fitch, though her shoes were of the same size and style as the other woman's, was nowhere near the place at that time. The mud on her soles and heels proved as much, because it originated from further along the coast, where the proportions of minerals in the alluvial deposits are somewhat different and consequently the colour and texture of the mud differs. The shoe prints by the pram were the main plank of the police's case against Miss Fitch, and once that collapsed, they had nothing left to charge her with."

"Why was she accused in the first place?"

"Merely because she had cooed over the infant earlier that day, while the parents were perambulating with it along the seafront. Subsequently the distraught couple gave her description to the police who, I'm afraid to say, were only too quick to pounce on her as a suspect. There is a great deal of prejudice among Eastbourne townsfolk against Winnicks. The fisher folk are held in the same low esteem as gypsies and tramps. They form an unfairly maligned underclass and are often the first to be blamed when there's trouble, which would account for their mistrust of outsiders."

"And this business of the mud in that case led you to take a deeper interest in the topic."

"Of course. I am only too happy to apply my mind to whatever new fields of interest take my fancy."

"Do you think there might even be a monograph in it?"

"I shouldn't be surprised."

Sometimes my friend seemed not to realise when I was gently ribbing him. That or he was perfectly well aware but would not deign to acknowledge it.

"How it is relevant in this instance," he said, "is that the mud on Patrick Mallinson's body is not the mud one finds in the shallows of a beach. It is not the loose, thin mud of the kind that Winnicks know as 'smeery' or 'stoach'. It is 'gawm' or 'slub', thicker and denser. Such mud comes from much further out to sea."

"Goodness. What might that signify?"

"Possibly nothing, possibly everything. It is a singular factor, at least. How does deep-sea mud get onto the body of someone who may have hurled himself off a cliff?"

"The tide could have dragged him further out than you think.

Or we could reconsider my theory that he fell from a boat."

"Yes, yes," said Holmes. "As yet we do not have sufficient data to draw any firm conclusions. We are too much in the dark. But there is always the prospect that something will come along to shed more light on the situation, and I would not be surprised if it happens soon."

CHAPTER ELEVEN

CRAIG MALLINSON, ESQUIRE

Further light did indeed come, that very afternoon. This was in the wake of a roast Sunday lunch at the Tiger Inn during which I did my utmost to dissuade Holmes from becoming embroiled to any greater extent in the affair of Patrick Mallinson's death.

"It really is none of our business," I insisted. "I feel that you very much want it to be. Your blood is up. But I would counsel you to steer clear. A man your age has better things to do with his time. You have been at pains to divest yourself of the stresses and strains of detective work. Why, then, be willing to take them on again, and with such avidity? Apprehending a jewel thief or a baby-snatcher is one thing. Those are relatively trivial exercises for someone of your powers. One could pass that off as merely keeping your hand in. But a mysterious death? That is altogether more serious and potentially more taxing."

"I am like the heavyweight prizefighter who reckons he has one more good bout in him," said Holmes. "He craves the challenge, so he re-enters the ring."

"To prove what? That he can be some young up-and-comer's punching-bag?"

"To prove to himself that he still has what it takes."

"But what if there is no case here? Or at any rate, nothing that warrants your involvement, nothing that the likes of Inspector Tasker can't handle."

"Then I will have roused myself from my state of torpor for no good reason. Should that happen, so be it. Sometimes the prospect of the hunt is as good as the hunt itself."

We had settled down in the sitting room at Holmes's cottage to digest our meal, and I was just closing my eyes for a well-earned and much-desired forty winks, when there came a loud rapping at the front door. Holmes was on his feet in a flash, and shortly was escorting in two visitors and inviting them to take a seat.

"Watson, vacate that chair, would you? There's a good chap."

I blearily and, I will admit, somewhat grumpily gave up my comfortable berth. Holmes found me a wooden dining chair to perch on, which did little to assuage the sourness of my mood. Aged bones like mine needed the consolation of upholstery.

I was none too cheered, either, by the fact that one of the two guests was Inspector Tasker, and that it was he who took occupancy of the very armchair I had been occupying. His demeanour was somewhat less officious than before, however. He was exhibiting more a kind of petulance now than anything, his air that of a schoolboy who has been dragooned into some errand by his headmaster on pain of a flogging.

The "headmaster" in this instance was a man far and away Tasker's social superior, a well-built, patrician individual wearing a box-pleated tweed Norfolk jacket with matching breeches and knee-length woollen stockings, the very picture of a prosperous country landowner. He had a fine head of raven-black hair, tufts of which also garnished the backs of his stubby fingers. His shoes were brown Oxford wingtip brogues of the latest fashion.

His face I would call sleekly handsome, his looks well preserved for a man in his fifties. Yet a shadow of beard stubble coated his jaw, and another kind of shadow, a subtler, sadder one, haunted his eyes. He looked, in short, haggard, someone who had been assailed by a recent calamity and who had forsaken the niceties of personal grooming even as he strove to keep his distress in check.

Had Holmes not made the formal introductions – "Watson, Inspector Tasker you already know, and the gentleman he has brought with him to see us is Craig Mallinson, Esquire." – I would nonetheless have intuited the stranger's identity. At the very least I would have wagered good money that here was the father of the drowned man on the beach.

"Mr Mallinson," I said. "Please accept my sincerest condolences. Your son… It is too dreadful to contemplate."

"I thank you, Dr Watson," said Mallinson. "The sentiments are appreciated. My grief is great. Patrick is – was – the younger of my two boys. He was always the apple of his mother's eye, and I had great hopes for him. He may not have been the most obedient of children, unlike his brother Clive, but there was nonetheless a deep and abiding affection between us that I believed could survive all rifts. But not this... This, the ultimate rift."

"His mother," said Holmes. "Is she...?"

Mallinson nodded. "Jocelyn died when Clive and Patrick were toddlers. She was taken by typhoid fever. We were living in Egypt at the time, where I have commercial interests. Her death impelled me to leave and return to England, and here I have remained ever since, being the best father I could to our sons, bringing them up as cultured, educated young men, just as she would have wanted. In a way, I am glad that she didn't live to see this."

Emotion choked Mallinson's voice. We all gave him time to collect himself.

"Even now I cannot quite believe it," he said. "I shan't see Patrick again, shan't sit across the dining table from him, shan't discuss politics and current affairs with him, as was our wont. To think that his future has been denied him."

Holmes fetched a glass of brandy, which Mallinson downed with trembling gratitude. It was pitiful to see someone so abundantly able and dignified so utterly unmanned.

"He never once begrudged me the string of governesses I hired to look after him while he was growing up," he continued. "Neither did Clive. They both understood that my work is important and that I needed to be away on business a great deal. I saw them as often as I could, as often as my commitments allowed. For all that, we were as close a family as could be."

"What, pray, is your occupation, Mr Mallinson?" Holmes enquired.

"Mining. Import."

Tasker piped up. "Fully a fifth of the rare minerals and chemical elements that enter this country from abroad arrive through Mr Mallinson's auspices. Is that statistic correct, sir?"

"Something in that region."

"Mr Mallinson is a well-regarded personage hereabouts," Tasker went on. "Most august and influential."

The inspector wanted us to know not only how important Mallinson was but also how important he himself was as the liaison between Mallinson and us.

"I have no doubt as to that," Holmes said. "Your estate near Alfriston covers several hundred acres, does it not, Mr Mallinson? I have skirted the bounds of your property many a time while I've been out on a ramble."

"I have the privilege of owning Settleholm Manor and its

attached land, yes," said Mallinson. "I purchased it off the Duke of Devonshire himself, inheriting the tied arable fields and grazing pastures as well."

"And never once have I received a complaint from any of his tenant farmers," Tasker interjected. "They have nothing but praise for him as a landlord. Treats them more than generously, he does."

"And your sons," said Holmes, "they were raised at Settleholm?"

"Yes," said Mallinson, "aside from spells at boarding school, first a preparatory in Kent, then Eton. Clive was always at his happiest here, though, and Patrick even more so. He adored the surrounding countryside. The Downs, the sea, the cliffs, the meander at Cuckmere Haven, they were his playground. Clive is somewhat more sophisticated in his tastes, less easily contented with the simpler things."

"Did contentment become an issue for Patrick later in life?"

"Whatever are you driving at?"

"Perhaps I should rephrase. Mr Mallinson, why have you come to visit? I do not suppose for one moment that this is a random social call. You are here about your son's death in some capacity or other."

"Yes. Yes, I am."

"Dr Watson and I had the great misfortune to chance upon the young man's body. My impression is that you had already spied it earlier, from the cockpit of your biplane."

"I did. I telephoned the Eastbourne police as soon as I landed and directed them to the precise location. I could not bear to go myself. From the air, the body I saw certainly looked like Patrick's, but I continued to hold out the vain hope that it was not. Finally Inspector Tasker came to Settleholm and delivered the message I had been praying not to hear. His words fell on my soul like a hammer blow."

"Among the many tasks that are a policeman's lot," said Tasker, "being the bearer of bad tidings is the one I relish the least. Yet I trust that I am sufficiently compassionate and sympathetic when I am called upon to execute it."

"Patrick had gone missing, then?" said Holmes.

"Since the day before yesterday," said Mallinson. "I was up in London all week and so I was unaware of his absence until I returned home on Saturday morning. It was supposed to be Friday evening but I was unavoidably detained. None of my household servants had seen Patrick since the previous afternoon. He had not appeared at dinner, nor had he returned home by the time they went to bed. When he did not come down for breakfast the next morning, the butler went up to his room to check on him. The bed had not been slept in. None of them was unduly perturbed, however. Patrick had stayed out late before, often lodging overnight at some friend's house and without leaving any note to indicate his whereabouts. I, on the other hand, *was* worried."

"For what reason?"

"Patrick had become restless and uneasy over the past few months. He was not himself. Deferring his place at Cambridge, that was one symptom of the malaise. He was due to read Classics at Corpus Christi, something he had worked tirelessly for at school. Yet over the summer he changed his mind, seeming to get cold feet. I tried to convince him that university was a golden opportunity, a place where he could meet new friends and where the course of the rest of his life would be set. I pointed out that Clive had been a great success as an undergraduate, gaining not only a double first but a rowing blue. Patrick, however, prevaricated and eventually wrote to the college Master requesting a year's grace. It was a decision I was not best pleased by, and I begged him on several occasions to reconsider."

"Do you have any idea what might have prompted it?"

"Some." Mallinson's expression darkened. "I cannot say irrefutably that the two things are connected, but I believe a major contributory factor may be found in Eastbourne itself."

"A girl."

"How did you guess?"

"I did not. It was beyond elementary. When a young man is troubled and begins to behave oddly and make imprudent choices, by far the likeliest cause is that he has contracted a relationship with a member of the fairer sex. Love can make fools of even the wisest among us, and wisdom is a quality seldom found in the young. So Patrick had become enthralled by a local lass. Do you know her?"

"Her path and mine have crossed."

"And your opinion of her?"

"Is irrelevant. Let us just say that she was unsuitable for my son on every level, over and above the effect she was having on him, distracting him from finishing his education."

"Ah," said Holmes. "And was your disapproval of her in any way a source of friction between you and Patrick?"

"I tried not to let it be. I tried to be as understanding and forgiving about the situation as I could. But to see him throw his place at Cambridge away for the sake of a mere dalliance..."

"You said he asked for a deferment."

"Which is as good as throwing it away. He was only pretending to want to postpone it, so that I would not be too aggrieved. I could tell, however, that he had no intention of going up."

"Patrick and you, in other words, were at loggerheads, and when you came down from town on Saturday and he was not at home, you began to fear the worst."

"Call it parental intuition. No matter how I tried, I could not shake the feeling that he had gone and done something drastic."

"It didn't occur to you that he might simply have left home

to go and stay with the object of his affections? That possibly they had even eloped?"

"No, Mr Holmes, for the simple reason that Patrick had told me just last week that he and she were on the outs."

"I see. They had broken off the affair. On whose wishes? His or hers?"

"Hers, as I understand it."

"Very well. So we have a lovelorn youth, deeply unhappy, suffering his first rebuff from a girl for whom he had been prepared to sacrifice everything. I can see now why, when confronted with his sudden disappearance, your thoughts may have turned to the worst possible outcome."

"I gave it one more night. I said to myself, 'Perhaps he has gone off to be on his own somewhere, to cool off, to take stock.' Yet I could not shake the impression that he had done himself harm. I barely slept. Yesterday afternoon my gamekeeper and I scoured the grounds of the estate looking for him. We had the dog out, and I was hoping against hope that Patrick was in an outbuilding, or sleeping rough in the woods. But we found no trace of him. Hence this morning I took out the plane in order to search further afield. I covered miles, quartering the Downs from Polegate to Firle Beacon, then proceeding to the coast, shuttling back and forth between Eastbourne and Seaford, all along the Seven Sisters. On my final pass, with my fuel running low, I… I spotted what could have been a body, by the foot of Beachy Head. And I knew. Patrick had done what so many have done before, other spurned lovers…"

At that point Mallinson broke down, unable to retain mastery of himself any longer. His sobs wrenched at the heart. He buried his face in his hands, and the tears leaked out between his fingers.

When at last he recovered, he apologised, but Holmes assured him that no apology was necessary.

"Tasker here mentioned that he had had the good fortune of

meeting you beside Patrick's body," Mallinson said. "The famous
Sherlock Holmes, our reclusive local celebrity."

I am quite sure that Tasker had not put it in those terms.
Judging by his behaviour during our first encounter, he would
have described Holmes much less flatteringly.

"I immediately desired to make your acquaintance," Mallinson
went on. "I would have telephoned, but when I tried, the switchboard
informed me that no one of your name is on the exchange."

"I do not own a telephone," said Holmes. "I am amenable to
being contacted by the traditional methods, or visited in person,
but I will not have a device in the house that can ring at any hour
of day or night and disturb my repose or my train of thought with
its jangling racket. I am not averse to any of the appurtenances of
the modern era, but having a telephone installed is where I draw
the line. No pun intended."

"Mr Mallinson enjoined me to come with him," said Inspector
Tasker. "It went against my instincts, but he was adamant, and I
am not one to turn down a request from a pillar of the community,
especially one so newly bereaved."

"I would like to keep this all above board," said Mallinson,
"and have the police involved at every step. You see, Mr Holmes,
I wish to engage your services. Whatever your going rate is, I will
pay you, and more. Money is no object."

My friend bowed cautiously. "I am prepared to consider it,
but what I fail to understand is how I can possibly be of help. Your
son committed suicide, Mr Mallinson. That is what you are telling
me. He threw himself off Beachy Head in a fit of despair, having
been jilted by a girl. Is that not all there is to it?"

"I expect so, Mr Holmes, but I need to know for absolute
certain. How to put this? I am a man of means, a man of
considerable worldly status. With that eminence comes renown
and also attention. When misfortune strikes one such as me, it

becomes a public matter. There are headlines. People pry. There is intrusion. Worse, my enemies and business rivals, of whom I have a fair few, get very excited. They start rubbing their hands with glee. They may perceive that I am weakened. They may reckon there is an opportunity to get the better of me. The industry I operate in is as cutthroat as any. It's every man for himself and devil take the hindmost."

"You wish to protect yourself."

"In a manner of speaking. I do not want Patrick's name – and consequently mine – to be dragged through the mud. I do not want even a hint of impropriety attached to his death. It could be the ruin of me."

"I cannot cover up the facts here, if that's what you're asking me. It would be entirely beyond me. Even if my silence were for sale, and Watson's, there are others who have seen the body, including Inspector Tasker's own men and some of the Winnick fisher folk. The former might be persuaded to keep a secret but not the latter. In short, not even through your best efforts can you hope to bury the truth."

"You misapprehend, sir," said Mallinson. "I am not trying to buy your or anyone's collusion. That is not my intent at all. What I would like you to do for me is prove beyond a shred of doubt that nothing more sinister has happened than appears to have. I don't want anyone to be able to insinuate that there is more to Patrick's death than the scenario I have laid out before you. If the revered Sherlock Holmes himself, having investigated, states that Patrick took his own life, then there can be no question but that it is so. The carpers and the gossipmongers won't have a leg to stand on. My company will be insulated from outside attack and I will be free to mourn in privacy and peace. It will not bring Patrick back, nor will it compensate me for what I have lost, but it will at least bring me a modicum of mental ease."

"I see," said Holmes. "A further question. Where is Clive right now? Is he at home?"

"Clive? No. The lad is abroad. Egypt. El Nuweiba, to be precise, in the eastern part of the Sinai Peninsula, beside the Gulf of Aqaba. He oversees business for me there, running the mines and ensuring the shipments of raw materials go out on time. My man on the ground, as it were."

"I take it you haven't informed him yet about Patrick."

"No, and I am dreading it. How can I send that telegram? How do I word it? What do I say? Clive doted on Patrick. They were inseparable, growing up. He was the perfect older brother, vigilant, protective. This will break his heart, Mr Holmes. Break it in two, as it has broken mine!"

"I imagine Clive won't make it back from Egypt in time for Patrick's funeral."

Mallinson shook his head sorrowfully. "It will take a day or two at least for the message to reach him. After that, he'll have to travel for at least two days by train to Alexandria, and another week and a half by boat to Dover. I wouldn't expect him home for a fortnight, and we cannot delay the ceremony that long. Poor Clive. He shan't even be here to see his brother interred."

The mining magnate fixed Holmes with an imploring look.

"Please, Mr Holmes," he said. "For the sake of Patrick's brother, if not mine, clear this matter up as soon as possible, will you? At least then Clive will be able to come back to a home transfigured by grief but not by scandal and dishonour."

CHAPTER TWELVE

AT TRIPP'S COSTUMIERS

"Let me see if I have it straight," I said to Holmes as we made our way on foot into town the next morning. "You have been hired to prove that a death which you happen to regard as suspicious is in fact anything but."

"That is the long and the short of it."

"And the irascible Inspector Tasker, who yesterday forbade you from interfering in any way, is now under constraint from Craig Mallinson to offer you all assistance he can."

"Irony heaped upon irony."

East Dean was situated a couple of miles to the west of Eastbourne, and the most direct route from one to the other was a deep-cut track of the kind known thereabouts as a "bostal". It climbed the hillside at a steep gradient, and I was quite out of puff when we reached the summit. Before us lay the town itself and, beyond, the flat scrubby expanse of the Pevensey Levels. Hastings was a pale hazy smudge along the far arm of the bay. The nip I had felt in the air the day before was quite marked this morning, and the majority of the trees within view had –

overnight, it seemed – turned from green to brown.

"Tasker's face," I said when I had regained my breath. "What a sight it was, when Mallinson demanded that he co-operate fully with you. He looked fit to explode."

"That is what you get when you kowtow to the members of the establishment," said Holmes. "You must acquiesce to their every whim, even at the expense of your own wishes. I do not think, though, that he will go out of his way to be helpful. He will do the bare minimum to be seen to be complying."

"Better than nothing."

"So many things are."

In town, we located our destination, a shop in a side street in the area nicknamed Little Chelsea, due south of the railway station. It was a costumier's called Tripp's, and its hoarding boasted *Fine Fanciful Wear for all Occasions*, while inside the window, painted in gold, was the legend:

Theatrical • Recreational • Historical
For Hire or Purchase
Made to Measure

The interior was a touch musty, and as the chime of the bell above the door faded I took in the display mannequins whose outfits ranged from a Hussar's uniform to some sort of fairy godmother ensemble complete with wand and gossamer wings. Fastened to the walls were masks – a whole Venetian masquerade of plumed dominos on the end of lorgnette-style sticks, grinning Harlequins and hook-nosed *Dottori* – which stared down at us with a vacancy I found unsettling. From clothes racks hung pirate, jester and minstrel costumes, and shelves bore such accessories as wigs, beards, moustaches and false noses, while on the counter was an array of makeup items.

"A treasure trove of disguise and dissimulation," said Holmes. "Why have I never visited this place before? I feel quite at home here."

"You always were something of an actor manqué," I said. "Your propensity for impersonation while on an investigation suggests to me that by becoming a detective you missed your true calling as a thespian."

My friend picked up a tub of greasepaint. "There is a lot to be said for losing oneself in the role of another. It is like taking a holiday, a respite from the pressures of who one is." He held the greasepaint aloft like Hamlet contemplating Yorick's skull. "Perhaps I have for too long tried to be another Sherlock Holmes, playing at being retired. Perhaps I am at last rediscovering my metier. Events are conspiring to steer me back onto my predestined path."

"Hogwash. You don't believe that any more than I do."

"You must at least allow me my fond indulgences." He set down the greasepaint and tapped the countertop bell. "Is there no one here? How many bell rings does it take to summon service?"

We heard activity from the backroom, and eventually a woman emerged, hastening into the shop with profuse apology. Her eyes were swollen and bloodshot from crying, and her flaxen hair somewhat dishevelled. Notwithstanding, she was a comely creature. I would put her age at thirty or thirty-one – though it is not polite to speculate on such things – and she had a fine narrow nose and a smooth slender throat. Her dress was in the latest mode, with a low neckline and shirtwaist bodice, to which she had added a few striking sartorial touches such as a profusion of bracelets on both wrists and unusually long earrings.

Dabbing at her eyes with a batik handkerchief, the lady enquired how she might be of assistance.

"Do I have the pleasure of addressing Miss Elizabeth Vandenbergh?" said Holmes.

"That you do. But you have me at a disadvantage, sir. You are…?"

"Sherlock Holmes, and this is Dr Watson."

I doffed my hat to her.

"Oh, I'm sorry," said Elizabeth Vandenbergh. "I feel I ought to have recognised you. You do not look much like you do in the *Strand*."

"I'm afraid I must put that down to the passage of the years, and also to the fact that Mr Paget chooses to depict me with a considerably higher forehead than I actually possess, as well as a sharper and more aquiline nose."

"No, now that I look more closely, Mr Holmes, I perceive that he has captured your likeness well."

"How we see ourselves is often not how we truly are," Holmes said philosophically. "Miss Vandenbergh, I beg your forgiveness for calling on you at what must be a difficult time. Watson and I came with a view to enquiring from a colleague as to your home address, whereupon we could present ourselves more formally at a time that suited you. We did not anticipate meeting you yourself on the premises. We imagined you would be elsewhere, having taken some time off in light of your present regrettable circumstances."

"A colleague?" said Elizabeth with a muted laugh. "I have none. I cannot afford to pay anyone's wages but my own. I run this business single-handed. And my premises are also my home address. I own the entire building, and live in a small flat on the upstairs floor. Being a costumier is not the most lucrative form of employment, especially in a small, out-of-the-way town such as Eastbourne. My margins are narrow. I keep body and soul together, but only just."

"There is no Tripp at Tripp's Costumiers, then?"

"I kept the name after I bought the business off Roderick Tripp, the previous proprietor, last year. Everything else here is all mine, and all my responsibility. I stitch, I sew, I work the till,

I sweep the floors, I do the accounts…" A delicate frown creased her brow. "But may I ask how you knew who I was, Mr Holmes, if you were not expecting to meet Elizabeth Vandenbergh?"

"Your tears gave you away. The woman Watson and I are looking for has recently undergone a bereavement."

Elizabeth, with an impressive effort, steeled herself. "That she has. And would that I could close up the shop and take time off to grieve, but such is the parlous state of my finances that I must stay open for whatever passing trade I can hope to attract. There are bills to be paid, and I need every farthing I can earn. Also, it is better to be busy than to sit idle and brood. That may all seem rather unfeeling of me, but as the saying goes, if your head is intact you can have a thousand turbans. In other words, when times are hard you must do whatever you have to in order to keep going. Everything else is unimportant."

"A noteworthy turn of phrase," said Holmes.

"So I have indeed shed tears, yes, but I must also get on with life." The phlegmatic tenor of her statement was belied by the catch in her voice as she spoke. Miss Elizabeth Vandenbergh was putting on a very brave face, but she remained manifestly distraught. "What's happened has happened. There are practicalities to consider. I just rather wish I hadn't found out the news in such a roundabout way. I overheard someone talking about it in the queue at the bakers this morning. Apparently it's all over town. Nobody, though, had the nerve to come to me in person and tell me. I had to learn it second-hand, as a rumour. Such is the regard in which I am held by certain persons."

"By certain persons you mean Craig Mallinson, I presume. After all, you are, or rather were, the paramour of Patrick Mallinson. That is correct?"

She moved her head from side to side, as though in embarrassment or discomfort. "Paramour. What a terribly pukka word. Patrick and I were, one might say, more than friends. Not for long, and not without complication, but we definitely formed a deep attachment. His father has sent you, I take it."

Holmes allowed that he had.

Elizabeth's lip curled. "What – am I to blame for Patrick's death? Has the high-and-mighty Craig Mallinson employed Mr Sherlock Holmes to build a case against me? Is this some petty act of vengeance on his part? If it is, sir, I should have you know that I am not a woman to be slighted or scorned. I am perfectly capable of defending my corner, like a fury if need be."

"Of that I have no doubt, madam," said Holmes. "While in India, you would have been exposed to some level of hardship. It has tempered you like steel. I do not know of anyone, not even a lady's companion, who has not returned from the subcontinent with an increased capacity for weathering the storms of life. Your disappointment in love while abroad has likewise inured you to storms of another kind – of the heart. The further reaches of the British Empire serve as a proving ground for all who go there. If it does not kill them, that is. Madras, was it?"

"Mysore, as a matter of fact. But how did you…?" Elizabeth shook her head with a rueful smile. "Either you have researched my background or you are applying your famous analytical reasoning. On balance, I think it is the second of the two."

"And you would be correct in your surmise."

"Let me see. What clues did I give?"

"For one thing –"

"No, Mr Holmes, it was a rhetorical question. I intend to analyse your analysis. I am curious to determine if I can match my wits against yours."

It amused me to see someone – a member of the opposite sex, moreover – halt Holmes mid-flow and elect to take him on at his own game. It amused Holmes too, but in a more abstruse, scientific way.

"My physical appearance would have been a factor," Elizabeth said. "My choice in jewellery – these earrings, these bangles – and my handkerchief. I suppose all of that would have been evident to you, although as a rule most males pay scant attention to the niceties of how a woman looks or dresses. They note the obvious but not the subtleties, the details. Then there was my use of the word 'pukka'. Doubtless that caught your attention."

"It is one of the many Hobson-Jobson loanwords that have entered our mother tongue from Hindi, via the Raj," said Holmes. "But whereas others such as 'pyjamas', 'verandah' and 'shampoo' are in common usage, 'pukka' remains more rarefied and tends to be in the vocabulary only of people who have actually lived and worked in India."

"I also quoted an Indian proverb. I have a store of those."

"Yes. 'A thousand turbans'. That certainly bolstered the impression I was forming of your background."

"But how did you know that I had been a lady's companion?"

"Is that another rhetorical question?"

"No, now I am genuinely asking. I can't imagine the job has qualities which are immediately obvious in one's bearing and speech."

"Here we come to the art of selecting the highest from a list of probabilities. Lady's companion seemed a logical occupation for one of your gender, age, social standing and unmarried status who has lived abroad. Now that I know you were in Mysore, one of the princely states rather than one of the presidencies or provinces, it is clear you were not in the employ of a governor's or lieutenant-governor's wife, so I am going to opt instead for the wife of someone in the mercantile professions – a plantation owner."

"Very good."

"A woman whose husband dealt in tea or rubber."

"Tea."

"And who would therefore have been living somewhere

rural and remote, where erudite English-speaking company was thin on the ground. You, with your obvious intelligence and accomplishment, were there to provide her with the society she would otherwise constantly have been in want of."

"But how could you tell I lived so far south? India is not a small country by any means, yet you alighted immediately on the region right at the tip of the landmass."

"The 'further reaches of the British Empire', as I said. You were away for a number of years – again, a deduction in part based on your current age, if I am not being too indelicate, madam – and you were not likely to have been there for so long if the southern parts of India weren't so much more inaccessible than the northern parts. One imagines that lady's companions come and go more readily in Sind or the Punjab than they do in Madras and Mysore. It is not worth the extra journeying time if you do not then stay for a goodly period – long enough, indeed, to pick up a healthy grasp of the vernacular and the local expressions."

"Most ingenious, Mr Holmes," said Elizabeth. "You are quite as clever as people say."

My friend responded with a nod that was halfway to being a bow. "There is a further indicator of your Indian sojourn that you may not be aware of, Miss Vandenbergh. You have adopted that peculiarly Indian mannerism of wobbling your head to show assent or acknowledgement. I am quite sure it is unconscious."

Elizabeth performed the action, knowingly. "How astute of you. If I do do that, I honestly don't realise it. There is one other thing, however. You spoke of a 'disappointment in love'. Was that a lucky guess? There can, after all, be few women who have not at some stage or other in their lives been let down by a man. Or am I to assume that the relatively sanguine face I am currently presenting to the world has some bearing on your inference?"

"I have never in my life made a lucky guess," said Holmes.

"It strikes me that you have been through worse than you are experiencing right now. I am not saying you are hard-hearted, but your heart *has* been hardened, your outlook made pragmatic by some previous difficulty related to a romantic liaison. Is that why you came back to England a year ago?"

Elizabeth's cheeks flushed a little. "The two events are not unconnected. I became... entangled with a local man while out there. He was high-caste, the son of a nawab. He lived in a palace in the hills, with views out across steaming jungle and the Kaveri river. Monkeys roamed free among the trees in the courtyard, and he kept mynahs in a cage. My visits to his home, though infrequent, were like trips to a tropical Eden. He was mentor as well as friend. He gave me lessons in swordplay, Indian-style. I am proficient with both *firangi* and *khanda*, and I am also versed in the principles of *kalaripayattu*, a martial art practised in the southern Indian states. I could have been happy with him, I could even have become his nawab begum, his memsahib..." She uttered a wistful sigh. "I don't know why I'm telling you all this."

"We have no objection to listening," I said.

"Good of you to say, doctor, but I have no wish to bore you with the sordid details of my past. To cut a long story short, my employer found out who I was consorting with and put a stop to it. He accused me of all sorts of vile sins, the least of which was that I had 'gone native'. He maintained that the brown man and the white woman were not meant to be together. It was an abomination, an affront to British dignity and the natural order. He vowed to besmirch my reputation if I did not end the relationship, and while a part of me could not have cared less what he did, another more conservative part recoiled at the threat. I acceded to his demands. I wish I had not. He put me on a train up to Bombay and thence on the first available steamship back home, and for every single one of the thousands of miles I travelled, I wept. Only as the ship put in at Southampton did I buck up and swear to myself that I would never again be that timid and easily cowed. Nobody but me would dictate whom I chose to fall in love with."

"An admirable sentiment," I said. "I applaud it."

"Poor Patrick, though," she said. "I never meant to hurt him, certainly not so badly that he would take his own life. In fact, by telling him we were not to see each other any more, I hoped to save him."

"How so?" said Holmes.

"It is complicated. Do you have time?"

"As much as you require."

"Then allow me to make you both some tea, and I shall unburden myself further to you."

CHAPTER THIRTEEN

THE ENCHANTED SUMMER

Elizabeth Vandenbergh flipped the sign hanging in the shop door from Open to Closed, saying, "I imagine my non-existent customers won't miss me for half an hour or so." Then she invited us into the back room.

Bolts of cloth lay in piles all around, sometimes stacked two or three deep against the wall. A treadle-powered sewing machine sat by the window. A dressmaker's dummy was clad in a maharajah's robes, which were festooned with pins and bearing the chalk marks that indicated where excess material was to be trimmed. The floor was littered with offcuts of fabric and twists of discarded thread.

Elizabeth managed to find seating for all of us: a couple of chairs and a stool from the curtained-off booth that served as a changing area. She boiled a kettle on a small coal-fired potbellied stove which also heated the room. The tea was good, fragrant but rich. I complimented her on it, and she replied that tea was her great weakness.

"I cannot abide anything but the highest-grade leaves, doctor," she said. "Drinking fresh-picked chai in India spoiled me. I have a tin of this orange pekoe Darjeeling blend posted to me once a month by a specialist importer up in Kensington. It is my one small treat for myself."

Holmes, impatient as ever with the niceties of social intercourse, said, "You claim you hoped to save Patrick, Miss Vandenbergh. How would spurning him achieve that?"

"I suppose spurning him was what I did," Elizabeth said. "But it was for his own good. I could perhaps have gone about it in a gentler, kinder way, but my plan was to startle Patrick, to bring him to his senses. I told him curtly that he was to leave me alone and never darken my door again. It was a calculated and I may say selfless strategy. I knew his feelings would be hurt, and deeply, but I had to risk it. I had already delivered several ultimatums. I had to resort to drastic measures."

"This was in connection with his decision to forgo Cambridge?"

"Oh no. Nothing to do with that. Admittedly it was silly of him to pass up a place at university for me, but it was a dramatic, romantic gesture typical of a young man. Patrick regarded it as a demonstration of the level of his affection. And I was flattered, although I was convinced, too, that distance need not be an obstacle to us and that I would be able to talk him into changing his mind, given time. Cambridge was not a bone of contention between us as it was between him and his father. There would have been ways around it."

"Then something else drove a wedge between the two of you."

"Perhaps I should relate first how Patrick and I met."

"If it has some bearing on your later estrangement from him."

"It does, I think. I first laid eyes on Patrick in June, when he called in at the shop wishing to buy a bespoke costume. It was an unusual commission, quite challenging, hardly run-of-the-mill."

"What sort of costume?"

"The Egyptian god Horus."

"Horus," I said. "Is he the one with the jackal's head?"

"No, that's Anubis, god of the dead," said Elizabeth. "Horus has the head of a falcon. He's a hunting god, among other things. I asked Patrick what he wanted the costume for, and he answered in vague terms. A fancy dress ball, I believe is what he said. I took his measurements, even though I am quite skilled at gauging clothing sizes at a glance. You, Mr Holmes, take an eleven collar, do you not? And you, Dr Watson, buy your trousers in a thirty-six waist, although I think a thirty-eight would be more appropriate."

I harrumphed, but she had me bang to rights. My wife had let out all my waistbands as far as they could go, and still the seams strained. However, I refused to admit defeat and order roomier trousers. It was a matter of personal pride.

Elizabeth continued, "Patrick said that money was no object where the costume was concerned. The more opulent, the better. So I made sure to use plenty of gold crêpe de Chine silk and rich blue and white cotton with a high thread count. The outfit consisted of a wrap-around pleated skirt, gathered at the front, and a variety of amulets, armlets and wristlets. The falcon head I constructed out of papier-mâché, painted white and black with gold accents. Finally there was a kind of criss-crossing assemblage of metal discs worn on the chest and attaching at the back. It's called a gorgerine. For that I stitched together hundreds of silvery sequins in a featherlike design on a crinoline backing. Using wood and gold paint I then fashioned a staff and ankh for the wearer to carry. They're Horus's signature symbolic regalia.

"In all, I fulfilled the commission rather well, and Patrick seemed pleased. But he seemed more interested in me than in the costume I had created. He was smitten. I knew the signs. And it was mutual. He was a darling boy, so good-looking, so fresh.

"I fought my emotions. I wrestled with my conscience. But

even after he had taken the costume home Patrick kept coming back to the shop, day after day, on the flimsiest of pretexts. Once he claimed a button had fallen off his blazer as he was passing, and would I mind sewing it back on? I could tell that the button had been detached by force, but I played along. He would stay, and we would chat.

"Soon he was explicitly declaring his ardour, and I – I resisted at first, but in the end could not demur. Even though he was a decade my junior, even though I knew people might frown, I reciprocated his advances. After all, had I not made a pact with myself that my own desires should come before all else? And, gentlemen, believe me, love is that little bit sweeter when there is an element of the forbidden to it, and when it carries within it the seeds of its own downfall. I knew what Patrick and I were entering into could not last indefinitely. Everything stood against us. I was determined, however, to enjoy it while I could and cherish the whole doomed impossibility of it."

I must confess that, had I been in Patrick Mallinson's shoes, I would have found Elizabeth Vandenbergh a hard proposition to resist. In my youth I had always found there to be something highly alluring about slightly older women. That greater experience of life, that graciousness that comes with maturity – it lent them a lustre and a ripeness which girls my own age seemed comparatively lacking in.

"Our first month together was bliss," Elizabeth said. "In fact, most of the summer seemed golden. Picnics on the clifftop. Ambles through the park. Clandestine trysts after nightfall. Patrick was attentive and enthusiastic. He learned much under my tutelage and, in every respect, became a man."

"You refer to matters of the boudoir," said Holmes.

"If you find my talk too frank, sir, you must understand that I belong to a different generation of females than you are used to. In these days of Women's Suffrage my gender has grown both more outspoken and more plainspoken. I will not apologise for that, especially mere months after Miss Emily Davison gave her life for the cause at the Epsom Derby. Our assertiveness is symptomatic of a timely shift towards equality, long overdue."

"I am no hidebound prude, Miss Vandenbergh. On the contrary, I welcome both the emancipation of women and a more relaxed approach to subjects normally considered taboo in polite company. I have, in my lifetime, seen sights which have left me now more or less unshockable. I could cite you numerous cases I have solved whose nature precludes Watson from recording them for publication in any respectable periodical, and if those experiences have taught me anything, it is that human depravity, like fungus, flourishes best in dark places. It is one of my hopes for this new century of ours that it sees people less inclined to hide their lusts in shame but rather allows them to acknowledge them overtly. All of us would benefit from less repression of the primal urges. Is that not what the neurologist Freud has been telling us?"

"You impress me, sir."

"You honour me by saying so, madam. But back to business. At some point during your enchanted summer together, things turned sour between you and Patrick. Is that right?"

"It began when Patrick missed one of our assignations. That was not like him. A note arrived at my flat the morning after, tendering his regrets. He had been unavoidably detained, he said. I thought nothing of it the first time, but then it happened again the following day. When we next met, I gave Patrick to know that he should not trifle with me. If he was no longer interested in pursuing our affair – if indeed he had found someone else, someone more appropriate – he should simply say so and there would be an end of it. 'An old maid like me,' I told him, 'cannot be expected to live at the mercy of her beau's whims.'"

"Old maid!" I snorted. "Hardly."

"Doctor, your gallantry is appreciated, but even by modern standards that is what I am. At any rate, Patrick was keen to make amends, and for a time all was as before. If anything, he was more assiduous than ever in his devotion to me."

"He offered no excuse for his failure to appear both times?" said Holmes.

Elizabeth shook her head. "I assumed he had been distracted in that way that young men are apt to be. Something had caught his fancy and he had lost track of the time. Then came the visit from his father."

"Mr Mallinson senior had got wind of your and Patrick's affair."

"An acquaintance of his had spied Patrick and me about town together. Mr Mallinson dropped by the shop and, in the plainest terms possible, advised me to leave his son alone. He did not want me ruining Patrick's prospects, matrimonial and otherwise. He said I was not a good match for him. A 'provincial shop girl' is what he called me, conveniently overlooking the fact that I am the owner of this business and that Patrick, for all his expensive education, was no less a product of the provinces than I am. Furthermore, I can trace my ancestry back to a family of respectable Dutch merchants, one branch of which emigrated to his country during the sixteenth century. I wonder if Mr Mallinson can lay claim to a lineage any more distinguished than mine."

"He affects a high-born diction," said Holmes, "but a stray flattened vowel here and there, and the occasional glottal stop, attest to humbler origins."

"I noticed that too, hence my scathing comment. I informed Mr Mallinson that Patrick was a grown man and could make his own choices, and also that there was one guaranteed way for a father to push a son closer to a woman he deems unacceptable, and that was to disapprove of her openly. This enraged Mr Mallinson, although he did not express his ire through violence or vituperation but instead through an offer of cold, hard cash.

"'How much would it cost,' he asked me, 'for you to walk out of Patrick's life forever?'

"'More than you could afford,' was my retort.

"'Every man has his price,' he said, 'and more so every woman.'

"'But this particular woman is not for sale.'

"'It would be a sum large enough for you to turn this failing enterprise of yours around,' he said, 'or even to close it down and relocate comfortably elsewhere.'

"'I was born in Eastbourne,' I said, 'and here I shall die.'

"He could see I was not to be bribed or browbeaten, and left in a state of high dudgeon. I now knew why Patrick had let me down on those two occasions. He had been in difficulties with his father. Craig Mallinson had forbidden him from seeing me again, but Patrick had then plucked up the nerve to defy his father's dictates and come anyway. This explained and excused everything – or so I thought."

"However…?"

"However, Mr Holmes, Patrick then defaulted on a rendezvous a third time, and when subsequently he and I met he refused to say why, in spite of my entreaties. I asked if it was his father's doing, and he denied it strenuously. He said his reasons were his own and I was not to pry. Once more I gave him the benefit of the doubt, but there was no question – Patrick had changed. His mood was different. His overall demeanour was not that of the happy-go-lucky boy who had walked into my shop two months earlier. He had become dark, withdrawn, perpetually preoccupied."

"Something was troubling him."

"But I had no notion what, and he would not vouchsafe any sort of explanation or justification. He became markedly more sullen and unforthcoming whenever I pressed him on the subject. For the rest of August we continued our association but it was not the same. I felt I was receiving only part of Patrick's attention. His thoughts were often elsewhere. More than once I told him to go home rather than remain with me. If he was only half present, he might as well not be present at all. Lord, but I have prattled on at such length! I trust I am not boring you, Mr Holmes."

"Not in the least," said my friend. "Can you tell us anything you might know about his brother?"

"Clive, you mean? Alas, I can't help you there. I have not met the man. Patrick would speak of him often, though. He clearly loved him, although there was also an element of strain in the relationship."

"In what way?"

"Simple jealousy, I think. Clive is the golden boy of the family. He was a great success at school and university, both academically and on the playing field, whereas Patrick was only ever an average student and sportsman. Clive helps their father run his mining company. He has an aptitude for business such as Patrick would never have. Patrick was always overshadowed by him even when they were boys, and their father did nothing to mitigate that. One is supposed to love one's children equally, but it's fair to say that Craig Mallinson had a distinct preference for Clive, at Patrick's expense."

"Do you feel that Clive may have had some involvement in the matter of the Horus costume? We know that he presently lives in Egypt."

"It seems hardly likely. Clive has not returned to England for four years. He and Patrick have occasionally communicated in that time, a letter here and there, nothing more. I do know that Clive once invited Patrick to come out and visit him, saying he missed his brother's company, but Patrick declined. Clive's aim may have been to acquaint Patrick with the ins and outs of mining potassium nitrate, sulphur and tantalite, with a view to getting him to take more of an interest in the family business. I doubt it would have worked, though. Patrick was just not that way inclined. Oh!"

Elizabeth raised a hand. A thought had just occurred to her.

"The incident of the hieroglyphs," she said. "I should have mentioned that earlier."

Holmes leaned forward in his seat, his hands pressed eagerly together. "Ah, now this sounds intriguing. Pray continue."

"One evening, I happened to observe markings on Patrick's chest and back. They were the traces of symbols that had been drawn on his bare flesh in pen, like some sort of temporary tattoo. He had done his best to scrub them off, but faint ink outlines still lingered, and reddish impressions had been left in his skin. Whoever had drawn them on him had scored him quite hard."

"Egyptian hieroglyphs?"

"That is how they looked to me. Because I had not long ago done research for the Horus costume, I wasn't unfamiliar with Egyptian ideographic script. There were feathers and eyes and open hands and ankhs and scarabs, all the common symbols. At least, in so far as I could discern. The moment I spotted the marks and voiced curiosity about them, Patrick immediately covered himself up with his shirt and denied their existence. My eyes must be deceiving me, he said. But I knew what I had seen. For a while he continued to insist adamantly that there was nothing there. Then he changed his tune somewhat and claimed the marks were just a rash. He had had a bad allergic reaction to a plate of whelks. I think that was the rationalisation he gave me, if memory serves."

"But the marks were no such thing."

"They were shapes, Mr Holmes. Most definitely. Not random, not spontaneous. Patterns. Somebody – maybe Patrick himself – had put them there on his body, and the process would not have been unpainful. I believe Patrick thought they had faded sufficiently that I would not notice them. To try and pass them off as a rash, though – that was just insulting. Whelks! As if I would be idiot enough to fall for that."

"So now you had an inkling that there was more to Patrick's aberrant behaviour than met the eye."

"I cannot honestly say what I thought it might all signify. The costume, the hieroglyphic imprints, Patrick's moodiness... All I knew was that I must do something about it, for my own self-preservation but also for Patrick's sake. I sensed he was heading down a strange, sinister path, becoming embroiled in some arcane business that could prove injurious to him."

"A secret society, you mean? Some sort of cabalistic cult?"

"Perhaps," said Elizabeth. "In hindsight, I realised that he had never again mentioned the 'fancy dress ball' which was his stated reason for ordering the Horus costume. Surely it would have been a grand event, and he had gone to it magnificently attired. Why, then, had he not furnished me with a detailed account of this party? Why had he not alluded to it, or to the costume, so much as once since making the purchase? To allay my misgivings, I asked him if anyone had complimented him on the outfit. That was when he flew into a rage."

"Did he hit you?" I said, bristling. To strike a member of the fairer sex was a cardinal sin in my book, and I would have nothing but contempt for any man who stooped to committing it.

"Goodness me, no. That is not how Patrick was. Not at all. Nor would he have dared, knowing I would give him back twice as good as I got. I have been a student of *kalaripayattu*, remember? There are over two hundred vulnerable pressure points on the body, any of which, hit correctly, can cause pain, temporary paralysis or even death. I am not saying that I am a master of the necessary techniques, but I'm sure I can give a good account of myself in a fight."

"I do not doubt it, madam," I said.

"Nonetheless Patrick harangued me and was wholeheartedly indignant, as though my question had been no casual, innocuous enquiry but an insult which struck to the very fibre of his being. Then he stormed out. Later he returned, ever so contrite, clutching a bunch of chrysanthemums from the florists, and we were reconciled. But it wasn't long before he grew withdrawn again, and I knew it was time to pull up sharply on the reins."

"Those ultimatums you spoke of," said Holmes.

"I gave him every chance. I told him he had a clear choice: come clean about whatever unsavoury habits he was dabbling in, or it was over between us. Patrick maintained that he had nothing to hide, he was merely tired, under strain, that was all. He and his father were trying to thrash out his future, he said. Things would settle one way or another in due course. But my threshold of tolerance for his shenanigans, already low to begin with, kept lowering further. At last I knew it was make-or-break time."

"The sudden shock of rejection would, you hoped, jolt the boy out of his weird, disordered mindset."

"I loved him. I thought it was the right course of action. How could I know, Mr Holmes – how could I even have suspected – that it would turn out so dreadfully wrong?"

CHAPTER FOURTEEN

A World of Sordid Ends and Human Blunder

"Well, Watson?" said Holmes as we left Tripp's Costumiers. "Your views on Miss Vandenbergh?"

"I admire her forthrightness and fire," I replied, adding, "And I would not say she was unattractive."

"Yes, you seemed quite taken with her."

"You seemed quite taken with her yourself."

"Ah, my friend, you know as well as I do that there has been, and will be, only ever one woman for me."

He was referring, of course, to *the* woman, Irene Adler, the erstwhile opera singer and sometime adventuress whose deftness in outwitting him a quarter of a century earlier had earned her his undying admiration and whose name he would habitually cite whenever the subject of the fairer sex arose. Against the vivacious and intelligent Miss Adler, all other females were judged and, in Holmes's estimation, found wanting.

"Although," he continued, "I would go so far as to say that Elizabeth Vandenbergh certainly runs her a close second."

"High praise indeed."

"Her account of her relationship with Patrick Mallinson has muddied the waters somewhat, wouldn't you agree?"

"I would," I said. "Do you think that Patrick Mallinson was a member of a heathen cult of some description?"

"There is a *prima facie* case for believing as much, yes."

"Something like Madame Blavatsky's Theosophists?"

"I am thinking more of Aleister Crowley and his Thelema society. You have heard of the fellow, of course."

"Crowley? A little, and none of it good," I said. "Isn't he some sort of devil worshipper and libertine?"

"So they say. The *Looking Glass* is forever attacking him on those grounds. 'One of the most blasphemous and cold-blooded villains of modern times,' it has called him, and that's among the less scathing epithets. It also implies that the degeneracy of his practices in his so-called temples is equalled only by the debauchery of his activities in the bedroom. It says that he pursues a doctrine of 'unbridled lust and licence.'"

"The *Looking Glass*, eh? I didn't realise you read such scandal rags."

Holmes smiled wryly. "When the latest *Punch* is unavailable in the dentist's waiting room, sometimes I err towards less edifying and more sensational reading matter. Crowley is also a one-time resident of Eastbourne, did you know that?"

"I confess I did not."

"Yes, he stayed here in the late 1880s as a lad, after having been thrown out of both Malvern College and Tonbridge School. He studied at Eastbourne College and also under a Plymouth Brethren tutor in the town, and famously climbed Beachy Head."

"Well, I suppose that beats falling off Beachy Head – although in Crowley's case that mightn't have been a bad thing."

"A libertine he undoubtedly is, but a devil worshipper? That depends. According to his writings, of which there are many and of which few are readable, let alone intelligible, his personal belief system has been influenced by the occultism of the Hermetic Order of the Golden Dawn, and also by the religious practices of Ancient Egypt."

"Ah. A link with the hieroglyphs on Patrick Mallinson's body and the Horus costume he commissioned."

"Yes. Crowley contends that he received psychic messages from an entity connected with Horus while he and his wife were staying in Cairo at the turn of the century. He wrote it all down in his *Book of the Law*, which he regards as a work of prophecy. He espouses a new era of enlightenment and self-determination for mankind, an 'Aeon of Horus', in which we throw off the shackles of patriarchal religions like Christianity and Judaism and become masters of our own destiny. Crowley's ritual magick – which he spells with a 'k' on the end in order to set it apart from any other kind of magic, including stage conjuring – is a means of communing with the powers of the cosmos and also of raising his own spiritual consciousness. His views may be heretical but they do not, as many claim, have any Satanic connotations."

"Nonetheless he does not sound like a man I would much care to meet. Did Patrick fall in with this Thelema lot, then? And could that account for his deteriorating conduct over the course of the summer?"

"Occult societies like Crowley's tend to lure in the disaffected and the disenchanted, and those with money as well, for fleecing adherents is one of the primary goals of sham religions. In both respects, disaffection and money, Patrick Mallinson fits the bill. And yet, to the best of my knowledge, there is no Thelema temple in the vicinity."

"With all due respect, Holmes, secret societies have a habit of being, well, secret. Just because you aren't aware of the existence of a Thelema temple round these parts doesn't mean there isn't one."

"Granted," said my companion, "which is why our next port of call is the police station, where I shall pick the brains of our new bosom friend Inspector Tasker."

"Pick his brains? I doubt that will take long."

Holmes chuckled. "Even a barren orchard may bear a single piece of fruit."

Tasker welcomed us into his office with no great show of delight. Holmes set to quizzing him about the presence of any secret societies or esoteric religious cults in Eastbourne.

"Aside from the Freemasons, you mean?" said Tasker. "Not that I'd call them secret. The local lodge is just down the road on South Street. You can't miss it. It's the one with 'Masonic Hall' painted in big black capitals above the door. Not that I hold with all that trouser-rolling malarkey myself."

"You are not 'on the square'?" said Holmes. "Rare for a policeman."

"Some coppers, the ambitious ones, see Freemasonry as a way of getting a leg up through the ranks, but me, I'd rather ascend by merit and the sweat of my own brow. As for religious cults, there's a synagogue over on Susans Road. Or do the Jews not match that description either?"

"I'm after less orthodox forms of worship."

"We've our fair share of table turners and mediums. How about that? Esoteric enough for you? Barely a street in Eastbourne doesn't have its own recreational spiritualist holding Sunday-afternoon salon séances. Get yourself invited to just about any posh tea party, Mr Holmes, and chances are you'll soon be holding hands in a circle and contacting the other side. Not forgetting the gypsy fortune teller on the pier. Cross her palm with silver, and you can bet the mists will be clearing in no time and messages coming through from the great beyond."

"I have the feeling, inspector, that you are not taking me entirely seriously."

"Whatever gave you that impression? On the contrary, I am being inordinately helpful, per Mr Mallinson's request. Has anyone been such a font of useful information as I?"

Holmes, with the utmost forbearance, changed tack. "Might you be so good as to tell me if the coroner's report on Patrick Mallinson is in?"

"I might."

"And is it?"

"It is."

"May we then see it?" Holmes said through clenched teeth. He looked tempted to punch the man, and I would not have held him back. Nothing would have pleased me more than to see a fist planted in the inspector's smug, obdurate face.

"I have it here somewhere," Tasker said, and proceeded to search the drawers of his desk at some length, before turning to rifle through the files and case folders which lined the shelves behind him. All the while he whistled tunelessly.

Eventually Holmes said, "Could that be it? The document sitting on the desk blotter right in front of you?"

Tasker turned back and feigned surprise. "Why, how observant of you. There it was all along. Silly me. It came in not half an hour ago. Ink's still wet on it, almost."

Holmes perused the coroner's findings, I reading over his shoulder. The autopsy had turned up little that we didn't already know. Judging by body livor, temperature, skin texture and degree of decomposition, the deceased had been in the sea for at least thirty-six hours before washing up on shore. There was seawater in the lungs, though not in any substantial quantity, suggesting that it had leaked in post mortem rather than been inhaled. The neck was broken, almost certainly the result of violent impact with rocks or the sea's surface.

"In sum," the report concluded, "death came about as a

consequence of injuries sustained from a fall from a height of 250 feet or more. The injuries are congruent with an act of voluntary or involuntary ejection from the cliffs at Beachy Head and environs. Instantaneous cessation of cerebral and cardiovascular function would have ensued on termination of said fall, such that the deceased did not drown but was dead upon the very moment of immersion."

"He fell, he died," Tasker said, spreading out his hands. "There's not much more to add."

"Except, how did he fall?" said Holmes. "And why?"

"Did he jump," I chimed in, "or was he pushed? That's a point the coroner raised – 'voluntary or *involuntary* ejection' – and one we haven't addressed yet." I realised that Holmes would have already been entertaining the idea of murder as a possible cause of death for young Patrick Mallinson. I know that I was always slower on the uptake than him, but I was also always slower to think the worst.

"Given young Patrick's disturbed frame of mind," said Tasker, "surely the question doesn't need asking, doctor, let alone answering. Patrick Mallinson had no enemies that we know of. He was universally well-liked. Why would anyone do him in?"

"His father has enemies," said Holmes. "He told us that yesterday. Rivals in the same industry as him."

"You think somebody may have murdered the son in order to – what? Enact revenge upon the father? Unhinge him? Destabilise his business empire?"

"It is not beyond the realms of possibility. Worse acts have been perpetrated in the name of profit."

"And where, exactly, do these cults and secret societies of yours fit in?" Tasker said. "Is there some dark Satanic conspiracy brewing against Craig Mallinson? Could it also involve Indian thuggees, perchance? Exotic poison on the tip of a blowpipe dart? A trained mongoose?"

The inspector's sneer of contempt was obnoxious to behold. Seldom had Sherlock Holmes been mocked with quite such disdain, and by an officer of the law, no less, someone who ought to have appreciated that the two of them shared a common cause.

"Oh yes, all those exotic, enigmatic crimes you used to investigate," Tasker went on, "all those twisting, turning cases. But this, Mr Holmes, isn't that world of yours – the world of Dr Watson's elaborately constructed narratives. This is the real world, *my* world, where a death is either a tragic accident or the end-product of a set of mundane circumstances. A world of sordid ends and human blunder. Nothing more, nothing less. And you and your outlandish hypotheses have no part in it. Now, if you will kindly show yourselves to the front door, gentlemen, I have work to be attending to, proper police work, and plenty of it. Thank you."

Outside on tree-lined Meads Road I gave vent to a torrent of invective about Tasker which I shall not reproduce here.

Holmes took a more sanguine view. "Irritating and arrogant though he is, Tasker has at least confirmed that the Thelema angle is not worth pursuing. If some disciple of Crowley's were operating in Eastbourne, Tasker would know. A man of his ilk keeps his ear to the ground. I doubt there is much that goes on in this town that he is not apprised of."

"How you can speak well of him when he holds you in such low regard, Holmes – it beggars belief."

"Where you see scorn, Watson, I see envy. Tasker feels threatened by me, so his instinct is to belittle and belabour."

"I could quite happily belabour him – with this." I brandished the sturdy hickory walking-stick which I had lately taken to carrying with me on longer jaunts.

"No, keeping relations cordial with Tasker is paramount," said Holmes. "We may have to call upon him for a favour in the near future – indeed the immediate future."

The import of this remark was lost on me then, and all did not become clear until much later in the day. During the afternoon I settled down on Holmes's sofa with a book, *The Insidious Dr Fu-Manchu*, the just-published account of the efforts of former colonial police commissioner Sir Denis Nayland Smith to thwart the machinations of an Oriental mastermind hell-bent on bringing about the downfall of civilised Western society. As I turned the pages I reflected upon how Nayland Smith always seemed to fall foul of Fu-Manchu's traps and schemes, relying on luck and his fists to get him and his somewhat colourless colleague Dr Petrie out of trouble. It was a far cry from Holmes's more artful and light-footed approach to tackling villainy.

Presently my eyes became heavy and I fell into a deep sleep, which lasted until well after sunset.

I awoke to the sound of Holmes bustling about the sitting room, opening cupboards and drawers, fetching out matches and lanterns.

At first I thought I must still be asleep and dreaming, for also present in the room with me was none other than Reptilio the Human Cobra.

"Holmes!" I spluttered. "What is the meaning of this? Why have you invited this – this ruffian into your home? How is it even possible that he's free from jail? What is going on here?"

"Calm yourself, Watson," said Holmes. "Think of your blood pressure. Reptilio – or Caleb Smith, to give him his proper name – has been released from police custody on temporary licence and on my recognisance. Tasker took some persuading to sanction it, believe me, but I was at pains to remind him of his pledge to Craig Mallinson, and eventually he relented."

"I took some persuading too, to be honest," said Reptilio. "Help the bloke who nailed me for the Barraclough's job? But Mr Holmes told me that if I did as asked, it would go well for me at my trial. In return for my co-operation he'd be willing to vouch on my behalf before the magistrate, and I might be in for a shorter stretch."

"Well, I… I…" I stammered. "I don't know what to make of it."

"Then don't make anything of it," said Holmes. "Just fortify yourself with some food. There's bread and cheese on the chiffonier in the kitchen and cold gala pie in the larder. Then gird your loins for a midnight excursion."

"A midnight…?"

I could see it in Holmes's grey eyes. They held a glint of excitement and anticipation that I recognised all too well.

The game, without question, was once more afoot.

CHAPTER FIFTEEN

A Living Lockpick

We hiked, the three of us, uphill to the turnoff for the Jevington road, which we then followed inland for two or three miles. The night was moonless, windless and clear, the stars out in profusion. An owl screeched, and a fox answered with its hoarse bark – lonely and forlorn sounds, both.

We diverted off the road onto a chalk footpath that glimmered like a silvery winding thread in the darkness. Holmes seemed to know his way around these rural byways as well as he had the back alleys and rookeries of London.

Soon we were in a forest, which enclosed us in primordial pitch-black silence and stillness. Here we deployed the lanterns. Tree roots underfoot were a perpetual tripping hazard. We moved in fragile haloes of light.

Reptilio began to talk, perhaps to combat the oppressively brooding atmosphere of the forest. He told me that he was not a bad person, just somebody whom providence had not given a fair shake. He had been a foundling, and his early life was a tale of orphanages, brutal education at the hands of strict Jesuit priests, and bouts of beggary, starvation and indigence, until his natural talent for serpent-like elasticity had brought him to the attention of McMahon the circus owner. He confided in me that he strongly suspected he was the illegitimate son of a nobleman, conceived with an actress. His father – a duke or an earl, he was sure – had no knowledge of his existence, else he would have come looking for him long ago and set him up in handsome lodgings with a stipend.

I refrained from commenting on the last. I had begun to feel pity for the man, this Caleb Smith. The credible parts of his story would have evoked compassion in even the hardest-hearted, and if his fantasy of aristocratic parentage brought him some comfort in his darker moments, so be it. And yet, that said, there could never be any excuse for criminality. No one need steal for a living while there was honest work, however menial, available.

Holmes instructed us to keep our voices lowered henceforth. "We are nearing our destination," he said. "Douse the lanterns. Follow me closely."

We arrived at the forest's edge, where a wooden post-and-rail fence bordered a large field.

"Whose property is this?" I whispered.

"Craig Mallinson's, of course. Who else?"

I had suspected as much but was still somewhat taken aback. "And we are here why precisely?"

"To gather evidence."

"Of what?"

"Malfeasance."

"I see. But this is looking awfully like an act of trespass."

"Wait," said Reptilio. "Did somebody just say trespass?"

"What did you think we were going to do, Mr Smith?" said Holmes. "Here we are, skulking about the countryside in the dead of night. Surely you must have had some inkling of the ultimate purpose of our journey."

"Well, yes, but you never said nothing about anything illegal."

"Why else would I have enlisted your aid if it wasn't to exploit your unique properties and the egregious use you have put them to?"

"I thought you were after a demonstration. But now I'm thinking you need me for breaking and entering."

"And you would be correct."

"But... But I'm supposed to get on the right side of the coppers by *breaking* the law? Where's the sense in that?"

"No one other than the three of us need ever know what transpires here tonight," said Holmes. "Perform as required, and I will back you to the hilt at your trial as promised, without ever breathing a word about any felony I may have asked you to conduct on my behalf. You have my solemn vow on that. Watson's full complicity you may also be assured of."

Reptilio was not placated. "But what'll I tell Inspector Tasker tomorrow, if he asks what I've been doing? He'll have a fit!"

"We shall concoct some suitable lie together. Watson is a great storyteller. I'm sure he can come up with a convincing fabrication. He does it often enough when turning my exploits into saleable fictions."

"I do not," I harrumphed. "I may embellish the truth on occasion, but fabricate? Holmes, you wound me."

"I don't know," said Reptilio dubiously. "It still seems wrong."

"Oh, this is not the time for scruples," snapped Holmes. "Perhaps if I were to increase the incentive... Watson? How much money do you have on you?"

"Ten shillings, I think."

"And I have fifteen. What do you say, Smith? Will twenty-five shillings sweeten the pot sufficiently?"

Simple greed lit up Reptilio's eyes, and he nodded to indicate that he would be able to overcome any compunction he had, in return for such a sum of money. Then he motioned with his fingers, the gesture of someone who would go no further without proof of earnest, and Holmes and I were obliged to take out our pocketbooks and hand over all the banknotes therein.

Reptilio's compliance now assured, we straddled the fence and proceeded to cross the field, which was broad, flattish and grassy, with here and there a thick tussock or a clump of thistle.

Halfway across, Holmes crouched to inspect a queer circular impression on the ground.

"What do you make of this, Watson?"

It was roughly the same diameter as a football and appeared to be a scorch mark of some kind. The grass within its circumference was blackened and brittle.

"Has a brazier stood here?" I wondered. "A stove?"

"And look, here is another one," Holmes said a few paces further on. "And another. They are positioned at intervals of fifteen yards, I'd estimate."

"Evidence of some pagan fire ritual?" I ventured, bearing in mind the younger Mallinson's Horus costume and Holmes's talk earlier that day about occult societies.

"Or something altogether less primitive," said my companion, but he would not be drawn to expand on this remark. Sherlock Holmes, as my readers will know all too well, could be highly reticent when it came to sharing his insights. More often than not he would wait until the most dramatic moment to do so, when the revelation would show him off to his best advantage or wrongfoot an opponent. He had a theatrical streak to rival Sir Henry Irving.

At the far end of the field lay a brick barn. It hulked up against the starlight, impressively large and impregnable-looking all the way to its pitched roof. Some distance beyond, through a stand of oaks, I could make out the lights of a house. This I took to be Settleholm Manor, Craig Mallinson's country seat. Despite the lateness of the hour, lamps were lit in several rooms, and I imagined the owner stalking the corridors and hallways, afflicted by the self-lacerating insomnia of the recently bereaved.

Thinking of Mallinson, I wondered what Holmes hoped to unearth in the barn and what relevance it had to the case.

As if reading my thoughts, Holmes said, "This is where he keeps his biplane. I have seen it once when passing by. It was sitting immediately outside, with Mallinson himself tinkering with the engine. The field serves as an airfield, affording him just enough room to effect take-off and landing."

He relit his lantern, narrowing the shutters so that only a thin beam of illumination was emitted. With it, he examined the large, heavy padlock which secured the hasp which in turn secured the barn doors.

"Ah yes," he said. "Alas, it is a Chubb four-lever detector, the bane of lock pickers everywhere, designed to jam automatically if anything but the correct key is inserted. Even if my fingers were as nimble and sensitive as they used to be, tickling open this particular brand of padlock would be the work of hours, perhaps even days. Which is why I have brought along someone for whom no gap, however slender, is impassable. Smith will be effectively our living lockpick. All we need do is apply brute force to one of the doors, like so, pushing it inwards as far as the bolt will allow. Watson? Your help, please. Put your shoulder to this with me, will you?"

I weighed in beside him, shoving against the door with all my might. Between us we contrived to create an aperture of perhaps seven inches in width.

"Quick, Smith!" Holmes urged. "Watson and I cannot keep this up forever. Slide yourself through while you can."

Reptilio inveigled his body into the gap in that sinuous, sinewy way of his. For several moments he appeared to be stuck, but with a bit of torsion and deft manoeuvring he contrived to wriggle further in, and then all at once, like a mouse into a crack in the wainscoting, he was inside, gone.

Holmes passed the lantern through to him. "You are my eyes now, Smith."

Reptilio retreated into the depths of the barn and returned almost immediately bearing a lump of firewood. This he inserted between the doors to keep them wedged apart, thus relieving Holmes and me of the strain of pushing.

"What do you want me to look at?" he asked.

"The biplane," came the reply. "I want you to inspect it carefully from end to end, every inch of it."

"To find what?"

"Anything that appears out of place. Anything that strikes you as abnormal."

"Abnormal?" Reptilio said. "I don't know the first ruddy thing about flying. How am I supposed to tell what's abnormal and what's not?"

"Try nonetheless. Make a mental record of all that you see, then report back."

Reptilio disappeared back into the barn, and was there for the next few minutes. Occasionally I caught glimpses of the Grahame-White as he shone the lantern beam over its framework. He was doing his best to be methodical, in accordance with Holmes's request: first the biplane's nose, then the wings, the cockpit, the propeller, all the way to the tailfin and back again.

The night's chill began to seep into my bones as Holmes and I waited. Many a long vigil had the two of us shared over the course of our acquaintance, staking out a room, a house, a lonely stretch of road. But I was older now, and more susceptible to cold and cramp. I could not stand stationary for lengthy periods as once I had been able. I was obliged to rub my hands together to warm them, and stamp my feet to keep the circulation going.

This irked Holmes but he withheld from voicing complaint. He himself flexed his fingers now and then, and shifted almost imperceptibly from foot to foot. His powers of self-regulation were tremendous even in old age. He once told me that, as old age encroached, plenty of fresh honey and royal jelly helped keep him in trim and preserve his stamina and constitution. "As a dietary supplement, Watson, nothing can beat the produce of the little striped gangs in my beehives." He had indeed devoted an entire chapter of his magnum opus, *The Practical Handbook of Bee Culture, with some Observations upon the Segregation of the Queen*, to the physiological benefits of honey, and had lectured on it to an audience made up of apiculturists and dieticians at the Royal Society, to some acclaim.

At last the discomfort grew intolerable, and I said, "Does he have to be much longer? I am anxious about being discovered here, loitering on someone else's property, but I am still more anxious about developing pneumonia. Damp night air is not kind to the pleural membranes, you know."

"Smith is being thorough," Holmes replied. "We must applaud him for that, and exercise patience."

"Your patience will render us hospital patients if we're not careful."

"If you're well enough to make dreadful puns, old chap, you're well enough to stay put a few minutes more."

"I am sure my puns would improve were I not –"

"*Hsst!*" Holmes dropped his voice to a barely audible whisper. "Did you hear that?"

I shook my head.

He cast his gaze about, peering into the darkness. I likewise scanned the vicinity. The grassy field, the low black band of forest, the distant sparks of the manor house lights… Nothing. Nothing unusual. Nothing different.

"Perhaps you were mist–" I began, but Holmes stopped my mouth with his fingertips.

It was then that I grew truly concerned. Thanks to my exposure to the din of rifle and cannon fire in Afghanistan, my hearing had always been less acute than Holmes's. If his ears had detected some unexpected sound, then I had no doubt but that it must exist.

His next four words were as faint as sighs, yet for all that they sent a shudder through me.

"We are not alone."

"Someone is watching?" I hissed.

"Yes. Someone practised in the art of stealth. He is but twenty yards from us."

The only place of concealment at that range was the stand of oaks.

"No. Do not look in his direction," Holmes warned.

"But he must realise we know he is watching."

"Not necessarily. Keep perfectly still. The lantern light in the barn is giving away Smith's presence, but we two are in the barn's shadow. He may not have noticed us yet."

My hand went reflexively to my pocket, groping for the service revolver that was not there and had not been there in nigh on a decade. I felt its absence more keenly then than if it had been a lost limb. How often had I relied on the gun to rescue me from trouble? I owed it my life several times over, all the way back to Kabul where I stopped one of the Khan's men in his tracks while I was in the midst of tending to an injured Sikh infantryman during the Siege of the Sherpur Cantonment. The Sikh later died of his wounds, and I would have joined him in oblivion had that sword-wielding Afghan maniac managed to plunge the blade of his *pulwar* into my breast, as he was so eager to do.

Sans revolver, I had no choice but to stand motionless as a statue. Holmes did likewise. Both of us hardly dared breathe.

Our only hope, as I saw it, was that our observer, whoever he was, did not belong on Mallinson's land any more than we did.

Perhaps he was a poacher and was surprised to find someone else engaged in nocturnal activities that were obviously as illicit as his own. His natural impulse would be to beat a hasty retreat. Certainly he would have no inclination to confront or challenge us.

This line of thinking, though mildly cheering, could not mitigate the fact that with poachers there was a tendency towards firearms.

Moments ticked by, and I waited for Holmes to relax and lower his guard, a signal that I might do so too. The tension that I was feeling at least made me forget about the cold and its effect on my person. With my heart racing and the adrenaline pumping, I was in fact almost warm.

Inside the barn, Reptilio had finally completed his examination of the biplane. He came to the doors to announce this fact, and though he addressed us *sotto voce*, he may as well have been shouting at the top of his lungs. Sound carries far at night, and our observer doubtless had his ears pricked, so that all at once he knew that the lantern-carrying man in the barn was not alone – he had associates outside.

In short, Reptilio had unwittingly given the game away.

"No alternative," said Holmes. "We must make a run for it."

He seized my elbow in order to drag me along with him. Meanwhile a startled Reptilio demanded to know what the matter was.

Then, from the oaks, a rough voice ordered us to halt, and the command was reinforced by the deafening blast of a shotgun.

CHAPTER SIXTEEN

THE GAMEKEEPER

Buckshot peppered the wall of the barn just above our heads. Holmes and I froze to the spot.

"And there's plenty more where that came from," the voice by the oaks growled. "Don't move a muscle, any of you. That includes you in the barn. This is a full-choke shotgun and I'm a damned good shot. I can clip a partridge at sixty yards, and I can take your head off even through that narrow gap."

A figure appeared from amid the trees, moving with easy, swaggering purpose. His shotgun, a double-barrelled twelve-bore, was aimed at us, levelled unwaveringly at our chests. I made out a bowler hat, knee-length boots and a leather pouch slung at the hip. The man's attire and authoritative bearing made it clear that this was no poacher. Rather, it was the poacher's nemesis, a gamekeeper.

"Devil knows what business you three are up to with Mr Mallinson's aeroplane," he continued, "but whether it's stealing or sabotage, you aren't getting away with it."

"It's neither, as a matter of fact," said Holmes. "We're acquainted with Craig Mallinson, as it happens, and if you were just to take us to him, I'm sure we could straighten the whole thing out."

"Acquainted, eh? Is that the truth?"

"Yes, so there's no need to keep pointing that weapon at us," I said. "This is all a misunderstanding, and we should deal with it like civilised people."

"Oh, I think there's *every* need to keep my gun trained on you," the gamekeeper said. Now that he was close to us I could see he was a medium-height fellow with a stocky build and extravagant muttonchop whiskers. His eyes were small and ferocious, and his nose was longer and sharper-tipped even than Holmes's own. The animal he most resembled physiologically was perhaps his commonest prey – a fox. "For all your fine gentlemanly talk, you look like squirrels ready to scarper. I don't intend to allow that to happen."

"You have one cartridge remaining," Holmes pointed out. "There are three of us. No matter how swiftly you reload, at least two of us would be able to get away."

"One of you dead is good enough." The gamekeeper swivelled the gun from me to Holmes to Reptilio in quick succession. "Which one wants the face full of pellets? Come on. You choose. It's no bother to me which."

"Very well," said Holmes. "You have us at your mercy. At the least, may we meet with Mr Mallinson, as I asked? You could march us to the house at gunpoint, and I give you my word we won't attempt to flee."

The gamekeeper cocked his head. "Your word? And is that worth much?"

"I am," said Holmes, "Sherlock Holmes. That must count for something."

"Not for me it doesn't. Never heard of you."

"Obviously no great reader," Holmes muttered aside to me. "Probably illiterate."

"What's that?" said the gamekeeper, scowling.

"Nothing, my good man. Nothing."

"Remember who has the gun here."

"How could we possibly forget?"

"So don't go cheeking me. I kill you, and no court of law will convict me. It's legitimate defence of property."

"Yes, don't antagonise him, Holmes," I said. "I for one prefer my brains where they are, in my head."

"Me too," said Reptilio. "I'm not with them, by the way," he told the gamekeeper. "I mean, I am, but not *with* them, if you follow."

The gamekeeper's frown said he didn't.

"I mean, yes, we're all of us in the same location, together in that sense, but I didn't come willingly. They forced me into it. Twisted my arm, like."

"You know what?" said the gamekeeper. "I don't care. Come out of the barn, and then we're all going down to the big house to see the boss."

"A capital idea," said Holmes. "Clever of you to think of it. Why didn't I come up with that?"

"Hoy! Quiet, you, Mr Hemlock Jones or whatever your name is. What did I tell you about cheeking me? Any more of your lip and it won't go well for you."

"Of course. One of my rules is that the man with the gun always sets the rules."

"Too right," said the gamekeeper. "Now move, all of you. And no funny business."

CHAPTER SEVENTEEN

Settleholm Manor

Settleholm Manor was a sprawling baronial hall, parts of which dated back to the 1700s. The main body of it was constructed of granite blocks and imposingly crenellated like a castle. Newer brick-built wings extended off to either side. Ivy covered most of its frontage, and the light spilling from the windows of the reception rooms picked out the leaves' autumnal blood-red hue. A large automobile was parked on the drive, a Humberette, its coachwork and brass trim giving off a host of gleaming reflections.

I would not call the manor beautiful by any means. Its size and grandeur, however, could not help but stir up in one a sense of appreciation. A sense of belittlement too, which perhaps was the point. We were all Davids before this architectural Goliath. It was a house designed to impress upon visitors its owner's lofty status and their comparative lowliness.

Up some stone steps we went to the porticoed entrance, and thence indoors, into a galleried hallway that was probably larger in itself than my and Mrs Watson's entire house. Certainly Holmes's cottage could have slotted snugly inside.

A staircase of oak, with matching banisters, swept to the upper storey like a soaring dragon. At its foot two suits of medieval armour stood sentinel, posed with their steel gauntlets resting on the pommels of their inverted swords. Portraits in gilt frames lined the walls, but none of the faces depicted resembled Craig Mallinson's. I imagine the paintings had come with the manor when he purchased it, generations of aristocracy immortalised in oil on canvas, held eternally hostage in their ancestral home, like ghosts.

The gamekeeper positioned Holmes, myself and Reptilio in the centre of the hall's chessboard-patterned floor, using the shotgun much as a shepherd might his crook when rounding up the flock. Then he called out to Mallinson in a loud voice.

"Sir! Intruders for you. What would you have me do with them?"

His employer appeared moments later. Mallinson was fully dressed rather than in nightwear, which bore out the supposition that he had been pacing the manor, unable to sleep; so, too, did his tired, reddened eyes. A black silk armband cinched his left sleeve.

"What's this, Jenks? Intruders you say?"

"Trespassers," the gamekeeper, Jenks, elaborated. "Found 'em snooping around your aeroplane up at the barn. Tampering with it, they seemed to be, and maybe liking to nick it."

"My God," said Mallinson, taking his first good look at us. "It's you, Mr Holmes. And your friend. And who's this other queer-looking fellow?"

"Someone who's got nothing to do with them, that's who," said Reptilio. "An innocent victim."

"Innocent to the tune of twenty-five shillings," I groused.

"And I am *not* queer-looking," Reptilio added, pouting.

"Jenks, drop your gun," said Mallinson. "These men are no threat to us."

"But sir, I caught them at it," Jenks protested. "Red-handed, as it were. Crept up on 'em and halted 'em in their tracks with a warning shot."

"That would account for the report I heard from out in the grounds just now. I assumed you were potting rabbits. But, whatever these men were doing, I will not have you waving that thing at them." Mallinson grasped the shotgun by the barrel and pushed it downward so that it pointed at the floor. "Could go off by accident, and then where would we be?"

Reptilio sighed audibly in relief, and I cannot deny that I felt like doing the same.

"We are grateful to you, sir," said Holmes. "And if I may be permitted to explain myself..."

"You'd damned well better had," said Mallinson crisply, "because, while I don't hold with shooting as prestigious a person as yourself, Mr Holmes, the fact remains that you are on my land without invitation and engaged in clandestine shenanigans of some sort, and I am not best pleased. It seems like a damned impertinence, if you ask me."

"I can see that that is how it might appear, but in as much as I am pursuing the matter of your son's death on your behalf, one could argue that I therefore, technically, *am* here by invitation."

"'Son's death'?" said Reptilio with a roll of the eyes. "This just gets worse and worse."

"Don't waste your sophistry on me, Mr Holmes," said Mallinson. "It won't wash. What, so your findings have led you to my door? Is that it?"

"To your aeroplane, strictly speaking. If we're going to be accurate."

"Ah," said the mining magnate. "And is there something about my Grahame-White that is germane to Patrick's death?"

"I wouldn't know. I haven't yet had a chance to confer with my colleague Mr Smith here about the state of the aircraft."

"I didn't see nothing," said Reptilio, addressing Mallinson. "Not a thing, sir. It was just a plane, and I'd be willing to swear that before a beak. Just a big old flying machine. Nothing peculiar about it at all."

"But *you* must reckon there is, Mr Holmes," said Mallinson. "You have suspicions – suspicions that have prompted you to come and take a look at the plane during the dead of night. Why is that, I wonder. Could you not have called round in the daytime and requested to see it? I'd have been more than willing to show you, and then there'd have been no need for any skulduggery, nor for Jenks to abandon his nocturnal patrol of the estate to bring you in."

"My motives were noble, I assure you," said Holmes suavely. "I had no wish to cause you further distress. I have at the moment only the merest glimmering of a theory about how Patrick died, and I hoped to furnish myself with proof or disproof without your ever knowing. Discourteous as it was for me and my associates to search your barn without permission, it would, I felt, have been a greater discourtesy to pay a call on you at such a sensitive time and give you cause to believe that I somehow suspected you of involvement in your son's demise."

"Too right!" Mallinson said with a flash of righteous fire in his eyes. "I should have taken a dim view of that indeed."

"Yes. On balance it seemed politer and more prudent for us to come 'snoop', as Mr Jenks puts it, then leave, with you none the wiser."

"Nonetheless, the upshot is here you are in my hallway, at a most inconsiderate hour. The discourtesy has been *de facto* done."

"Regrettably, yes."

At that moment a second man entered the hallway, via the same door that Mallinson had used. He was tall and slightly stooped, handsome in a rakish manner, with a stare of hawklike intensity. His hairline was receding, making a natural widow's peak look even sharper and more pronounced. In many ways he reminded me of Holmes.

"You're taking your time, Craig," he said. He had a glass of wine in his hand and his words were ever so slightly slurred. "Who are these fellows? What's all the fuss?"

"Nothing to concern yourself about, Josiah. I'm handling it."

"Sir Josiah Partlin-Gray?" said Holmes.

"I am he," said the new arrival. "Who might you be?"

"This is Mr Sherlock Holmes," said Mallinson. "You know, the private detective. I told you about him. I've hired him to look into... what happened to Patrick."

"Ah yes, the great, the famous Sherlock Holmes," said Partlin-Gray. "May I shake you by the hand? An honour."

"The honour is all mine," said Holmes. "I recognised you from the newspapers. I had no idea Mr Mallinson was friends with so eminent a personage as yourself."

"You flatter me, sir. Craig and I go back a long way. When I learned about his son's appalling mishap, I journeyed down to Sussex post haste. Craig proved a great comfort to me during a dark period in my life. I hope I can be of similar use to him in his own time of trial."

Holmes turned to me. "This is my friend Dr John Watson, who likewise has seen me through many a dark period, and also been by my side at my moments of greatest triumph."

I shook hands with Partlin-Gray, who had a remarkably strong grip. I, too, recognised the fellow, if only by name. Sir Josiah Partlin-Gray was a steel millionaire, one of the most illustrious in all the land, if not *the* most illustrious. There were few industrialists who could compete with him in terms of income or eminence. He owned steel mills all over the world, not just in England, and he was also patron of numerous charities and a philanthropist *par excellence*, annually donating thousands of pounds of his own money to worthy causes. Queen Victoria herself had knighted him at the turn of the century, one of the last such titles she conferred before her death.

"And I'm Caleb Smith," said Reptilio, pushing in. "You can call me Reptilio. An honour to meet you, my good sir. I've not been in the same room as an actual knight before."

Partlin-Gray shook hands with the snake-featured contortionist circumspectly, throwing a glance at Mallinson as if to say, *What on earth is an oddity like this doing here?*

"You are, I see, not just friends," said Holmes to the two plutocrats. "You are also members of the same Mayfair club. The Colonial and Overseas, if I'm not mistaken."

"How did you know that?" Partlin-Gray asked.

"It is as plain as anything. Mr Mallinson has on the club tie. Those blue and green stripes, with the emblem of the globe embroidered just below the knot, make it readily identifiable. You yourself sport cufflinks with the same emblem upon them."

"Of course, of course," said Partlin-Gray. "I see your famous powers of observation remain as acute as ever."

"I hope so," said Holmes. "It makes sense that you're both in the Colonial and Overseas, since you both have another thing in common. You both have significant business interests outside Britain's borders, which is one of the criteria for membership of that particular establishment. Mr Mallinson mines minerals in several countries, one of his principal sources of income being the vast quantities of potassium nitrate, sulphur and tantalite he unearths in Egypt. You meanwhile, Sir Josiah, run steel mills on more or less every continent, but most notably in Scandinavia, where your wife hails from. I'm sorry, I should say your late wife."

Partlin-Gray cast down his gaze and shifted his feet uncomfortably.

"I beg your pardon, that was tactless of me," said Holmes.

"No. No. It's quite all right."

"She died only this summer, in her native Norway. This was the 'dark period' to which you referred a moment ago."

Partlin-Gray moved across the hallway to stand by a massive oak sideboard on which stood a pair of elaborately branching candelabras. He clasped his hands stiffly behind his back. "As I said, Craig helped me through that very difficult time. Inga's sudden death nearly unhinged me, but he was a rock. If I can be half as helpful to him now as he mourns for poor young Patrick..."

"You already have been, Josiah," Mallinson said, "and will, I'm sure, continue to be. Now listen here, Mr Holmes. A moment ago you spoke of discourtesy. I will respond only with courtesy, though I do not feel you deserve it. You wish to see my biplane? Very well. I will show it to you myself."

"Now?" said Holmes.

"Yes, now. No time like the present. Josiah, if you'll excuse us?"

Partlin-Gray waved a hand. "Do as you wish, Craig. Occupy one's mind and one's time, and one will dwell less on one's loss."

CHAPTER EIGHTEEN

THE DREAMS OF ICARUS

Thus it was that we found ourselves back at the barn, escorted there by Mallinson himself and also by Jenks, who lit our way with a battery-powered tungsten filament torch. The gamekeeper kept his shotgun to hand, broken over the crook of his arm, with a fresh cartridge loaded in the empty barrel, just in case.

"Take as long as you like," Mallinson said, undoing the padlock. "Snoop away. Be my guest. I don't know what you're hoping to find, but I am confident you'll turn up nothing untoward."

The aircraft, at close hand, was even larger than I had imagined. Its upper wing spanned nearly thirty feet, and its length from stem to stern was not much less than that. The smells of canvas, engine oil and wood varnish that radiated from it were strong, almost overcoming the barn's more traditional smells of hay, earth and timber. I saw canisters of fuel sitting in what had once been a loosebox, along with tools, spare parts and various greasy rags. It occurred to me that all of this made the barn a terrific fire hazard. One stray spark, and the place would go up like a tinder box. I did my best to banish the thought.

Jenks set his torch down on an empty feed trough, its beam pointing squarely at the biplane, and by its brilliant light Holmes commenced his scrutiny. He traipsed back and forth beside the Grahame-White, and sometimes went up on tiptoe and at other times down on his haunches. At one stage he even crawled beneath the machine.

"How fast does she fly?" he asked Mallinson.

"That's a three-cylinder, fifty-horsepower engine. Top speed is supposed to be fifty miles per hour but I reckon I've had her up to sixty."

"And her endurance?"

"The longest I've had her out is three and a half hours."

"She's a pusher rather than a tractor type. How does that affect performance?"

Mallinson looked quizzical but also pleasantly surprised. "Why, Mr Holmes, I seem to have come across a fellow aviation enthusiast."

"More of an informed bystander."

"But you clearly know about aeroplanes."

"A little. I have an enquiring mind."

And, I thought to myself, a mind that knows how to disarm others and gain their allegiance by establishing a common bond, however tenuous and contrived.

"A rear-mounted pusher prop, all agree, gives a smoother flight," said Mallinson. "The Type Seven is a beast at take-off. You need heavy rudder input to counteract the P-factor – that is, the torque from the moving propeller which puts asymmetrical thrust on the airframe when there's a high angle of incidence and makes her yaw slightly. But once she's up and levelled out, she's fine. Three pounds per square inch wingloading means she dances in the air like a ballerina. Though, like a ballerina, she can be temperamental and highly strung at times. She certainly doesn't like a cross-wind much, but then show me the kite that does."

"Manned flight is a science, isn't it?" said Holmes, running a hand along one of the rear booms. "So much knowledge is required."

"Yet once the technicalities are mastered, it becomes an art form. Aeroplanes are a harbinger of the future, Mr Holmes. That is part of my fascination with them. We are on the cusp of a glorious era of mechanisation, our inventiveness proceeding in leaps and bounds, in aviation and in many other disciplines. With aircraft we have begun to realise the dreams of Icarus. Who knows what we might next achieve in that sphere? I would not be surprised if one day dirigibles are crossing between here and America as commonly as ships, and in half the time. Nor is a transatlantic multiple-occupancy heavier-than-air aircraft, carrying both passengers and cargo, beyond the realms of possibility."

"The dreams of Icarus," Holmes echoed. "A ringing turn of phrase. I note, by the way, that your Grahame-White is itself multiple-occupancy. It has the capacity to seat two people."

"It does. Few Type Sevens have been made in that configuration. Mine is something of a rarity."

"The passenger, or perhaps navigator, sits here." Holmes indicated a space just to the fore of the upper wing, fitted with a crude, skeletal chair. "In front. The pilot goes behind, nearer the engine."

"That way the control wires do not have to pass around or through the passenger's section of the cockpit. The connection from joystick and pedals to engine and ailerons is direct, without risk of being impeded."

"Of course. And both passenger and pilot have harnesses to keep them secured during flight."

"A necessary precaution. Let us say that a sudden wind shear catches the pilot unawares. He momentarily loses control. The plane tips over. There is a very good chance of being ejected. Centrifugal force keeps one in place during a sustained aerobatic manoeuvre of the kind that the Frenchman Adolphe Pégoud and the Russian

Pyotr Nesterov are so fond of demonstrating, such as a barrel roll or a loop-the-loop. But it does not have the same effect during a sudden, chaotic lurch that throws the plane off its horizontal axis. Those harnesses have saved many a life, let me tell you."

"Quite, quite."

"Well, have you seen enough?"

Briefly Holmes studied a stack of clay plant pots ranged against one wall. Then he said, "I believe I have."

"Then," said Mallinson, "would you be so good as to share with us the reason for this expedition?"

"No."

"I beg your pardon?"

"I said no. I have been testing a theory. I have come to a conclusion. That is all."

Mallinson's face darkened. "Do not trifle with me, Mr Holmes. You have put me to some inconvenience. You have disturbed me at a godforsaken hour, during a time of great personal trial. Now you are being evasive. I have neither the leisure nor the patience to indulge your games. You looked at my plane for a reason, and I demand to know what it is."

"You perhaps won't want to hear it."

"I most certainly do. And if I have to order Jenks to cock his gun and put it to this man's head in order to force an answer out of you, then by heaven, sir, I will."

Mallinson was pointing at Reptilio, who quailed at the threat.

Holmes shrugged. "You would be wasting your time. Mr Smith is of no concern to me. You heard him speak of his lack of affiliation to me. Shoot away."

Reptilio let out a squeal of protest, little appreciating that, by disavowing him, Holmes had put him out of danger.

"Fair enough," said Mallinson, "but I suspect the same isn't true of Dr Watson."

"Indeed not," said Holmes, with a solicitous glance at me. "I would not have Watson's life jeopardised for all the world. Very well. Here is the theory. It is my belief that standing before us here, stowed in this barn, in the guise of an aircraft, is a murder weapon."

CHAPTER NINETEEN

FIREPOTS

Silence ensued, during which Mallinson's face darkened further, like clouds presaging a storm.

Eventually he said, in a voice far quieter than the thunder I had been expecting, "You had better qualify that statement, Mr Holmes, and the explanation had better be phenomenally good. Is this what I have hired you for? To accuse me of the murder of my own son?"

"Did I say that?" replied Holmes. "I am accusing *you* of nothing. I merely averred that your Grahame-White may well be implicated in Patrick's death."

"But what nonsense is this? Patrick jumped from Beachy Head. We all know that."

"Patrick fell into the sea from a great height, that is what we know beyond all reasonable doubt. He could as easily have plummeted from an aeroplane as from a clifftop. If so, why not this very aeroplane?"

"I don't see how it is even possible," said Mallinson. "Are you telling me he went up in her, flew her over the Channel, and leapt out? My son, Mr Holmes, did not even know how to fly. The whole idea is preposterous."

"I agree. For how would the plane have returned to land safely after Patrick leapt out? It's not as if it is a homing pigeon. If, however, someone else were in the pilot's seat and caused Patrick to be thrown out – that is altogether a more viable proposition."

"It is not viable. It is barely sane."

"I admit it pushes the limits of plausibility," said Holmes. "That is why I was so reluctant to voice the idea, until you insisted with such vehemence that I did. A theory that is not yet fully formed is little better than no theory at all."

"Who was the pilot in this fantastic scenario of yours? Not me, I can assure you."

"No, not you. It couldn't have been. The coroner has estimated the time of death to have been Friday night. This is borne out by Patrick's disappearance from home on that same night. You have told us that you were up in London then, returning to Sussex the following morning. I have no doubt that this is so."

"It absolutely is, and I can prove it," said Mallinson, adding, "Not that I should have to. I spent all of Friday evening in the company of several esteemed colleagues at the Colonial and Overseas, not least among them Sir Josiah."

"Ah."

"Yes. Together, we dined, drank and played cards until well into the small hours. A few hands of euchre, then several rubbers of bridge, if you must know. Any number of other members of the club can attest to my presence there that night. I can give you names if you would like to check."

"I wouldn't want to put you to the trouble. Besides, the club must keep records of all comings and goings. A quick look at the attendance ledger for Friday night would, I am sure, incontrovertibly shore up your claim. However, there is still the matter of the scorch marks out on the airfield."

"I can account for those."

"As can I," said Holmes. "Firepots."

"Firepots?" I said.

"Earthenware containers for fire."

"I know what they are, Holmes. But what is their relevance here?"

"Did you not observe these?" my friend said, gesturing at the stack of what I had taken to be plant pots.

"I saw them," I said. "I did not think anything of them."

Holmes rolled his eyes. Still, after all these years, he was exercised by my inability to spot what he thought were obvious clues. "Most of them bear smut marks around the rim. They will have held naphtha gel, inset with a wick, generating a clear bright flame that will burn for several hours. Spaced out in a line, they may be used to illuminate a pathway – or indeed a runway. To facilitate night flying. Is that not so, Mr Mallinson?"

"Very shrewdly deduced, Mr Holmes," said Mallinson. "I have been known to venture aloft on moonlit nights. It is possibly a greater thrill even than daytime flying. One truly feels one is among the stars, part of the universe."

"A greater risk too, surely. Without landmarks being clearly visible, how do you navigate?"

"Practice. Repetition. Familiarisation. I know most of the towns hereabouts by the pattern of their lights, recognising one from another by size and street layout. Newhaven, for instance, looks quite distinct from Hastings or Hailsham, or even Eastbourne itself. The shape of each is unique, like a constellation. Then there are the actual constellations. They help. The North Star invariably restores my sense of direction, should I by chance become disorientated mid-flight. I am also versed in the intervals and repetitions of the various lighthouses along the coast."

"And once you are close to Settleholm again, the firepots guide you back in to land."

"Just so." Mallinson looked wistful for a moment as he considered the uncomplicated delights of aviation in the midst of his present misery. I felt for the man. All the assurances of his world had, it seemed, been snatched away from him in one fell swoop.

His stern demeanour reasserted itself. "Your contention, Mr Holmes, is that somebody, without my knowledge or say-so, flew my plane the night before last, having inveigled Patrick into being its passenger. This person was then somehow able to – to eject Patrick? Is that what you reckon?"

"Sending him down to his death somewhere out in the Channel, where the seabed mud is different from the mud closer to shore."

"The mud?"

"The mud clinging to his body. The tide then washed him back in a day and a half later."

"Well then, I suppose the obvious question is who. Who did this?"

"That I cannot say."

"Cannot because you refuse to, or cannot because you do not know?"

"The latter," said Holmes. "Can you think of anyone, Mr Mallinson, who disliked Patrick enough to kill him?"

"In the manner you're suggesting? No."

"You are certain?"

"Utterly."

"But you yourself, you have enemies."

"Business rivals. One doesn't get to the position that I'm in without treading on a few toes along the way. Nobody, though, hates me *that* much, I am quite convinced of it. More to the point, I have no enemy that I know of who could have pulled off the elaborate feat you're outlining. Availing himself of my Type Seven, taking Patrick up in it... A simple knife in the dark would have done the trick. A bullet in the back. Mowing him down with a car. There are any number of ways my boy could have been assassinated, none involving night flying and my very own plane. So why go to such lengths?"

"Yes," Holmes admitted, "put like that my case rather falls apart."

"Falls apart? I would say I had demolished it."

"Unless the aim was to make Patrick's death look like suicide."

"But why bother?"

"To throw off suspicion, obviously."

"Surely blatant murder would have sent a blunter message."

"The result, either way, would be the same: a devastated father. The purpose need not be a message, merely the destabilisation of yourself and your company."

"Mr Holmes..." Mallinson appeared at a loss for words. "I am made of tough stuff. I will survive this. Mallinson Mining Limited will survive this. Anyone who knows me at all would know that. It is my opinion, and I am quite firm in it, that you are looking in the wrong direction. Have you considered the possibility that a certain Miss Elizabeth Vandenbergh might be the guilty party? Have you even spoken to the woman?"

"I have."

"And? Did she not strike you as the forceful, vengeful type? Could she not have lured Patrick up to the cliffs, perhaps on the pretext of begging for reconciliation after she thought better of spurning him? The woman is crafty, if you ask me. Rapacious, too. The gold-digging sort. No money of her own to speak of, just a failing costumier business that's leaking funds like a sieve. Perhaps she saw Patrick as her ticket to prosperity. I could have – should have – warned him about girls like her. They would have been a particular hazard for him at Cambridge, frequenting the undergraduates' favourite watering holes and attending college functions and balls in the hope of snaring a well-to-do husband with prospects. Patrick, naive and rich – he would have been catnip to the more scheming kind of female up there. Clive spent all of three years of his degree course sidestepping unwelcome advances from just such women. He viewed them not least as a distraction from his academic and sporting endeavours. And yet, with tragic irony, Patrick managed to fall into the clutches of one right here on his doorstep."

"Miss Vandenbergh pushed Patrick off Beachy Head?" I said.

"It would have been easily done, while Patrick's guard was down."

"To what end?" said Holmes. "Was Miss Vandenbergh not the one who rejected him? She was hardly, in that sense, 'a woman scorned'."

"Patrick's sudden cooling towards her," I said. "Remember she mentioned that? How he became evasive and secretive?"

"Exactly," said Mallinson, seizing upon my words. "That could be construed as being scorned. A woman is a subtle, complex creature, her motives often inscrutable. Perhaps she expected Patrick to fight to regain her affections and was bitterly disappointed when he did not. *Cherchez la femme*, Mr Holmes. Our French cousins know a thing or two about the duplicity and dangerousness of the opposite sex. Seek the lady."

CHAPTER TWENTY

A Murmuration of Starlings

Before we left Settleholm Manor it was agreed that the matter of our break-in at the barn would remain solely between ourselves – that is to say, between Holmes, Mallinson, Reptilio, Jenks and me. Mallinson had behaved with remarkable reasonableness throughout the episode, not once succumbing to the temptation to be outraged, although he had every right to be and had veered close. He agreed to write off our expedition onto his estate as an aberration and a wild goose chase. No blame would attach to us for it. This came as a special relief to Reptilio, who had the most to lose by being involved in a further felony.

"Inspector Tasker shall be none the wiser as to what transpired here tonight," Mallinson promised.

"I couldn't ask for more than that," was Holmes's reply, and we all parted on fairly good terms, Jenks the only truly disgruntled one among us. I imagined he felt that we three trespassers had got away with more than we deserved. His eyes said he would not have been quite so magnanimous as his employer.

Holmes was sunk deep in thought as we trudged back through the dark to East Dean.

When I enquired what was preoccupying him, his somewhat unexpected reply was, "Scuff marks."

"What?"

"Perhaps you noticed. No, what am I saying? Of course you didn't. When Sir Josiah crossed the hallway to stand by the sideboard, I observed scuff marks on the floor tiles by his feet. They formed a curve from the legs of the sideboard, suggesting the thing has been moved lately."

"Moved? Whatever for?"

"That's just it. I don't know."

"Perhaps an object fell behind and the sideboard was pulled out from the wall in order to facilitate its retrieval."

"Perhaps," said Holmes. "Perhaps it was just that. It may mean nothing at all."

"It would have been small but valuable, the thing that fell behind," I said. "That sideboard must weigh several hundred pounds. I would not want to shunt it aside without good reason."

"Watson, as ever you speak sense. I should probably not waste any more time thinking about the matter."

At the cottage, I retired upstairs to bed while Holmes remained down in the sitting room, keeping watch over Reptilio in case he attempted to sneak away.

Early the next morning, two police constables came to collect the contortionist and return him to his cell.

With Reptilio gone, Holmes lapsed back into his funk. I couldn't tell if he was angry, stymied, or just thinking hard. It was difficult to know with Holmes. When his shutters came down, they came down firmly, and there was no penetrating them. He sat in his armchair stuffing black shag into his pipe and puffing away with a brooding determination that bordered on mania. I couldn't elicit a single word from him, and soon gave up trying.

"I'm off for a stroll," I said, fastening the buttons of my overcoat and fetching my walking-stick. "I may be a while. Goodbye."

Holmes's only response was an airy flap of the hand that was not so much a farewell as a dismissal. I was, at that moment, nothing other than an irritant, a buzzing gnat.

Leaving him lost in smoke and contemplation, I bought that day's *Times* from the village shop, then set off cross-country with the newspaper tucked in my pocket. Soon I was descending the slope into Eastbourne over sheep-grazed downland that was smooth and uninterrupted save for the occasional thicket of hazel or wind-warped briar.

A cool, pale sun was emerging through the morning's hazy overcast as I circumvented a chalk pit and joined the seafront promenade at its western end, not far from the natural spring called Holywell that leapt from a cleft in the cliffside. A low onshore breeze blew steadily and strongly, stirring the waves to a chop. The Channel was the white-streaked grey of a much used blackboard.

I passed the stately Grand Hotel and continued on along the lower parade, tipping my hat to my fellow promenaders. The weather might not have been of the warmest but Eastbourne's seafront afforded such a pleasing aspect that it drew people to it in all conditions short of a full-blown storm. The buildings ranged from Italianate stucco terraces to individual houses and hotels in the Flemish Renaissance and Regency styles, a delightful variety. Well-kept municipal lawns and flowerbeds added a dash of colour. Then there were features such as the bandstand, which projected out over the beach on stilts like some great glass birdcage, and of course the ornate pier, my intended destination. Not for nothing was this town nicknamed "the Empress of Watering Places".

The beach's bathing machines were all drawn up above the tideline, for this was not a day for casual swimming. However, a handful of young men were preparing themselves for immersion, and I stopped to watch, marvelling at their fortitude and foolhardiness. Some of them performed jumping jacks and similar warm-up exercises to get the blood pumping while others smeared grease on their bare limbs to insulate against the cold. I overheard a passer-by say that these were members of an endurance swimming club and their goal was to cross all the way to Pevensey Bay – some two miles as the crow flies – and back in under an hour. The young men, in their woollen bathing costumes, proceeded to tiptoe down the shingles and enter the water, whereupon with yelps and exhortations they launched themselves into the surf like seals and struck out from land. Soon they had taken a left turn and were forging eastward, parallel with the shore.

Rather them than me, I thought.

I stopped at a shop to buy a postcard and a stick of rock. I planned to send the former to Mrs Watson and, when I returned home, present her with the latter as a gift. Thus she would know that she was never far from my thoughts.

I continued on towards the pier.

I was, and remain, terribly fond of Eastbourne Pier. Any pleasure pier is a splendid folly, in my opinion – a structure jutting boldly out over the sea with no purpose other than to look jaunty and gay and be a venue for recreation and entertainment. There is something peculiarly affecting, not to say peculiarly British, about their elaborateness and sheer frivolity. Eastbourne's is no exception, and as I paid my fee at the entrance kiosk and strode through the turnstile I felt a smile forming on my face. Last night's shenanigans, Holmes's brown study, my own tiredness due to lack of sleep – all seemed to melt away with every resonant thud of my feet on the boardwalk.

With the windbreak screens shielding me from the worst of the buffeting breeze, I headed towards the structure that dominated the pier's seaward end, the Kursaal. Named after the "cure halls" found in fashionable German spa towns, the Kursaal was a two-storey fantasy of cast-iron pillars, balconies, balustrades, domes, cupolas and finials. Inside, it contained a theatre, bars, offices, and last but not least a rather good tearoom, where I claimed a table beside the window and shortly was tucking into a late breakfast of eggs, bacon, fried bread, sautéed mushrooms and black pudding, washed down with strong coffee.

Stomach replete, I wrote the postcard to my wife, confining myself to a few innocuous comments about the weather and expressions of affection, and making no mention at all that Holmes and I seemed to be involved in a case, of sorts. The second Mrs Watson did not wholeheartedly approve of my crime-solving activities with Holmes and had often expressed how glad she was that he, and therefore by extension I, had abandoned the habit. She preferred a husband who kept regular hours performing a regular job and didn't go, in her words, "gallivanting around, risking his neck chasing after villains".

I then spent the next half an hour perusing *The Times*. Usually this was an agreeable occupation, but on that particular day the news was unduly dispiriting. There were massacres and disasters far afield, such as an attack by Libyan tribesmen on a garrison of occupying Italian soldiers which resulted in over thirty deaths and the bombing of a train in Mexico by terrorists which resulted in over fifty. Closer to home, though, there were the continued ominous rumblings of something much worse, a catastrophe in the making which nobody, it seemed, either was willing or knew how to avoid.

A second war in the Balkans was under way, hot on the heels of the last one. Bulgaria had provoked Greece and Serbia, and was reaping the consequences. Meanwhile tensions in the rest of Europe, already simmering, were rising to the boil. The continent's great powers – the Triple Entente of Britain, Russia and France on one side, the Triple Alliance of Germany, Italy and Austria-Hungary on the other – were at loggerheads, their imperial fiefdoms in a state of continuous competition and flux, each seeking advantage over their rivals, keen to expand their spheres of influence. Russia was ramping up her military might, mobilising troops and amassing matériel like never before. Germany was doing likewise in alarmed response, and also increasing the size of her navy, vying with Britain on that front as she had been since the invasion of the Transvaal in 1896. France, for its part, was behaving in a provocatively cocksure manner, in the grip of a nationalistic fervour which had been stoked by recent setbacks resulting from its colonial crises in Morocco.

It was clear to an old soldier like me, and to anyone with even the loosest grasp of international politics, that Europe was on a knife edge. It was the proverbial powder keg awaiting a spark. All this diplomatic growling, this aggressive jockeying for position, could not carry on indefinitely. Matters would come to a head sooner or later, and one could not help but think that the resolution would be a far from peaceful one. Many commentators foresaw a spasm of violence unlike any the world had hitherto witnessed, an entire continent at war, tearing itself apart. How many millions of deaths might that mean? The level of destruction and devastation would surely be unprecedented.

These thoughts cast a pall of gloom over me. I left the tearoom and walked to the very end of the pier hoping to find consolation in the view out to sea. The sun had by now fully shaken off its veil of cloud, and the water had gone from grey to pearly green, like nephrite marble. Seagulls haunted the air, pinned on the wind with their wings spread, yet they were outnumbered by starlings, of which there were many hundreds, congregated in the sky in that ever-shifting mass known as a murmuration.

It swooped and twisted, this bird cluster, directly above the pier. It flexed and folded in on itself as though it were a single sentient entity, a vast amoeba gifted with secret intelligence.

The starlings were flocking in readiness to migrate south to Africa. The pier was a landmark, a rallying point which they returned to by instinct year after year. I knew these facts, yet that did not vitiate the wonder of the phenomenon. Countless individual creatures acting as one, moving in concert as though choreographed – it offered at once a mesmerising display and a salutary reminder that Nature was above the affairs of men, indifferent to our scrambles for territory and our propensity for conflict. We and our squabbles were transitory. Nature had its rhythms and its rituals, eternally recurring. Nature abided.

Leaning on the pier railing, with the waves crashing against the support pylons some thirty feet below me, I observed the starlings and felt my dread begin to ebb away. I did not believe for a moment that all would be well. I was too old and jaded to harbour that hope. However, I did at least feel that there was some stability in the world, that some things were constant and immutable. The ever-changing murmuration was, paradoxically, a symbol of permanence.

I had thought I was alone at the end of the pier, but then all at once hands seized me roughly from behind. A brutal, powerful grip took hold of my left arm, another of my right thigh. I felt myself being upended, pivoted over the railing.

I struck backwards with my walking-stick, a clumsy flailing blow, but the handle of the stick must have connected with some part of my unseen attacker, for I felt a sharp impact and heard a furious grunt.

It did not deter him, however. With a terrible, remorseless strength he continued to tip me over.

I was upside down. The sea seethed below. The waves seemed terribly far away and at the same time terrifyingly close. I tried to utter a cry for help but somehow my throat was stopped, my tongue blocking my larynx.

The only thing preventing me from falling was my assailant's grip on me.

This he relinquished, and down I went, head-first.

CHAPTER TWENTY-ONE

One Brush with Death after Another

Helplessly I fell, and on the way down my shoulder collided with one of the pier's pylons, which not only sent a savage jolt of pain through me but set me spinning. I crashed into the water at an angle, mostly on my back, with enough force to drive the air from my lungs and render me halfway insensible.

All that I recall of the next few desperate moments was the roar of bubbles in my ears and the horrendous, sickening sensation of being unable to tell up from down. Underwater, I thrashed toward what I hoped was the surface, but I seemed to be getting no closer to it and feared that, in my efforts to save myself, I might instead be going in the opposite direction, sinking deeper. Panic overcame me; I heard myself howling in the back of my throat, and my exertions grew more frenzied but also less focused. The harder I fought to keep from drowning, the more remote my chances of success seemed.

My chest ached. My lungs burned. My shoulder felt jagged like broken glass. I began to think I would never be able to extricate myself from the sea's clutches. My clothes had become sodden and heavy, their weight bearing me down. I resigned myself to the inevitable. In a moment of weird stillness and clarity I thought of Sherlock Holmes, and of the current Mrs Watson, and of my darling lost Mary, the three people who were nearest and dearest to me, the pillars of my life. I realised how much I had relied on them and leaned on them over the course of my life, and I prayed that I had been as good to them as it was in my power to be.

Then a pair of hands fastened on to me, and in my stunned, hypoxic daze I imagined they must be the same hands responsible for hurling me off the pier, so I writhed against them, trying to shake off their inimical grasp.

But they insisted on maintaining their hold, and there came more of them, at least three pairs now, and they were hauling me, cradling me, and I remember wondering, dimly, if they belonged to angels and I was being carried to my final reward.

Then my face broke the surface, and through reflex I opened my mouth and sucked in air.

A wave crashed over me mid-inhalation, and I spluttered and gagged, and someone nearby shouted, "Keep his head up!" and another replied, "What do you blooming well think I'm trying to do?"

I felt myself being borne bodily through the water, enfolded by strong arms, the focus of commotion and communal effort. All at once my heels were scraping through gritty seabed sand, and then I was laid out on my back, on pebbles, looking up, gasping. I was aware of a dozen faces around me, peering solicitously down. I was numb and shuddering. I sat up and regurgitated a quantity of mucus and salt water, before lying back down again in a swoon. Voices became distant, the daylight dim. I suspect I passed out for a brief while.

Back in the land of the living again, I found myself swaddled in blankets provided by I know not whom – some kind local hotelier most likely. A mug of hot milk was thrust into my hands.

My rescuers turned out to be the self same swimming club members whom I had seen earlier venturing out towards Pevensey. By immense good fortune they had been on the last leg of their return journey, almost back where they had started, when one of them had spied me toppling from the pier. Exhausted though they were, they had spared no time, nor the final ergs of their energy, diving down to retrieve me from the depths and bring me safely to shore.

I thanked the young men profusely and enquired if any of them had got a look at the rogue who had propelled me into the sea. None had. It was impossible to see up onto the pier from down in the water right beside it, where they had been. The angle was too steep.

I asked the same question of the small crowd that had gathered around us, again fruitlessly. Several of these onlookers' faces registered scepticism, as though they didn't believe that I had been the victim of an attempted murder. They assumed I was just some doddery old man who had somehow managed to slip over the railing and was now trying to cover up his clumsiness and retain some dignity by pretending another party had been involved.

Truth be told, I could scarcely believe it myself. Someone had tried to kill me. A man had sneaked up behind me and sent me plunging into the waves, his goal patently my death. What for? What had he hoped to gain?

I resolved to inform Sherlock Holmes about the incident straight away. It could not be mere coincidence. There had to be some connection with Patrick Mallinson. The lad had died after a fall into the sea; so too had I, nearly. The similarity was alarming. Had the assassin been a member of the secret society Patrick had belonged to? Was Holmes's and my investigation getting a little too close to the truth? Was the cult coming after us now? Was Holmes too in mortal danger?

One of the swimmers owned a car, which was parked nearby, and he offered to drive me home. I accepted gratefully, and once the young man had towelled himself off, got changed, and then spent a couple of minutes cranking the car's starting handle until the motor grudgingly turned over, we were on our way.

His little open-topped tourer, a "bullnose" Morris Oxford, chuntered gamely along the seafront, and tackled Duke's Drive, the winding hill road at the end, with gusto if not with speed. Descending the steep gradient on the other side towards East Dean, it began accelerating at a disconcerting rate and the driver fought hard with the steering wheel to keep us from skidding off into the ditch. He laughed all the while, blithe in the face of peril as only the young can be, whereas his passenger clung to the dashboard and prayed. So soon after one brush with death I wasn't keen on another.

We reached the village in one piece, I'm glad to relate, and exiting the car on unsteady legs I made my way to Holmes's cottage.

My friend was not in, but he had left me a note:

My dear Watson,

This case is proving most perplexing. I seem to be going round in circles and getting nowhere. With each new dead end, complication mounts.

I'm afraid, therefore, that I am going to have to absent myself from your company for a day or so. There are avenues of enquiry which may only be pursued elsewhere, and alone.

I deeply regret interrupting your visit in this way. You will think me very antisocial, and you would be correct. I shall endeavour to return to your side as soon as possible. In the meantime, Mrs Tuppen will take care of you. I have asked her to accord you the same courtesies and care as she would me,

Your friend, as ever,
Sherlock Holmes

I changed out of my damp clothes, wrung them out and hung them up to dry. The postcard for my wife, which had been in my jacket pocket, was just so much fibrous mulch now. The stick of rock was likewise ruined.

As I performed these tasks, I mentally cursed Holmes. Of all the times to go running off on his own! Little did he appreciate that we had been targeted by a mysterious and ruthless adversary. There was a sinister cult in the vicinity, so secret that not even the local police knew of its existence, and its members did not wish us to pry into their affairs and would stop at nothing to discourage us. If they knew who I was, they definitely knew who Holmes was. My friend's life was at risk, and he seemed entirely oblivious to the fact.

Sherlock Holmes was a wily and perceptive man, I reminded myself. Many an enemy had tried to eliminate him and failed. He had faced the worst that the criminal fraternity could throw at him and lived to tell the tale. Even Professor Moriarty, the deadliest malefactor this world has ever produced, was unable to vanquish him, though not for want of trying.

Yet the Holmes of 1913 was not the Holmes of yesteryear. He was more erratic, possibly more prone to error.

I was deeply worried for him.

CHAPTER TWENTY-TWO

FLORENCE NIGHTINGALE AND MRS BEETON ROLLED INTO ONE

Mrs Tuppen showed up that afternoon, a stout, formidable woman with a broad, pleasant face marred somewhat by a plethora of warts on her chin and cheeks.

By the time she arrived, I had established two facts.

The first fact was that my shoulder, though severely bruised from hitting the pier pylon, was not broken or even dislocated. It felt damnably sore but exhibited full rotation, impeded only by the muscular discomfort of moving it. My other shoulder was the one that had taken a Jezail bullet back in 1880, so that, for the moment, I had a matching pair, both of them stiffened and achy.

The second fact was that I had caught a chill from being dunked in the sea and it was fast developing into a fever. My brow was hot, but I felt cold, cold to the marrow of my bones, and however much I stoked the fire in the sitting room I could not seem to get warm. I fashioned a damp compress from a teacloth and swaddled myself in as many layers of clothing as I could, but the fever would not slacken its hold. On the contrary, as the hours went by it merely worsened, until soon I was shivering uncontrollably, my teeth chattering.

Mrs Tuppen took one look at me and ordered me to bed. "White as a sheet you are, sir, and hollow-eyed like a skeleton. I'll brook no ifs or buts. You do as I say."

She brought a bowl of chicken broth up to my room and, when I proved incapable of feeding myself because my hands were shaking too much, spooned the stuff into my mouth.

That night, and the whole of the following day, Hettie Tuppen was my guardian angel. I don't know how I would have coped without her. I might even have perished. She was Florence Nightingale and Mrs Beeton rolled into one. I hovered in and out of consciousness, lucid one moment, debilitated the next. Mrs Tuppen mopped my forehead, kept me fed and watered, and was a constant fussing presence by my bedside.

I cannot fault her nursing skills other than that she insisted on dosing me regularly with a foul-tasting, home-brewed concoction, a tincture of herbs and tree bark whose recipe had been in her family for generations and whose restorative properties she was adamant were second to none.

"Unfailingly efficacious in lowering temperature and soothing inflammation," she said of this nostrum of hers, sounding like the text of a newspaper advertisement for the latest pharmaceutical wonder remedy.

I myself would have been happier with simple aspirin, but I dutifully gulped down the bitter liquid. In my experience it did one no favours to argue with the person caring for one. As a doctor, I had always found that compliant, obedient patients healed faster than those who were troublesome and contrary. As a patient myself, I elected to submit to the given course of treatment rather than resist. I had no wish to cause Mrs Tuppen to take umbrage, not when I was relying on her to restore me to health.

Strangely enough, it seemed that her homemade medicine

was indeed as potent as she claimed. My fever broke only twenty-four hours after it had set in. That evening I was feeling considerably better, almost human again, and by the next morning, the Thursday, I was positively bristling with renewed vigour. I bounced out of bed and wolfed down the substantial spread Mrs Tuppen laid on for breakfast, eating as though I had been on starvation rations for weeks.

"My dear woman, you are a miracle worker," I told her. I was feeling almost giddy from the rapidity and completeness of my recovery. "I am forever in your debt."

"Just don't go over-exerting yourself, doctor," she said. "At your age, you must learn to take things easy. However did you let yourself get in such a state in the first place? I found all that damp clothing of yours. Were you caught out in the rain?"

"Something like that." The woman did not need to know about my near-murder. It would only upset her. "Tell me, I don't suppose Holmes put in an appearance while I was laid up."

"I've seen neither hide nor hair of Mr Holmes since he called round at my house on Tuesday morning, valise in hand, to say that he was taking a leave of absence and that I was to look after you while he was gone."

"He offered no clue as to where he might be off to?"

"None whatsoever, and it wasn't my place to ask. Gent wishes to come and go as he pleases, that's his business. I'm surprised he didn't tell *you* anything, though, you being such a friend of his."

"Sherlock Holmes moves in mysterious ways, Mrs Tuppen, his wonders to perform. I have lost count of the number of times he has pulled a vanishing act on me like this. Usually he turns up again soon enough, and more often than not feeling pretty pleased with himself."

The confidence with which I spoke belied my true emotions, however. Doubt and misgiving gnawed at me. Holmes's note had talked of him being away "for a day or so". Yet two full days had elapsed since he wrote it. Surely he ought to be back by now. What was keeping him?

As the morning progressed, I found it hard to settle. A book was no distraction, and Mrs Tuppen's company began to grate, for although Holmes's housekeeper was a decent enough woman and a demonstrably skilled amateur physician, she was also an inveterate chatterbox. I dropped several hints that she should feel free to go home. She must surely be tired, I suggested, having kept watch over me round the clock. What about Mr Tuppen? Was he not curious as to where his wife had got to?

"Oh, my Billy can look after himself," she replied, "and besides, there's a barmaid at the Tiger he's taken a shine to and would rather be spending the time with. Not that a young thing like her is going to give a clapped-out old fool like him anything more than a nice smile and a bat of her eyelashes." Then on she went with her near-unceasing prattle about her neighbours and their carryings-on and about the shenanigans got up to by members of her extended and somewhat startlingly misbehaved family.

When I could endure no more, I announced that I was heading out to search for Holmes. It was impulsive of me, but I would rather have been doing something active than sit around twiddling my thumbs, waiting for him to return.

Eastbourne was the obvious place to look first. I roved the town, ever cautious and on my guard, for the man who had attacked me on the pier must know that I had survived his attempt on my life and might be keeping an eye out for me with a view to trying again. At least this time I was armed, albeit only with Holmes's jack-knife which I had taken from his writing desk. It was no pistol but it would do in a pinch.

After a couple of hours spent trawling the streets in vain, I decided to turn my footsteps towards Little Chelsea and pay a call on Miss Elizabeth Vandenbergh at Tripp's Costumiers. It was a long shot, but Holmes may have called in on her yesterday or earlier today.

You may imagine my shock and amazement when I rounded the corner onto the road where Tripp's lay, only to find a fire engine parked outside the premises and a small crowd of onlookers gathered nearby. These people were chattering animatedly with one another and gesticulating towards the shop, which was, I saw to my dismay, a charred, gutted ruin. Every window was blackened and shattered, and smoke was still emanating from the upstairs rooms, trailing thinly upward. The pavement in front was littered with debris and slick with water.

I scanned the faces of the crowd but could not see Elizabeth among them. Feeling a pang of dread, I hurried over and introduced myself to the nearest of the firemen. He and his colleagues were busy lowering their ladder and furling the rubberised hose onto the back of their appliance.

"What has happened?" I asked. I could feel heat radiating from the brickwork of the shop.

"Isn't it obvious?" said the fireman. "Place went up in flames. Early this morning the butcher across the road spotted smoke coming out from under the front door. He tried to enter the building, but the smoke was too dense and beat him back. So he sent his errand boy off on his bicycle to fetch us. We got here as fast as we could, but it was already too late. The fire had taken hold and spread to the upper storeys. All we could hope to do was contain it and stop it spreading to the houses next door."

"But was it an accident?" I said, aghast.

The fireman shrugged and scratched his head beneath his brass helmet. "In all likelihood, yes. A stray spark from a fire, an untended oven... We'd have to go in and take a look around to know for certain, but we can't do that as yet. The building's still too hot inside, and too unstable. The ceilings or floors could give way at any time."

"So it might have been arson."

"Who can say? Possible, I suppose. Might I ask what your interest in this is, sir?"

"I am acquainted with the lady who owns the shop," I said.

"Then," the fireman said, looking rueful, "I would prepare yourself for the possibility of bad news."

"Good Lord. You don't mean to say…?"

"I'm given to understand that the owner lived on the premises."

"Yes. She has a flat above."

"And nobody here saw her escape, or has seen her since. The reasonable assumption would be that she perished. Nothing is confirmed," he added quickly. "Unless or until we find a body, one should not assume the worst. But to be frank, I wouldn't get your hopes up if I were you. In my experience, there's almost always a victim in incidents like this. They pass out from smoke inhalation before they can get to safety, and the flames do the rest."

I reeled under the weight of these grim tidings. Elizabeth Vandenbergh – dead? And meeting her end in the most horrendous fashion, by being burned alive? "A stray spark from a fire," the fireman had said, "an untended oven…" I remembered the potbellied stove in the shop's backroom. Perhaps it had been responsible. With those bolts of cloth nearby, it would only take an ember falling out through the firebox grating and lying unnoticed amid the flammable cotton, smouldering, until all at once: inferno.

Or was there something more sinister going on here? Could Elizabeth have fallen prey to the same occult society which had taken her lover Patrick from her? Did she know more about them than she had let on? Were they scared of her in some way? Did they think she might cause them trouble, perhaps threaten to expose them, and thus they felt their only recourse was to do away with her?

In which case, it seemed likelier than ever that Sherlock Holmes, too, had become their victim.

The police station lay not far from the costumiers. Inspector Tasker was hardly the most receptive or sympathetic of audiences, but he was a police officer first and foremost. He had a duty to follow up any report of suspected criminal activity. At the very least it seemed prudent to lodge an official report about Holmes's absence and recruit the Eastbourne constabulary in the hunt for him.

CHAPTER TWENTY-THREE

THE TELL-TALE BRUISE

Tasker made me sit for nearly half an hour in the antechamber to his office before inviting me in. While I waited, drumming my fingers on the handle of my walking-stick, I turned over recent events in my mind: my near-murder, Holmes's prolonged disappearance, the devastating fire at Tripp's. Holmes himself would no doubt have been able to divine the common thread linking these things. But I was not Holmes, and the more I badgered and beleaguered my poor brain, the less sense I could make of it all.

When Tasker finally deigned to see me, the first thing I noticed about him was a swelling on his left cheek, a contusion just below the eye. To judge by the colouration – it was blackish purple with a yellow corona – it was a good two days old.

"Ah, you've spotted my little shiner," Tasker said.

To be honest, I could hardly tear my gaze from it. Already a small, awful thought was forming in my mind, a seed of suspicion that swiftly germinated and blossomed.

"Got it manhandling a drunkard the day before last," Tasker went on. "We were taking him in on charges of vandalism, public indecency and affray. He'd got into a fight at the Counting House on Star Road, threatened the landlord, smashed a window, then as he was departing performed an unmentionable act in the doorway. He was a big brute – a merchant sailor – so it took four of us to subdue him. He caught me a lucky blow." Tasker fingered the bruise carefully. "Needless to say he paid for it. The demon drink, eh, doctor? The harm I've seen it do to lives. It's enough to make one join the Temperance Society. Anyway, what can I do for you?"

"I don't know," I said hesitantly.

Was it possible? Could I be sitting across the room from the very man who had tried to kill me? The bruise on Tasker's face could easily have been the result of a blow from the handle of my walking-stick. It was about the right size and in the likely location.

All that flummery about being punched by a drunken sailor resisting arrest – Tasker had recited the tale slickly, inserting enough detail to lend it accuracy and credibility. A little too much detail perhaps? Liars were apt to over-ornament their accounts in order to confer a ring of authenticity.

From there my thoughts kept spiralling further into distrust and even paranoia. Tasker had denied all knowledge of there being an occult society in Eastbourne, but then he would say that – if he were a member of that occult society himself. He did not belong to the Freemasons, which was unusual in a policeman – but then why would he align himself with one shady, secretive cabal when he already had links with another that was shadier and even more secretive?

Tasker had recognised Patrick Mallinson's body the moment he set eyes on it on the beach. Granted, Patrick had been a familiar face around town, but was it not conceivable that Tasker had known him in another capacity? That the Horus-related cult Patrick had been inveigled into joining counted Tasker too among its initiates?

Furthermore, the inspector had come in to work on a Sunday,

the very day Patrick's body washed ashore. Was that not a tad fortuitous? It ensured he would be the one summoned to the scene, the officer charged with heading up the enquiry into the death, which would put him in a position to falsify evidence if need be and steer the investigation away from any hint of wrongdoing. In other words, he was ideally placed to cover up a ritual killing committed by his colleagues in the cult.

Hadn't he been consistently hostile and obstructive towards Holmes and me? He had only agreed to help us after Craig Mallinson strong-armed him into it, and even then he hadn't exactly fallen over himself to be useful. All that rigmarole with the coroner's report, for example. He had let us look at it, but he clearly would have preferred us not to, in case it rendered up some incriminating clue. He had also roundly pooh-poohed the suggestion that Patrick's demise might have been something other than suicide.

Here, before me, was a would-be murderer and an accomplice to murder, in the guise of a sworn upholder of the law.

The notion made the blood drain from my head and pool somewhere in the pit of my stomach.

"…anything the matter, doctor?" Tasker was saying. "Doctor? Hello?"

I realised I had drifted off and not been paying attention to the conversation.

"Yes, no, all is well," I said, but the knot in my gut was insisting otherwise. I had unwittingly walked straight into the lion's den. Worse – I was all but putting my head in the beast's maw.

"You seem distracted."

"Tired, that is all. This sea air. I am a Londoner. Perhaps I am hyper-stimulated from all the unwonted oxygen."

"You haven't been swimming, have you? At this time of year, and at your time of life, that would be unadvisable."

Swimming? Now, surely, Tasker was mocking me.

Yes, for the grin with which he accompanied the remark was sly and taunting, even feral. No doubt he had worn just such a grin as he dogged my footsteps through town on Tuesday and then, spying his chance at the pier, crept up on me and sent me to what he had hoped would be a watery grave.

The effrontery of him, the gall! To let me into his office and make no effort to hide the tell-tale bruise, knowing that there was every chance I would deduce its provenance.

That was how powerful this cult was. How untouchable. They could murder with impunity, for they had representatives everywhere, in the highest echelons of authority. And they laughed at us when we challenged them and were prepared to wipe us out like vermin.

Did they have Sherlock Holmes in their clutches even now?

I very much thought that they did, and this was the final straw, the clinching blow.

I stood up, shunting my chair back. I staggered for the door.

"Dr Watson?" said Tasker. "Where are you going?"

"Nowhere. Out. I'm leaving."

"But you haven't yet stated your business. You were waiting out there long enough. Why did you wish to see me?"

"No reason." My hand was on the doorknob, the palm slick with perspiration. "I happened to be passing."

"I doubt that. Do you have something to report? Or have you just been wasting my time? If the latter, that would be a pity. For you. Wasting police time is an offence, you know."

I stumbled out of his office. His voice followed me through the anteroom and down the corridor like a cackling phantom.

"Come back when you've remembered what you were going to tell me. Or don't come back at all. Either's fine with me. You and Mr Holmes can keep barking up any number of wrong trees.

You won't get anywhere. An open-and-shut case, doctor. Open-and-shut. Why not admit it and spare yourselves the effort? It's over. You've tried and failed. Over!"

CHAPTER TWENTY-FOUR

THE FOLLOWER IN THE SEA FRET

It was mid-afternoon, but already the daylight was weakening. A sea fret had moved in over the town, wreathing everything in a gauzy haze. The mist brought an eerie stillness and silence to the streets. Voices and footfalls became muffled. Pedestrians drifted along like ghosts.

Lamplighters set about their duties early, as was the custom on the coast when mist or fog rolled in. Electrification had yet to come to Eastbourne's municipal infrastructure, so one after another the streetlamps were ignited by hand and began to shed their gibbous yellow glow.

Yet the sea fret only thickened, as though contemptuous of men's efforts to ward off its occluding embrace. It wrapped itself over shopfronts and rooftops. It coiled around railings and awnings. It blanketed the world like snow.

Soon visibility was reduced to a couple of dozen yards. People on the pavement became mere grey outlines who gained detail and solidity as they passed by, before reverting to shadows again and finally disappearing altogether. Carriages rolled down the roads all but inaudibly, as though wheels and hooves were bandaged in cotton wool.

And I, I kept walking. Through this town which had been made alien and phantasmagorical by the fret, I kept walking, without aim or direction, simply so as to remain in motion, to feel as though I had a purpose even if I had none other than to keep questing vainly, hopefully, after Sherlock Holmes.

In hindsight I can see that I was still not wholly delivered from the fever's influence. Some small residue of it lingered within me, disordering my brain. What seemed to me an eminently sensible course of action – plodding on with my one-man search for Holmes – was in fact anything but. I should have found myself somewhere warm to take refuge in, a public house, a restaurant, a hotel lounge. That or made my way back to East Dean by the shortest possible route.

Instead I remained out in the open, criss-crossing Eastbourne like a lost lamb. Every face that loomed towards me out of the mist, I scrutinised. Could that be Holmes? That one? That one? Even women. Even children. For my friend was a known master of disguise. He could make himself look like anything, from an aged seaman to an Italian priest, from a French plumber to a Chinese coolie. Perhaps he had spent the past two days in camouflage, plastered in enough makeup to render him wholly unrecognisable, scouring the town for a lead, evidence, some clue which might yield up the existence and whereabouts of the Horus cult.

After a while the streets were deserted, people driven indoors by the impenetrable, confounding mist. I wandered on, doubtless looking as demented and gimlet-eyed as the Ancient Mariner.

Then I began to discern a set of footfalls behind me. I was on the seafront, and at first I thought that what I was hearing was the echo of my own boot soles, over and above the sound of the surf whispering softly, invisibly, to my left.

It became clear, however, that the second set of footfalls wasn't a perfect match for mine. They shuffled. They were irregular.

I darted a stealthy look over my shoulder but spied no one – nothing but the swirling tendrils of the sea fret, as dense as any London pea-souper. I strode on, then paused. The other paused too. I quickened my pace; so did he.

A pursuer, then. Someone was following me.

My nerves tingled. Was it a cult member? Inspector Tasker himself, perhaps, stalking me once again? Coming to finish what he had started the day before yesterday?

My hand closed around the jack-knife in my pocket. All at once I no longer felt the stiffness in either shoulder, nor any symptom of my advanced age. My heartbeat was as loud as timpani in my ears. I was alert and on my mettle, made young and hale again by excitement.

Whoever was behind me, if he wished me ill, would not find me such an easy mark as at the pier. I would fend off any assault with all my might. He would rue the day he crossed Dr John H. Watson, decorated war veteran.

Near the disused Napoleonic-era coastal fortification known as the Wish Tower, I took the steps down from the Grand Parade to the Lower. This was so as to draw my unseen pursuer after me, the better to expose him.

Sure enough, the mysterious footfalls descended behind me. I had him. There was no question now but that he was following me with malign intent.

The sun was sinking from its zenith, a pallid disc no brighter than the moon. Save for the man on my tail, I was alone. I would survive this encounter, I vowed to myself. I had only my wits and courage to rely on, plus Holmes's knife, but by God, I would survive.

The Lower Parade boasted shelters positioned along it at intervals, embedded against the sloping rocky base of the promenade.

These were built in the mock-Tudor fashion, with thatched roofs. In them one could find shade and respite from the sun on hot days, and rest one's weary bones on a wooden bench seat.

I ducked into the first of the shelters I came to. I set down my walking-stick, then slipped out the jack-knife and levered the blade from the clasp. Holmes had not looked after it well. There were spots of rust on the metal, and the edge did not appear as sharp as it might be. Yet the knife was still fearsome enough. It would serve. The sight of it alone ought to intimidate anyone with any sense.

The footfalls drew nearer, hesitant now, faltering. My pursuer was unsure what had become of me. Where could I have gone? Had I ventured up one of the steep, zigzagging pathways which led back to the Grand Parade? Had he somehow lost track of his quarry?

I waited, tense.

Then the moment came. A figure manifested in the shelter entrance, framed there. I emerged like a snake from its den, my "fang" flashing in my hand. I grabbed the fellow from behind in a chokehold. I poised the tip of the knife an inch from his eye.

"Do not move," I said in a guttural growl. "Do not struggle. I will gladly carve you open and feel not one whit of remorse."

In my ferment of fear and anger, I meant every word. At that precise instant I was sure that the outcome of this confrontation was my life or his, and I would not allow it to be mine. I would slay the fellow without compunction if I had to, just as he or one of his cohorts had tried to slay me.

"Now, I need answers," I said, "and quickly. Who are you people? Where are you headquartered? And what in God's name have you done with Sherlock Holmes?"

"Sherlock who?" came the quavering reply. "I ain't heard of nobody by that name."

"Come off it. Don't play the ignoramus with me. You have him captive, don't you? You and your ghastly irreligious associates."

"Me and my what? I don't know what you're talking about, sir. I ain't got any 'associates' as such, just a few blokes what I go boozing with from time to time, and bunking down with too. I don't know as you'd call any of them irreligious, excepting maybe Charlie Nine-Fingers. To hear him curse, you'd think he had a personal grudge against the Almighty. Now would you kindly take that knife away, I beg you. I ain't done nothing. I was just coming after you because you looked like a swell gent and I was hoping to touch you for a half-crown or maybe even a shilling when I caught up with you."

It was only then that I became conscious of the malodorousness of the man whom I was holding at knifepoint, and of the shabbiness of his clothing. He reeked of stale beer and of a body that had not felt the benefit of soap and water in many a moon. His garments were ill-fitting and gone-to-seed – a tattered topcoat, a threadbare flat cap, boots whose heels were worn down and whose uppers were parting company from their soles. His beard was bushy and matted, and his long, lank hair hung over his shirt collar in rat-tails.

This was no assassin. This was a tramp, the proverbial gentleman of the road.

I lowered the knife but not my guard. For the tramp could still pose a danger to me. Indeed, his rough talk and poverty-stricken appearance could be a disguise, a carefully calculated feint. These cultists were devilishly cunning, were they not?

I spun him round and looked him in the rheumy eye.

Suddenly everything became clear.

"Holmes!" I blurted out in a transport of delight. "It's you! Of course it is. Oh, you sly old dog. Trailing me like that. You had me thinking your intentions were hostile, when all along you simply wished to get us to a secluded spot so that we might have words."

Holmes feigned incomprehension. "Who is this Holmes

person you keep yammering on about? It surely isn't me."

"Come now. That nose of yours is unmistakable. However much putty you put on it to change its shape, it sticks out a mile."

"This is my own nose, sir," he said, fingering the swollen, strawberry-like appendage. "Every bit of it."

"And the stench of you. Good grief! What must you have done to conjure an aroma as authentically foetid as that? How can you bear it?"

"I admit I may not smell of the nicest, but it ain't easy for a bloke in my position to keep clean, you know."

"I have much to tell you, my good man. And you no doubt have much to tell me."

"For heaven's sake!" the other exclaimed, backing away. "What is wrong with you? I am not this Mr Holmes, whoever he may be. You're making a mistake."

I lunged for his artificial beard, in order to pull it off and prove my point. I refused to have Holmes continue with his imposture now that I had penetrated it. It seemed to me the height of perversity.

I batted aside his feeble attempts to resist and tugged hard on the beard.

It did not come off.

"Overdone it with the spirit gum, eh?" I said, and tugged harder.

"Owww!"

The cry sounded so plaintive, and so full of genuine pain, that it stopped me in my tracks.

The truth dawned.

Not Holmes at all. The tramp was exactly what he appeared to be.

"You flipping lunatic!" he expostulated. "First a knife, then you try to wrench half my ruddy face off. Who the hell do you think you are? Get away from me, you maniac. Leave me alone. I only wanted a spot of money, a bit of a handout, and you blooming well lay into me."

"I do beg your pardon," I said, shamefaced.

"It's people like you what give toffs a bad name. You belong in a lunatic asylum, you do!"

"Look, please, I'm sorry. Here, how about a sixpence for your trouble?"

I fumbled for my wallet, but the tramp was having none of it.

"I don't want your ruddy money now," he said. "I wouldn't take a penny from a crackpot like you. I have my standards."

With that, and a toss of his head which spoke of deeply wounded dignity, the tramp stomped off into the mist.

I was left feeling every kind of idiot. What had come over me? Threatening an innocent person like that. Ready to slit his throat if necessary. That was not me. I was not myself, not in my right mind. This damnable murder. The fear of this occult society. The fire at Tripp's Costumiers. Tasker's arrogant, triumphal crowing. Holmes's prolonged absquatulation.

I sat down inside the shelter and ordered myself to be calm.

"Think, Watson," I said aloud. "Think like Sherlock Holmes. You've known the man more than half your life. You know how his mind works. Reason things out. Be logical. Analytical."

It was hard, because I had so little information to go on.

I tried to put myself in Holmes's shoes. If I were he, where would I be now? If I wasn't the captive of some sinister organisation, that is.

"I would be…" I said, racking my brains. "I would be sifting through evidence. Amassing data. Going over the scene of the crime again."

The scene of the crime was the shoreline below Beachy Head. I contemplated the prospect of going there in this mist, negotiating my way along the uneven sweeps of pebble and skirting the chalk boulders that had tumbled from the cliffs due to erosion. I wasn't even sure I would be able to find the correct spot. Any useful landmarks, not least the brow of Beachy Head itself, would be lost in the fret.

Besides, as far as Holmes was concerned, the crime had occurred elsewhere: up in the sky, in Mallinson's biplane.

The plane.

That would still be of interest to Holmes, wouldn't it?

It was a slender thread but it was all I had. If I hoped to have a chance of locating my friend, Settleholm Manor was the only place left to look.

CHAPTER TWENTY-FIVE

To the Manor Borne

I doubted I would be able to find my way to the manor unaided. However, I had in the past availed myself of the hansoms which waited in a rank outside Eastbourne station. I prayed that cab drivers would still be touting for business despite the inclement weather, and as luck would have it one man was indeed on duty still, hunched in his seat with a drooping-headed nag in the traces before him. He didn't seem too glad of a customer, grumbling that he could barely see his hand in front of his face so how could he be expected to find his way anywhere? He was, of course, simply preying upon my sympathies so that I would be inclined to pay him more generously, and since I was in no position to do otherwise, I told him that an extra florin would be his if he took me where I wanted to go. This perked the man up somewhat, although he demanded to see the colour of my money before he applied the whip to the horse.

Thus, at considerable financial cost, I had transport to Settleholm. The hansom picked its way through the hushed streets, heading north out of town on the Willingdon Road. Then we were clip-clopping along lanes where the mist seemed to glide against the blackberry bushes and the hawthorn hedgerows like some fast-flowing river of condensation rolling between its banks. Now and then the driver, mounted at the rear of the cab, would mutter about the difficulty he was experiencing with seeing, the which complaints, though he kept his voice low, I was nonetheless expected to hear. I bit my tongue, thinking that if he resented being out in these conditions so much, why hadn't he simply gone home when the sea fret first manifested?

I had asked him to give me notice when we were a stone's throw from the manor entrance, and sure enough he rapped on the roof when the time came, announcing that we were almost there.

"Stop the cab," I told him. "I shall walk from here."

"You're the boss," the driver replied indifferently, and pulled on the reins.

As I stepped out, he indicated that I should continue on ahead. "Great big set of gates on the right. You can't miss it." Then he clucked his tongue to gee up the horse and began the process of turning the cab round in a series of laborious back-and-forth manoeuvres.

I raised the latch that secured the pair of immense, heavy iron gates. Hinges creaked faintly as I pushed one of them open and closed it behind me. A broad, packed-earth driveway spread in front of me, winding through an avenue of linden trees. I followed it for perhaps half a mile until at last I caught sight of the house itself, which reared up out of the mist like some forbidding fairytale castle. I noted that parked outside it, alongside Mallinson's Humberette, there was a second car. Evidently he had a guest, perhaps guests plural.

Orientating myself from memory, I turned off in the direction of the barn where the Grahame-White was stored. From time to time I had to pause to get my bearings, even as the manor grew dimmer and more nebulous in the distance. I recognised the stand of oaks ahead and made that my next point of reference.

Halfway there, I noticed an insistent squeaking sound, and then to my right I spotted someone headed my way, pushing something before him.

It was a gardener with a wheelbarrow. The wheel's axle was in need of oil, hence the squeak, and now I could hear an accompanying humming from the gardener himself. He was singing "Greensleeves" wordlessly under his breath in a reedy baritone as he trundled his load – rolls of turf and a shovel – across the lawn.

I darted as swiftly and stealthily as I could away from this rustic-looking member of Mallinson's staff. A nearby rhododendron bush seemed to afford some cover. I hid behind it, peering out. The gardener carried on by, oblivious. He stopped momentarily to straighten up and press a thickly gloved hand into the small of his back, uttering a soft groan. Then he bent to the wheelbarrow's handles and was off once more.

The mist swallowed him up. I let out a breath I hadn't realised I was holding.

I resumed my course towards the oaks. My close encounter with the gardener had reminded me that I was an interloper on the estate, as I had been the last time with Holmes and Reptilio. That occasion had nearly turned out very badly for us, and I had no desire for another run-in with Jenks the gamekeeper.

Moreover, it was beginning to sink in just how futile an exercise this was. Did I honestly think I would bump into Holmes somewhere by the barn? That was assuming he was even here at the manor at all. The odds against such an eventuality were astronomical. I was more likely to come up empty-handed, and then what would I have to show for my trouble? I would be stuck out in the middle of the countryside, in thick mist, with evening fast falling. What would be my next move? Strike out for the nearest village? I did not even know in what direction it might lie. Go up to the front door and throw myself on Craig Mallinson's mercy? Possibly. I could claim I had been walking in the area and had lost my way, until I passed Settleholm Manor. That seemed plausible enough, and Mallinson was a decent cove. It was doubtful that he would refuse me hospitality and turn me out on my ear. As long as I acted the part of the wayward, stranded traveller well, he would have no cause to doubt my veracity. He might even offer me a bed for the night, in the expectation that the fret would diminish and the air be clear again by morning.

From the oaks I could just make out the shape of the barn. It was time to see this misbegotten venture through to its end.

I had gone no more than three steps when a familiar coarse voice thundered, "You there! Halt!"

I barely needed to look round. What appalling wretched luck. The one thing had happened that I had hoped would not.

I had been caught by Jenks.

The unmistakable silhouette of the gamekeeper was approaching through the mist. He unshouldered his shotgun as he came, thumbing back the hammers on both barrels.

Briefly, wildly, I considered running. But what would be the use? I was not fleet of foot, and if Jenks was half as good a shot as he professed to be, he would have a round of pellets in me before I'd gone five yards, mist or no mist.

I would have to devise some other way out of this predicament. My best bet seemed to be gentle dissuasion.

"Jenks…" I began.

"As I live and breathe, it's Dr Watson," said he. "Well I never. Back on Mr Mallinson's property, and up to no good again, I'll be bound."

Now he was close enough for me to discern his features.

My jaw dropped.

For Jenks, like Inspector Tasker, sported a large, prominent bruise. It was on his forehead, just by the temple.

We looked at each other, he and I, for several taut seconds.

Then I said, "You."

And he said, "Indeed. Me."

I could see that he knew there was no point denying it. He was the one who had thrown me off the end of the pier. The evidence was as plain as the bruise on his face. His lopsided, unabashed smile clinched it. I was in the presence of my would-be killer.

And he had a loaded gun levelled at me.

CHAPTER TWENTY-SIX

A Stiff Upper Lip and a Belly Full of British Pluck

"You survived," he said. It was a statement, not an interrogative. He was not expressing surprise. "I watched those blasted swimmers rescue you. Not a ruddy thing I could do about it. Such rotten timing. If only I'd waited another five minutes, they would have been too far past."

"Jenks, listen," I said, "I have no idea why you want me dead, but I am not one to hold a grudge. Put the gun away. I'm sure we can settle this amicably, without resorting to bloodshed."

"And now you have the nerve to come sniffing round here again," Jenks said, as though I had not spoken. "Funny thing is, I had a hunch you might. Where's your chum Holmes? He's got to be somewhere nearby. You're keeping lookout for him, that's it, isn't it?"

"Yes," I said, and then more firmly, "Yes. Sherlock Holmes is around. So you'd better watch out. In this mist, he could be anywhere."

The bluff had no impact. "Well, wherever he is, he won't be fast enough to save you, if that's what you're hoping. This can be done with in the time it takes to pull a trigger. But first, put aside that walking-stick of yours. I'll not have you catching me another lucky blow with it like last time, or trying any other funny business."

I dropped the stick as requested. "There. Satisfied?"

"Good. I just want you to know, doctor, that it's nothing personal. You've been too inquisitive, that's all. Shoving you in the water was meant to put Mr Holmes off. Had you died, it would have made the point clear as day. He would realise he should leave things well alone. As it is, he should at least have taken the hint, as should you. You're meddling with forces greater than you comprehend."

"You should know that I am not a man to 'take a hint', and even less so is Sherlock Holmes. In fact, were you at all familiar with the man and his deeds, you would realise that the more you try to deter him, the more determined he becomes. Had you succeeded in killing me at the pier, you would have made yourself an implacable enemy. Holmes would not rest until he saw you swinging from the hangman's noose. The same applies now."

"Is that so?" said Jenks. "Well, perhaps we should put it to the test. I failed last time, but this time I have you bang to rights."

His finger coiled round the trigger.

"Emphasis on 'bang'," he added with a cruel leer.

I steeled myself. I stared him in the eye. I had faced death before, many times, and learned that it must be met with boldness and courage, for that is how you rob it of its power. When it cannot be evaded or parlayed, then it can only be confronted head on.

That was the soldier in me, ready to meet his end with a stiff upper lip and a belly full of British pluck.

Jenks hesitated, cocking his head.

Both of us had detected a repetitive, insistent squeaking, which got rapidly louder and clearer. Jenks lowered the shotgun part-way, then all the way.

"Now who the devil…?" he murmured, irritated.

The gardener came into view, pushing his wheelbarrow as

before. He was a venerable, whiskery sort, with a red spotted neckerchief fastened around his throat and an unlit clay pipe clenched between his teeth. The brim of his felt hat shaded a pair of lively eyes.

"Afternoon, Mr Jenks," he said in a thick rural burr, touching finger to forehead. "Begging your pardon, sorr. Don't mean as to interrupt your chitchat with this gent, but where's Mr Mallinson wanting this here stack of sod to be laid? Only oi can't seem to find the bare patch oi'm meant to be looking for. Was it the croquet lawn?"

"How am I supposed to know?" said Jenks testily. "Ask Daykin, the head gardener. It's his job."

"Right you are, sorr. You wouldn't happen to know where he be, would you? Mr Daykin, that is."

"No, I would not. Now be off with you."

"Aye, sorr. Whatever you say, sorr." The gardener hoisted up the wheelbarrow handles, but then abruptly let out a hiss of pain and dropped them. The barrow tipped over, landing on its side and disgorging its contents. Several rolls of turf unravelled, half burying the shovel among them.

"Oh, fiddlesticks!" he exclaimed. "How clumsy can a fellow be? It's me back, see. Me lumbago. It keeps giving me these abominable twinges. Now look at what oi've gone and done."

He knelt to start gathering up the turf. I tried to catch his eye and give him a look that would convey that I was in distress, but he was too involved in his task to notice. Jenks's shotgun was no longer pointing straight at me. There was no way the gardener could have inferred the true import of the situation, how things actually stood between me and Jenks. To him it looked as though the gamekeeper and I had merely been engaged in casual conversation when he happened by. Doubtless he assumed from my dress and deportment that I was a houseguest of Craig Mallinson's, perhaps the owner of that second car.

If I could somehow get him to notice that something was awry here…

But then that might endanger him too.

At any rate, he continued to pay me no heed. Jenks watched impatiently, and I impotently, as the old man righted the wheelbarrow and loaded the turf back into it. It was absurd – farcical, even. This cackhanded yokel was holding us up, keeping us from concluding our business. Unfortunately for me, that business was my being murdered in cold blood.

Jenks peered intently at the gardener. "I don't know you, do I?" he said. "Haven't seen you around before."

"Oi be a recent hire," came the reply. "Only started as of last week. Tuppen's the name."

"How come you know *my* name, then? Seeing as we've never met."

"Everyone in Mr Mallinson's employ be knowing Mr Jenks the gamekeeper. Besides, Fanny the chambermaid pointed you out yesterday as you was passing in the distance. 'That's Mr Jenks,' she said, all admiringly like, in such a wise that oi could tell she be nursing a special fancy for you."

"Fanny, eh? Well, I don't deny that she's a pretty young thing. Shapely, too. There's just one problem."

"Oh arr?"

"I wasn't here yesterday. Wednesdays are my day off."

"Then it must've been the day before," said the gardener. "Oi gets muddled, see. Me age, sorr. Memory isn't what it was. Oi can remember scrumping apples from farmer Evans's orchard as a nipper, clear as anything, but ask me what the missus served for supper last night and oi couldn't tell you."

Jenks raised the shotgun again, only now it was aimed not at me but at the gardener.

"Stand up," he said.

"Sorr?"

"You heard."

Before the gardener did as bidden, his hand stole towards the shovel.

In that instant I perceived the full picture. It should have been obvious but, as Holmes was fond of pointing out, too often I *saw* but failed to *observe*.

I made my lunge for Jenks even as the gardener moved too, with startling swiftness for a man of his years who professed to suffer from chronic lumbago. The shovel came sweeping upwards, connecting with the shotgun barrel. Jenks's finger involuntarily tightened on the trigger. The gun boomed, discharging into the sky. At the same time I collided bodily with Jenks in a sort of bearhug-cum-rugby-tackle which, I regret to say, had greater consequence for me than it did for him. He was strong, more muscular than I had given him credit for. He shrugged me off as though I were a child.

The gardener swung the shovel again, and this time the flat of its blade struck Jenks's right hand. The gamekeeper bellowed in pain and his firearm fell to the ground. Clutching his right hand in his left, he seethed and swore, spittle flecking his lips. The gardener whirled the shovel as though it were a golf club, hitting the shotgun where it lay and sending it skidding across the grass, out of immediate reach.

In the event, the gamekeeper ran at him like a charging bull. The gardener danced backwards with alacrity, then thrust the shovel at Jenks's midriff like a lance, the blade end-on. Jenks arched away defensively, but in a surprising move, one that the gardener had not foreseen, he seized the shovel blade and pushed hard. The butt of the handle was driven forcefully into the gardener's belly. He managed to brace himself, but the blow clearly still hurt.

I launched myself back into the fray, somewhat more

circumspectly than before. I clouted Jenks on the side of the head. Who could have predicted that he would possess such a thick skull? I reeled away feeling that every finger in my hand was broken. Jenks, for his part, was barely fazed. He and the gardener continued to grapple with the shovel, which lay between them like the rope in a particularly vicious tug-of-war.

"Watson," said the gardener, his bumpkin accent gone, "I would truly appreciate some help."

"I'm trying," I replied, shaking out my bruised hand.

"Well, try harder."

Grimacing and gasping, the two men fought to wrest the shovel from each other's clutches. Jenks was half as old as his opponent – as Sherlock Holmes, I should say, for the secret of the gardener's true identity was now out. Jenks, furthermore, was in prime physical condition, only to be expected in a man who engaged in outdoor activity all day long. There seemed little doubt but that he would prevail in the contest with Holmes.

That, apparently, was Holmes's conclusion too, because all at once he loosened his grip on the shovel.

Jenks was caught unawares and teetered backwards several steps, off-balance. Holmes pressed at him, hoping to topple him entirely, but Jenks regained his footing.

This left the two of them nose to nose, with the shovel now turned sideways between them, so that in a strange manner they resembled a pair of dogs squabbling over a hambone.

I, meanwhile, made for the discarded shotgun. I picked it up, only to find that my right hand, the one I had punched Jenks with, was too painful to use properly. I had badly bruised the knuckles with that ill-advised blow, perhaps even torn a ligament or two, and my index finger refused to bend sufficiently to be inserted inside the trigger guard.

Still, I could hold the gun, and that meant I could employ it as a striking weapon. Gripping the forestock with both hands, I approached Jenks from behind. Holmes, spotting me, gave a brief, tight nod. One white sideburn had partly peeled away from his face, revealing a familiar gaunt cheek.

Jenks, alas, sensed my presence, perhaps alerted by Holmes's surreptitious nod. He wheeled round just as I was preparing to ram the shotgun butt down onto his crown. He dragged Holmes in a half-circle with him, and it was only by dint of sudden self-correction that I avoided clubbing my friend with the gun instead of Jenks.

Holmes still had that clay pipe in his mouth, and as a last resort he spat it out hard. It flew into Jenks's eye, and in that split second, while the gamekeeper was distracted, I saw that I had been given a fresh opportunity. I slammed the gun into Jenks's face. The impact was not as powerful as I would have liked, but I didn't have much time to steady myself for the blow and I was delivering it at an awkward angle, over Holmes's shoulder. It was enough, all the same, both to send Jenks reeling and to release the hammer on the second barrel. Another gunshot blast rent the air, deafeningly loud, and the gun itself bucked so hard in my hands that I dropped it.

We all staggered apart in different directions, Holmes, Jenks and myself, dizzied and panting, ears ringing. Of the three of us, it was hard to tell who was in the worst shape, although Jenks, unlike Holmes or me, was cut. A trickle of blood was issuing from the small gash that I had put in his forehead.

I realised the shotgun was at my feet. So, at the same instant, did Jenks. With a sudden, atavistic growl he sprang for it and snatched it up. I admit I did not react nearly fast enough, but in my defence, I had not thought the gamekeeper capable of such a turn of speed just then. He was less stunned than he had seemed.

With practised facility Jenks broke the shotgun open, ejected the spent cartridges and produced a fresh pair from his pouch.

Holmes looked at me and said, "Watson, I believe the time has come for us to practise the better part of valour."

"Meaning run?"

"Meaning run."

CHAPTER TWENTY-SEVEN

YOUNG BUCKS, OLD CROCKS

It wasn't so much a run as a stiff-kneed canter, but we did our best, putting distance between ourselves and Jenks as fast as we were able. Once the gamekeeper had slotted the two new cartridges in place he hastened after us, but by then we had become engulfed by the mist. We heard him cursing and raging behind us, his voice gradually dwindling.

A few minutes later, after we had gone the best part of half a mile, I begged Holmes to be allowed to stop and rest. He consented, and I stood with my hands braced on my thighs, heaving for breath. I felt sick and lightheaded and my heart laboured within my breast. Holmes, though not quite as fatigued as I, was nonetheless red in the face and puffing hard.

"What fit young bucks we once were," he said with a rueful grimace, "and what broken old crocks we are now. There was a time when a dash like that would have left us barely winded at all."

"Speak for yourself, old chap," I said, forcing the words out between stertorous gasps. "I am in as fine a fettle as a racehorse. I would have gone faster, but I didn't want to show you up."

"Funny, I was about to say the same thing."

"Deuced good to see you, though."

"And you, you great inimitable oaf. You somewhat ruined my stakeout, you know, forcing me to break cover, but I shall forgive you."

"I was frantic with worry. I had no idea what had become of you. I even thought you might be dead."

"Not yet, Watson. I am as alive as can be – and also stuffed to the gills with new information. But that must wait. It is imperative that we carry on going and get as far from Settleholm as we possibly can."

"Why? We have shaken off Jenks, and there is precious little chance of him finding us, not in this mist. Surely we are safe."

"That is where you are wrong, I'm afraid. We are anything but safe."

The seriousness with which my companion said this put me on edge. "Would you care to elaborate?"

"First, let us resume our flight."

We set off again, not attempting to run this time but adopting a loping pace that was somewhere between a walk and a trot. The mist had begun to darken and turn grey, becoming yet more impenetrable. Somewhere to the west the sun was creeping towards the horizon.

"You see," said Holmes, "Jenks may choose to pursue us still, and if he does, it will not be without assistance."

"He will set up a hue-and-cry and dragoon in others from the estate staff to form a search party?"

"Not as such. He would not wish to involve witnesses. At least, not any who can talk."

"I don't understand."

"How rarely you do."

"Perhaps if you were to be less exasperatingly cryptic…"

"Very well. Cast your mind back, Watson, to when Craig

Mallinson was telling us about the hunt for his missing son."

I did my best to recollect the conversation. "Are you suggesting Jenks might come looking for us in Mallinson's aeroplane? But that would be absurd. He would be no more likely to see us from above, in this mist, than on the ground. Besides, he would be flying blind, as it were, and that would be suicidally risky."

"No. Think harder. Mallinson was describing how he and Jenks scoured the grounds of the estate."

"I'm sorry, old fellow, but just at this moment I'm drawing a complete blank."

"Are your powers of recall really so poor?" Holmes snorted. "No wonder so many inconsistencies and discrepancies crop up in your published oeuvre. Mallinson said that he hoped Patrick was in an outbuilding or the woods, so he –"

Holmes was interrupted by a far-off noise, one which I myself found unduly hackle-raising.

It was the barking of an enormous hound.

CHAPTER TWENTY-EIGHT

THE HOUND OF THE MALLINSONS

"A dog," I breathed.

"Indeed," said Holmes. "I spied its kennel earlier today in a courtyard at the rear of the house. The creature was ensconced within and I failed to get a good look at it. I can tell you, though, that a thick chain led into the kennel and the other end was fastened to the ground by an iron stake. And when I say kennel, it was actually more like a small shed."

"My God..."

"A sizeable beast," my friend said with a confirmatory nod, "and probably not of the most amiable temperament. What's more, we must assume it has been trained to follow a scent. Regrettably you have left your walking-stick behind. Years of use will have imprinted your smell on the handle."

"I am an idiot."

"I wouldn't go that far. But the set of circumstances you have helped to create is not ideal. We may yet be able to shake the hound off, but for that to happen we will have to find the Cuckmere river."

"Which is where?"

"Somewhere to the south, the way we are currently headed," Holmes said, but did I discern a faint note of uncertainty in his voice? Was he trying to sound more confident than he genuinely was?

We hurried onward through the dreary, darkening haze, while to our rear those gruff, ferocious barks continued, unabated. Sometimes they seemed near, other times far away, but it was hard to know if this was truth or just a trick of the mist. The conditions seemed designed to confound one's every perception. Holmes kept taking a bearing from the position of the sun, but it was, I thought, an imprecise method of reckoning direction, for all he really had to go on was a paler stretch of the sky, a broad expanse where the gloom was slightly less intense. As long as that was to our right, then notionally we were travelling southward, but the margin for error was considerable.

We passed from field to field, using gates or stiles where we could find them but otherwise cleaving through hedgerows by brute force. In many instances the earth underfoot had been ploughed and we had to trudge through the furrows, our boots becoming clogged and heavy with mud; or else there was stubble to stumble over, or late-season root crops whose leaves entwined around our ankles. In short, it was slow, cumbersome going, and the unseen dog's ever-present barking made it seem all the slower and more cumbersome. I had had nightmares like this, where I was being pursued by some marauding monster and could make little headway, my feet becoming ever more bogged down in swampy ground.

The present situation was all too horribly reminiscent of that night in 1889 when, at the Grimpen Mire on Dartmoor, Stapleton's dreadful coal-black hound would have savaged Sir Henry Baskerville to death had Holmes and I not managed to shoot it in time. I recalled my friend's scorn at the Tiger Inn just a few days back when his talk of an eldritch black dog had sparked an involuntary shudder in me. Now my fear was even greater, and justified, because it had a solid grounding in reality. Jenks's dog was flesh-and-blood, and it was leading its master to us, and in the unlikely event that it wasn't the sort of animal that was capable of killing a man, the gun its master carried certainly could.

In the distance a church bell tolled the hour – six o'clock.

"St Andrew's at Alfriston," said Holmes. "It can only be. The peal of a bell with a side clapper is distinct from that with an internal clapper, and St Andrew's has the only side clapper bell in the area."

"Is this good news?"

"It is. It confirms we are on the correct course."

"Can we not head for the village and find sanctuary there?"

"We have passed it already. The bell was behind us. To double back now might prove fatal."

On we forged, as the daylight waned still further. It felt as though the world was disappearing around us bit by bit, leaving us in a benighted limbo.

Then at last came the susurration of running water.

"The Cuckmere," said Holmes, veering off towards it. "Come along, old chap. One final push."

I was at a low ebb and Holmes knew it. He coaxed and cajoled me along. Shortly we reached the river bank, down whose grassy slope we slipped and slithered, landing in shin-deep water at the bottom. We set off across to the other bank, which was only just visible from this side. The water deepened until it was up to our thighs, but thankfully, though the river was tidal at this point, the tide was low and the current not strong. Each supporting the other, we waded across without incident or mishap.

Climbing the other bank proved problematic. It was steep, and thick with brambles and stinging nettles. Our boot soles could not obtain easy purchase. We scrambled up on all fours like rats, and eventually – scratched, stung, sodden – we gained the top. I lay there panting, wishing I could just go to sleep on the spot. Sleep would be such sweet oblivion.

Holmes, however, urged me to my feet. "No rest yet."

"Why not? Hasn't fording the river destroyed our scent trail?"

"It is far from guaranteed. Remember Toby, Mr Sherman's spaniel-lurcher cross? How he tracked that wooden-legged fiend Jonathan Small halfway across London, following the scent even over one of the city's busiest, most heavily trafficked roads? Never underestimate the power of the canine nose, Watson. It is many orders of magnitude more sensitive than our own. Besides, we have left spoor on the opposite bank. An experienced countryman like Jenks may have little trouble inferring what we have done."

"Then perhaps you should leave me here," I said, "and carry on without me. It is my scent the dog has caught. You will be able to get away scot-free without me holding you back. Live to fight another day."

"Don't be ridiculous, Watson. You insult me simply by saying that. Now come on, up with you."

Wearily I allowed myself to be led across several further fields. A chalk footpath offered itself to us but Holmes eschewed it. "Too obvious," he said. "It's safe to assume that Jenks is intimately familiar with the lie of the land round here and believes that we are not. Therefore he would think us liable to take a path if we find one, and for that very reason we shouldn't. We must not make his task any easier for him."

Jenks's dog began baying that very moment. Whether this was in excitement or frustration, I could not tell. I hoped that the sound signified that it had lost our trail and was venting its dismay, but I feared the opposite – that Jenks and the dog had traversed the Cuckmere too and were hot on our heels once more.

The last of the daylight leaked from the sky like the embers of a fire dying out. Holmes and I had nothing on us to illuminate our way, not even a pocket lantern. We were surrounded by an infinite, impenetrably dense blackness. Every step we took, we took more or less blind, groping our way forward as though we were condemned prisoners with sacks on our heads. The smallest rock, the slightest declivity in the ground, could trip us up, and did.

All the while, Jenks's hound kept up its eager ululation, and there was no question but that the two of them, man and dog, were getting closer to us now. Not only were the dog's howls growing in volume, and moreover exultancy, but we also caught glimpses of a beam of light flickering intermittently like a firefly. Jenks's electric torch.

"How?" I said. "How can we possibly escape? We cannot see, and Jenks can. We've done our best to foil the hound, to no avail. It's hopeless."

"Do not despair, Watson. We have been in tighter scrapes than this and lived to tell the tale. Have I ever steered you wrong? Let you down?"

"Never."

"Then trust in me once again. If my calculations are correct, very soon we shall have guidance. After all, what does a ship's captain do when he's close to shore on a night as murky and fogbound as this?"

I could not fathom an answer to this riddle just then. I wondered if Holmes was perhaps trying to divert my mind from the futility of our predicament, the way one distracts and soothes a fretful child by focusing its attention elsewhere.

Within moments, however, all was explained as I perceived a distant, ponderous sweep of light, a moving glow which sustained itself for several seconds before fading out. It came again, and then again, filling the mist with enough lambency that I could make out the contours of the landscape and essay my next few steps with confidence.

"The lighthouse," said Holmes. "Beachy Head lighthouse. We are not far from East Dean and safety."

But not near enough, as it turned out. Our ordeal was not yet at an end. Several further trials awaited us that night.

CHAPTER TWENTY-NINE

Fallen Angel

"Take care," said Holmes. "We are close to the cliff edge now. It is not simply that one misstep might mean your undoing. Chalk is a friable substance. Parts of the cliff have been known to break away spontaneously, and where there is an overhang, often all it requires is the weight of a human being to cause it to give way."

I would have asked why we needed to be so near the cliffs at all, but Holmes had already expounded his reasoning. The illumination from the lighthouse was better up here. The pulses from its revolving lamp array revealed more. Therefore we could make quicker progress.

There was, however, a corollary, namely that we ourselves became more visible. Our silhouettes would stand proud every time the light came round. Holmes was gambling that thanks to the lighthouse we could keep sufficiently far ahead of Jenks for this not to matter. Jenks's shotgun, given that it had full-choke barrels, was accurate and effective up to sixty yards, the maximum range for such a weapon. As long as we stayed beyond that, the chance of being hit was remote.

The dog, of course, was another matter.

The terrain undulated. We were travelling across the craggy shoulders of the Seven Sisters, tracing the cliffs' series of rises and falls. At our backs Jenks's hound was setting up a damnable frenzy of yips and howls, knowing that its quarry was almost within reach. The only reason I could posit as to why Jenks had not let the animal off the leash yet was that without it he might very easily lose track of us. Until he himself could see us and keep us within sight, the dog was serving as his eyes.

All at once, I was alone. Holmes was not to be found. Somewhere our paths had diverged.

I called his name softly. No answer. As the light from the lighthouse flared, I gazed all around, seeking his shape amid the thickets of mist. Nothing. No sign of him.

I fell prey to a deep pang of dread. Not only did I feel abandoned, cast adrift like a marooned mariner, but I entertained the notion that Holmes had succumbed to the very danger he had warned me against. His footsteps had taken him accidentally over the cliff edge, whereupon he had plunged to his death without a sound. Awful memories of the Reichenbach Falls went parading through my head.

I froze, terrified of following him to the same fate. I felt hapless and helpless.

Then, to compound my alarm, I saw the bright flash of Jenks's torch. It could not have been more than a hundred yards away.

Abruptly the dog ceased to cry.

That could mean only one thing.

Sure enough, I heard the galloping thump of paws on grass. They sounded as loud as a horse's hooves.

Next I knew, a hunched, massive animal was before me, a hulking beast as large as any dog I had seen – larger, even, than *that* dog, the Baskerville hound. There was mastiff in its ancestry, and Alsatian, and perhaps Rhodesian ridgeback as well, to judge by the bristle of fur along its spine. In short, it was made up from a whole gallimaufry of breeds that were prized for their size, muscularity and ferocity.

It was phenomenally ugly, too. Dr Frankenstein himself could not have sewn together an atrocity as misshapen and grotesque-looking as this. Folds of skin drooped around a pair of baleful bloodshot eyes. Jowls dangled either side of its maw, dripping threads of drool. Lower teeth protruded up over its muzzle, the canines each as long as my little finger, the incisors not much smaller and certainly not much less sharp. I have seen pleasanter sights in the paintings of Hieronymus Bosch.

Ears pricked, tail hung low, this *thing* pounded to a halt in front of me. It regarded me for several long seconds, and then emitted from its throat a growl that resembled the rumble of an earthquake.

I nearly lost all control of myself. It was as much as I could do to keep from whimpering.

The dog took another couple of steps closer. Unthinkingly I moved the same number of steps back. I was heedless of my proximity to the cliff edge. I simply wanted to maintain a decent gap between me and this enormous, hideous creature.

Again the dog growled, and at the same time bared all of its teeth. There were more fangs in its mouth than one would have thought possible for any single animal to own. I felt that I was looking at an arsenal of ivory daggers.

"Angel!" Jenks called out from somewhere not far removed.

The dog stiffened and replied with a short, sharp bark.

"Hold, Angel. Keep 'em pinned. I'll be right there."

Jenks knew that his hound, so inaptly named, had at least one of us at bay, if not both. How many poachers must he have apprehended in this way, working in perfect concert with the dog? The animal was clearly practised at cornering people and intimidating them into immobility while it awaited the arrival of its master.

I retreated a little further. Angel padded forwards. The dog must have a fixed pouncing distance, I realised, a span it knew it could cover in a single leap. It was trained not to let me get out of range.

I heard Jenks's heavy breathing as he laboured upslope to join the dog. He gave a whistle, and Angel barked to help orientate him.

It was only then that I remembered the jack-knife in my pocket. Did I dare to try and slip it out somehow? Or would the dog consider this a provocative act and respond with aggression? Would I even have time to get the knife open before the beast's jaws closed on me? I doubted it.

Then there was a thump; a crash; the sounds of a scuffle.

Angel twitched and half turned round.

I made a desperate bid for freedom while the dog's attention was not fully on me. I darted to one side.

A strangled shout came from the mist: "Angel, attack!"

The dog spun and lumbered after me. Such was its bulk that it took several paces to get up to full speed from a standing start. Yet, once it was running flat out, it easily outstripped me.

I heard its paws thundering at my heels. I swear I could feel its hot breath on my back.

The hound sprang.

At the self-same moment, someone bore down on me, bringing me sprawling to the ground.

The dog shot above me, open jaws just missing my head.

It landed without a sound.

Or rather, it didn't land at all. It hurtled out into empty space, legs flailing. There was a whine of sheer terror, followed by a couple of seconds of silence and then a heavy wet impact far below.

I half sat up. Holmes was beside me. It was he who had been

my saviour, knocking me down at the last instant so that the dog had sailed over me and then over the cliff edge, which lay mere inches to my right.

"But you were fighting Jenks a moment ago, weren't you?" I said when my heart rate had returned to something approaching normal.

"True. I used his torch like a beacon, to guide me to him. When he whistled to the dog, that was when I knew I had him once and for all."

"Then how were you able to reach me so swiftly, if you were engaging him?"

"As soon as he gave the attack command, I delivered the coup de grâce and ran like the wind to intercept you," said he. "I had, you see, been hoping to provoke Jenks into just such a precipitate action."

"You mean I was bait? I was there to lure the dog away, a sitting duck?"

"A regrettable but unavoidable exigency. I needed to separate the two of them so that I might tackle Jenks one-to-one. He is currently lying unconscious, felled by a *baritsu* palm-heel strike to the nerve cluster just below the jawline. He will live, but the same, I am glad to say, cannot be said of his dog."

"Angel," I said with spite and venom.

"A fallen Angel now."

"And good riddance. Dash it all, Holmes! You could have told me what you were planning."

"Would you have volunteered to participate if I had?"

"Well, no," I admitted. "Probably not. But I would rather not be made to feel like a pawn that can be sacrificed at will."

"I would never sacrifice you, Watson. You are far too valuable a piece on the board. But that isn't to say I wouldn't use you to tempt my opponent into committing one of his own pieces."

He was jesting, but I was not mollified. "What if you hadn't got to me before the dog did? What if you had been too slow, or misgauged your leap to flatten me? What if that damned animal had –"

I never finished the sentence, for just then a deep vibrant groan resounded through the patch of cliff we were perched on, and suddenly I was falling.

CHAPTER THIRTY

CLIFFHANGER

The cliff had given way. We were, it transpired, atop one of those overhangs Holmes had referred to. It had cracked under our weight and was now shearing off. I was about to meet the same end as the devil-dog Angel.

It is an horrific sensation, to feel solid ground crumble beneath you, to feel gravity abruptly claim you when you thought you had nothing to fear from it. I remember letting out a high-pitched cry that had as much indignation in it as alarm, as though Mother Nature had just played a rotten prank on me. In a way, I suppose she had.

That I didn't plummet to my doom can be ascribed to two factors. The first was that Sherlock Holmes had been lying inland from me, just the other side of the fissure along which the cliff had cracked. The second was that his reflexes were so spectacularly swift.

He seized my right wrist with both hands, arresting my fall. My momentum dragged him after me but he dug his knees and elbows in and managed to keep most of his body still on the clifftop. With all of the strength in him he kept me suspended, even as several large chunks of chalk tumbled below us to the beach, crashing onto the pebbles in a rocky avalanche.

I dangled by one arm, Holmes my only anchor.

"Now listen, old chap," my friend said. His teeth were clenched with the incredible physical effort of supporting me. "I cannot hold you like this for long. Use your feet. Find a toehold. Take some of the weight."

"I can't," I said in a paroxysm of terror. "I can't. Don't – don't let go."

"I'm not going to let go, but you will slip out of my grasp if you do not do as I say. Just in front of you is a crevice, level with your knee. Place your foot there. Concentrate! Do it!"

I somehow wedged my foot into the space. Holmes adjusted his grip. I could feel the sweat lining his palms, making them slick. He was digging his fingers into my wrist to compensate, and it hurt but I didn't care. My injured shoulder was complaining, too, adding a throbbing bass note to my overall cacophony of pain and panic.

"Good," said Holmes. "Now, you must push yourself up while I pull. We shall have only one shot at this, so we need to get it right. If we fail, I doubt I can do anything but drop you. Do you understand?"

My only response was a frantic nod.

"On my mark. Three. Two. One. Go!"

I kicked down into the crevice. Holmes heaved with all his might. For a moment I seemed to hang in midair. I was all too conscious of the abyss beneath me, the waves throwing themselves hungrily at the shoreline, the imminence of a two-second plunge that would truncate my life abruptly and very messily.

Then I was sprawled on the clifftop, half of me, my legs still angled out over the edge. Holmes hauled on my sleeve, my coattail, my waistband, anything to help tug me the rest of the way onto the cliff. I clawed the turf with my hands.

Finally I was fully on land again, but I kept going, scrambling along on my belly like a sea lion until I reached what I considered was a safe distance from the cliff edge. I had never been so grateful to feel wet grass under me. I wanted to kiss it.

Holmes left me there to recover while he went to check on Jenks. He returned looking aggrieved.

"He has gone," he said. "Upped and ran while we were otherwise engaged."

"I thought you knocked him out."

"I did. He is made of steel, it would seem. Nigh on impervious to harm."

"Is he still out there?" I scanned the mist trepidatiously.

"He appears to have fled. His footprints were uneven, indicating that he is limping or at any rate unsteady on his legs, groggy after the blow I struck. He still has his shotgun but it would appear that, despite his remarkable powers of recuperation, he is in no mood to confront us again. Not yet."

Holmes shook out his arms, wincing.

"Are you all right?" I asked.

"Yes. A touch of muscle strain. Would you do me a favour, Watson?"

"Anything, old man. You just saved my life."

"Lose some weight before you next go gallivanting off the side of a cliff, would you?"

I chuckled, in spite of everything. "Mrs Watson nags me about my expanding girth. Now you too. It is like having two wives."

"The inestimable Mrs Watson is a well-put-together woman," said Holmes. "I doubt, however, that she has had the task of bearing your entire bulk by means of her arms alone, which makes my plea more impassioned and pertinent than hers."

"I think the solution to the problem may not be going on a diet but rather avoiding pursuit by a dangerous dog so close to a precipice."

"A situation I pray we shall never find ourselves in again."

"Seconded. Heartily."

CHAPTER THIRTY-ONE

SAFE ROOM

Dirty, battered, bedraggled, both of us feeling as though we had gone several rounds in the ring with "Gentleman Jim" Corbett, Holmes and I fetched up back at his cottage late that night.

I immediately began to make preparations for drawing a bath, but Holmes stopped me.

"No time," he said. "We are not out of danger yet."

"Surely in your own home we can at least pause and take stock. My feet are soaked and could do with being warmed before a fire."

"Later. First, we must take steps to render ourselves secure. Given what I have gleaned over the past two days, we are up against villains whose audacity is matched only by their ruthlessness."

"Then you propose we lock all the doors, barricade the windows and so forth?"

"I can go one better than that," said my friend, and he made for the new bookcase which had drawn my notice on Sunday morning. He reached for a single volume on the shelves, the one whose spine bore the name Samuel Chatwood, and pulled it down by the upper edge. It proved not to be a real book at all; rather, a false one attached to the shelf by a hinge. Tugging on it triggered a spring mechanism which released a catch. The entire bookcase swung outwards, revealing a doorway and a set of steeply descending steps, more like a ladder than stairs.

"It occurred to me not long ago," said Holmes as he invited me to climb down first, "that I have a fair few foes left in the world, and that many of those criminals whom I was instrumental in capturing will just now be coming to the end of their jail sentences. They are the sort of men who are apt to hold a grudge, and their resentment will have had years to fester as they sat in their cells. It is likely, then, that one or more of them may come seeking retribution. My whereabouts are hardly a secret. Per my request you have kept the location of this house vague in your writings and called it a farm rather than what it is, a smallholding at best. Nonetheless you have left sufficient clues that anyone of average intelligence might be able to pinpoint this village as my place of retirement, and it would not be difficult then to identify the house itself, since the locals are well aware who I am and have no qualms about mentioning their 'famous' neighbour to all and sundry. Hence it seemed prudent to take precautions."

"What is down here?" I said as I set foot on a flagged floor. I could make out the dim outlines of a subterranean chamber perhaps fifteen feet long by ten wide. "Some kind of cellar?"

"And more," said Holmes, lowering himself down after me. "I must confess I live in particular fear of reprisals from Colonel Sebastian Moran, Professor Moriarty's main accomplice."

"Ugh. That wretch."

"He remains at large, somehow managing to evade the efforts of countless national police forces to catch him. Last I heard, he was suspected of being at the heart of several major scandals and conspiracies in Europe and, skipping ahead of the long arm of the law, has decamped to Australia where he is wreaking his own kind of havoc in Queensland and the Northern Territories. He belongs there in that land of convicts and ruffians, but that isn't to say he might not choose to return to England sometime and come looking for me. I doubt that time and age have diminished his hatred of me. Old soldiers never forget – especially foot soldiers of the Napoleon of Crime."

Holmes reached for a wall-mounted lever which brought the bookcase-door clanging shut. Simultaneously a gas lamp ignited and I was able to discern my surroundings with clarity.

"I engaged a builder from the Midlands," he continued. "I told him I wanted a wine cellar. He came down with an assistant to do the excavating, shore up the walls and ceiling, and lay the flagstones. I employed nobody from the immediate area, so as to keep the job a secret. The rest of the work, the carpentry and so forth, I performed myself."

The chamber was furnished with a cot, a chair, books, and a goodly supply of canned foodstuffs, enough to last one man a fortnight. There was a small sink with a tap, and, screened off by a low partition, a toilet. I noted a rack of knife-switches beside the lever which operated the door, and next to them the lower end of a periscope, the shaft of which penetrated up through the ceiling.

"Samuel Chatwood," I said, referring to the false book. "As in Chatwoods the safe makers."

"My little joke. I call this place my 'safe room'. It has something of the prison cell about it, I grant you, or perhaps more accurately the priest's hole, but one could easily cope with being down here for a week or so, especially if the alternative was death. Fresh air is supplied via that pipe up there, a conduit leading to a hidden grating in the garden. Things might get a little stuffy with the two of us breathing, but we shan't suffocate."

"You said you had been in consultation with Fred Tilling. Now I know why."

"He assisted with the general design of the place and answered a couple of engineering-related queries I had."

"And how long do you intend we take refuge here?"

"As long as need be," said Holmes. "I expect, however, that we shall receive a hostile visitation ere long. Would you care to tell me why you and Jenks were talking about 'swimmers' and a 'lucky blow' from your walking-stick? I'm afraid I caught only the tail end of your conversation at Settleholm."

I explained about my near-drowning and also about my subsequent fever and the fire at Tripp's.

"Tut, poor Watson!" my friend exclaimed. "I regret even more that I absented myself the way I did, leaving you to your own devices."

"It was somewhat brusque of you. Might you not have waited until I had come back, instead of just scribbling a brief note and dashing off?"

"Forgive my impoliteness and my intemperate haste, but I felt that time was slipping away and I simply couldn't sit still a moment longer. I had to act. And a fire at Tripp's, you say? But no body has been discovered."

"None to my knowledge, although a fireman at the scene did not espouse any great optimism. For my part, I would like to believe that Miss Vandenbergh is alive and well. She is a resourceful lady. If she could possibly have escaped from the burning building, she would have. And if she did, it would make sense for her to lie low, so that no one would know the attempt on her life had failed."

"You think it was an act of arson?"

"I strongly suspect it was, and I strongly suspect that this Horus cult are to blame. Don't you? They are covering their tracks, eliminating all witnesses."

"Interesting," said Holmes. "Well, it seems you have been kept very busy. So have I. Would you like to know what I have been up to while I was away?"

"Very much so."

"I warn you, it is a long story."

I glanced around the confines of the safe room. "I don't appear to be going anywhere in a hurry, and neither do you. How else are we going to pass the time?"

CHAPTER THIRTY-TWO

THE COLONIAL AND OVERSEAS CLUB

"London was my first port of call," said Holmes. "To be precise, the Colonial and Overseas Club."

"Mallinson's club."

"The very same. It's one of the grander institutions on Pall Mall, with Doric columns beneath the portico and a liveried ex-serviceman on the door to deter the riffraff. I arrived there shortly after luncheon on Tuesday and was soon able to ingratiate myself with the lobby clerk."

"How much did this ingratiation cost you?"

"Watson, you are too cynical. The fact is he recognised me."

"Ah, as the famous detective."

"No, as the brother of Mycroft Holmes, whose reputation still carries weight in Mayfair. Mycroft was a generous tipper, which endeared him to the ancillary staff of all the clubs he frequented, not just the Diogenes. The lobby clerk at the Colonial and Overseas remembered him with fondness and said that for the brother of 'that great man' he might be willing to bend the rules."

"*Might* be. So money did change hands."

"A ten-bob note secured me quarter of an hour alone with the attendance ledger in a backroom," Holmes said, with a touch of chagrin.

"You wished to verify Mallinson's alibi."

"I did, and it proved to be watertight. He arrived at the club at seven-thirty last Friday night and left shortly after two in the morning. The ledger had not been tampered with or falsified; the clerk himself confirmed the timings. It is still conceivable that Mallinson journeyed to Sussex that same night, although not by rail, since the last train to Eastbourne departs at eleven-twenty."

"He drove down in his car, you mean."

"Except that he didn't. Just today, while posing as a gardener at the manor, I made surreptitious enquiries among the domestic staff. Mr Mallinson never travels any great distance by car, and definitely not to and from London. It is too unreliable a mode of transport, apt to break down en route. His Humberette remained at the house all last week."

"Someone else might have driven him in another car."

"Possible. But I am inclined to think Mallinson did not return to Settleholm until Saturday, as he has said. The manor house staff would know if he had, and none of them saw him before the Saturday morning."

"Well, I, for one, am glad to hear it," I said. "For a moment there, it seemed as though you still fancied him for the killing of Patrick. Filicide – surely the most heinous form of murder."

"No. I firmly believe Mallinson to be innocent of that crime." The emphasis Holmes laid on the word "that" suggested to me that Craig Mallinson might be implicated in some other nefarious deed. "I was simply being thorough. The attendance register confirmed, too, that Sir Josiah Partlin-Gray was also at the club that night, as Mallinson asserted. Also at the Colonial and Overseas that night was another plutocrat, Victor Anstruther."

"The name does not ring a bell."

"Cars, Watson. Buses and lorries too. He owns the Mercury marque. You have heard of that, presumably."

"Ah yes. My next-door neighbour owns a Mercury motorcycle, a Velocity. Ghastly noisy thing. Whenever he starts it up in the street, the windows rattle in their frames and I fear the panes might shatter. Mrs Watson curses it every time. Once, our housemaid Jemima dropped a dinner plate she was drying, so startled was she by the racket. She said she thought a bomb had gone off."

"Inestimably popular, though, are Mercury cars," said Holmes. "Anstruther's manufacturing plants run along the production line principle pioneered by Henry Ford in America. Fifty thousand vehicles per annum roll out of his factories and onto the roads. He has a contract to provide vans for the Royal Mail, among other things. Recently he has moved into building steam locomotives and rolling stock, but automobiles remain his primary focus of interest. He considers them the future of transportation, and foresees a world where the internal combustion engine dominates."

"I have no doubt that he is correct. It would be a shame to see the age of steam come to an end, but I fear steam's louder, brasher upstart cousin is here to stay and will in time usurp. H.G. Wells, the great prognosticator himself, has stated that a tide of increasing mechanisation is upon us, threatening to engulf us, and that the motor car is at the forefront of it. The car will grant us each an unprecedented level of personal freedom when it comes to travel, and yet will enslave us with its costs and demands."

"Wells is a peculiar mix of optimist and doomsayer," said Holmes, "never happier than when he is extolling the wonders of science and at the same time warning of its dangers. His Socialist and pacifist tendencies show that he thinks the best of mankind – perhaps somewhat naively – but I am pleased to say that he stands staunchly opposed to Germany's current aggressive imperialism.

He believes that that nation's *Hohenzollern* stance – 'blood and iron' – will inevitably drag Europe into all-out war and that this war must be fought if democracy is to prevail."

"I believe that too."

"As, alas, do I."

My friend was lost briefly in sombre contemplation. I chose that moment to remind him that he was still wearing his gardener disguise. With a self-upbraiding cry he began peeling off his artificial sideburns and putty nose.

"Beg pardon, sorr," he said in his rustic accent. "Most neglectful oi be."

When he had washed the last of the makeup off at the sink and looked more or less like himself again, he resumed his narrative.

"The lobby clerk told me that Anstruther, along with Partlin-Gray, made up two of Mallinson's companions for cards on the evening in question. They're longstanding bridge partners, Partlin-Gray and Anstruther. Mallinson himself was partnered by a Conservative member of parliament, Fowlkes by name. Represents a Home Counties constituency, not sure which. Unimportant fellow. One of those backbenchers who seldom turn up for votes or do much except prop up the bar in the Pugin Room and hobnob with the wealthy in their spare time."

"With the likes of Mallinson and Partlin-Gray."

"Perhaps he has an eye on a seat on the board of directors with one of their companies. Politics, for him, would appear to be merely a stepping stone to a more lucrative post. At any rate, Fowlkes need not detain us, a mere rank-and-file public servant with aspirations that lie beyond the House of Commons. We can look on him as simply making up a four. It is Mallinson, Partlin-Gray and Anstruther who matter."

"How so?"

"They are supremely powerful and influential individuals.

Mallinson and Partlin-Gray we already know are firm friends, but they are also intimate with Anstruther. Furthermore these three are, according to the lobby clerk, regularly to be found consorting together at the club with a fourth of their ilk, Lord Eustace Harington."

"I don't know of him either," I said.

"Medicines," said Holmes, "that's his line. Owns several large pharmaceutical firms. You will have doubtless prescribed his products to your patients and used many of them yourself. Lord Harington has a warrant to supply the royal household with all their medicinal needs, and has patents on a host of drugs, including, a universal vitamin pill made from extracts of rabbit gall bladder and a brand of radium-infused water which purports to lift one's mood and boost flagging virility."

"He flirts with quackery, then."

"His lordship is not immune to dabbling in the more fanciful areas of the health industry, it is true. According to *Debrett's* he has travelled extensively throughout South America and brought back a range of 'miracle cures' which he picked up from witch doctors in remote corners of Amazonia. Yet this accounts for only a small fraction of his business. For the most part he produces things like bandages, splints and tongue depressors. That's his bread and butter. That and tablets containing active ingredients such as acetaminophen, sodium bromide and bisacodyl whose effectiveness has been scientifically proven."

"He could add Mrs Tuppen's homemade fever remedy to his menu of miracle cures," I said, not entirely without sincerity. "If he were somehow able to make it palatable."

"Eustace Harington – Lord Harington of Barnstaple and Knowstone, to give him his full title – can trace his lineage all the way back to the fourteenth century. Burke's *Peerage* states that he is descended from Sir Nigel Loring, a Knight of the Garter who distinguished himself during the Hundred Years' War, most notably at the battles of Crécy, Poitiers and Nájera."

"I have read of Sir Nigel's exploits," I said. "He was chamberlain to the Prince of Wales as well, was he not?"

"His wife gave him only daughters, one of whom married a Sir Robert Harington, a baron. The Haringtons were, and remain, prominent landowners in north Devon, but before Eustace came along the family had become somewhat impecunious, as is sometimes the way with aristocracy. Idleness, inbreeding and a lack of initiative had seen their fortune dwindle to a rump, with nothing but a crumbling stately pile, a title and accumulated debts to pass on down through the generations. Eustace has succeeded in reversing this decline by means of his entrepreneurial flair. He now ranks not far below Partlin-Gray in the list of Britain's highest earners. Together these four – Mallinson, Partlin-Gray, Anstruther, Harington – represent a good one per cent of our nation's net wealth."

I let out a soft whistle. Until then, I had not fully appreciated just how rich a man Craig Mallinson was.

"And," Holmes went on, "they are habitually to be found at the Colonial and Overseas. I checked. In the past twelve months alone, each has called in at the club on no fewer than two dozen occasions. Quite often their attendances have coincided, so that at least three of them have been there at once, if not all four."

"So? They are friends. They are wealthy. They enjoy card games and the conviviality of a club environment. They have a great deal in common with one another. Like is drawn to like. Nothing intrinsically wrong with that. I don't see the significance of any of this."

"How would you? Neither did I initially. Yet there was something about the four names that niggled at me. I was certain that something united this quartet more than just the Colonial and Overseas and a fondness for bridge – more, even, than an enviable bank balance. What this shared factor was, though, my aged grey cells refused to divulge. The connection was there, like a word on the tip of one's tongue, but would not make itself known."

I could hear the frustration in Holmes's voice. This man, whose ability to retain facts and retrieve them at will had once been second to none, was angry that his powers had temporarily deserted him. When he had chided me earlier about the discrepancies in my writings, perhaps he had also been rebuking himself.

"At any rate," he said, "I jotted down a note of the dates and times of the four men's comings and goings at the club before returning the ledger to the lobby clerk. I asked him if he could tell me anything more about them, and at that point a metaphorical portcullis came down."

"What do you mean?"

"The lobby clerk became tight-lipped, with the full taciturnity and inscrutability required of one in his position. 'I have stretched the boundaries of club discretion as far as I dare, sir,' said he, 'in honour of your brother's memory. Please do not try and make me reveal anything more about any of our members. I value my job too highly.' I apologised and handed him a couple of extra shillings, a token gesture to atone for my tactlessness and the embarrassment it had caused him. We parted on good terms, and I headed out into the chill of a London afternoon.

"For a while I just walked, ruminating. It felt strange to be back in the capital after so long. Much had changed. Mechanisation has indeed made its mark on the city. The streets are noisier, with all the motorised vehicles, but also less pungent, with fewer horses to foul the roadways. The crowds seemed denser than I remembered, faster-moving, although that could be because I have spent so much time in the provinces that I no longer recall what a truly busy thoroughfare looks like. And so many of the theatres and concert halls you and I once haunted have been turned into moving-picture palaces!

"Yet, for all that, it was at heart the same old London, dank and dark and stalwart. I took tea in a Joe Lyons Corner House in the West End, almost a mechanised procedure in itself, so brisk and no-nonsense was the service; the waitresses more than lived up to their nickname, 'nippies'. Then I continued on my way to the British Library, with a view to conducting some research in the newspaper archive.

"It was there that I finally hit upon the missing connection between the four men, the one I had not been quite able to summon up. And Watson, it is a sinister, tragic thing indeed."

CHAPTER THIRTY-THREE

A Concatenation of Deaths

"I passed the remainder of that afternoon and much of the following morning at the library," Holmes continued, "spending the intervening night at a cheap, anonymous hotel in Bloomsbury. I pored over countless bound volumes of papers and periodicals from this year and last, searching for references to our fabulously affluent foursome.

"Here and there one of their names might crop up in the Court and Social sections, to no great consequence. Mallinson's aviation hobby earned him a captioned picture in *The Illustrated London News*, him looking keen and intrepid in goggles and leather flying helmet, and I learned courtesy of the *Graphic* that Victor Anstruther is something of an expert on Ancient Greece. He has given talks on Sparta and the Second Peloponnesian War at the Royal Historical Society and in 1907 published a scholarly tome on the life and work of Thucydides, which was the subject of a fawning review in the *Journal of Hellenic Studies* from a Cambridge don clearly far more impressed by the author's worldly status than by his marshalling of facts and presentation of opinions.

"Then I came upon the first clue, the first link in a chain I diligently and painstakingly began to assemble. It was a small headline low down on an inside page of *The Times*, quite unobtrusive. One could easily have overlooked it. 'Pharmaceutical Tycoon's Father Dies After Long Illness.'"

"Lord Harington's father," I said.

"The very same. The previous Lord Harington passed away at the end of last year, shortly before Christmas. The cause of death was a stroke, a severe cerebral haemorrhage. It followed another similar stroke a few months before which had left him partially paralysed on one side and with his speech hampered. He was seventy-nine."

"Regrettable but not surprising in a man of that age."

"No, but what I found noteworthy about the article was that Eustace Harington was mentioned as having been personally involved in his father's treatment."

"Is that so surprising either, given his line of work?"

"Perhaps not, but Eustace was administering a specially concocted nerve tonic to the old man while he was convalescing from the first stroke. It had, apparently, been having a remarkable influence on his recuperation."

"He was getting better?"

"So it would seem. Then he had a sudden relapse and died. The physician attending to him, a Dr Wilcox, attested to the upturn in Harington senior's health and professed himself disappointed and dismayed that the patient went into such a steep decline when the prognosis had seemed so encouraging."

"It can happen," I said. "Once a haemorrhage has caused a weakening in the wall of a cranial artery, it is perfectly possible that a second rupture will occur, often with more devastating results than the first. Harington's nerve tonic may or may not have assisted with the father's recovery. The recovery may, equally, have been entirely spontaneous – and the same goes for his subsequent death."

"My feelings too," said Holmes. "But, as a doctor yourself, would you allow the son of a gravely ill patient to dose that patient with an untried form of remedy you knew nothing about?"

"I might if I saw that it was effecting an improvement, or at any rate not injuring the patient. Even if it was functioning as no more than a placebo, that would not be undesirable. He who believes his therapy is progressing well has more chance of regaining his health than he who does not. It's the psychological factor. I imagine, too, that this Dr Wilcox was more than a little in awe of his aristocratic clients and unwilling to question or dispute Eustace Harington's authority in matters medicinal."

"But what if the nerve tonic gave only the illusion of beneficiality? What if it were actually, secretly, causing more harm than good? Can you think of a substance which confers liveliness upon mind and body while at the same time placing chronic strain upon one's constitution, Watson? I can."

It took me a moment to follow his train of thought. When I realised that he was speaking from first-hand experience, I alighted upon the answer in a flash.

"Cocaine," I said.

My friend gave a tight nod of the head. "I did, as you know only too well, fall under the spell of that drug for a time. It seemed to provide me with everything I craved: stimulation, vigour, an acceleration of the mental processes. And yet in between injections, what lassitude overcame me, what depths of depression and torpor I sank into. Under its influence I felt on top of the world; without it, as though the world was on top of me. You yourself saw how cocaine ravaged me. I well recall your hectoring lectures about my use of it."

"Hectoring lectures? Concerned admonitions, surely."

"You warned me that I should count the cost. You told

me cocaine addiction is a 'pathological and morbid process, which involves increased tissue change, and may at least leave a permanent weakness'. Your very words. And in the end I heeded your warnings and was able to rid myself of my dependency on the needle and the seven-per-cent solution, thanks to your persistent efforts to wean me off it, and thanks to my own willpower too. I was a young man back then, in my prime, so there were no lasting physical, mental or emotional effects. But if someone in his late seventies were fed repeated quantities of cocaine, in a disguised form, might he not show the exact same pathology and symptoms as Eustace Harington's father?"

"I agree. Cocaine-induced hypertension alone would be liable to trigger a second stroke, but until then the effect of the drug would be to enliven the fellow and give every indication that he was recuperating well."

"The nerve tonic, incidentally, went by the name 'Peruvian Gold'. We know that Lord Harington likes his South American native cures, and what plant is used more often for medicinal purposes in South America than the coca leaf, the source of cocaine? It is chewed in the Andes to overcome altitude sickness and is used among primitive Indian jungle tribes as a means of anaesthesia."

"Now hold on here," I said. "You're telling me that Eustace Harington wilfully killed his own father? To me the thing looks at best like death by misadventure. His lordship may sincerely have believed that his Peruvian Gold was the ideal pick-me-up for the old man. We don't even know that the stuff *did* contain cocaine."

"No, we don't. Nor would there have been an autopsy which might have revealed the drug's presence in Harington senior's system. The death would in no way be deemed suspicious."

"One could always track down Dr Wilcox, I suppose. See if he harbours any misgivings about it."

"One could, were he still alive," said Holmes. "Wilcox was

a Harley Street practitioner, a specialist in circulatory diseases. I thumbed through back-issues of the *British Medical Journal*, looking for his name, and found a reference to his obituary. He died in a road accident shortly after New Year, three weeks after Harington senior was laid to rest in the family tomb. A singular coincidence, wouldn't you say?"

"By which you mean no coincidence at all."

"I am inclined to think it a somewhat convenient state of affairs, the doctor perishing so soon after the patient. Especially since he was struck down late at night outside his house in Marylebone by a motorist who failed to stop and help but simply drove on, leaving the poor man to bleed his last onto the cobbles."

"Accidents happen."

"And yet do you remember Mallinson describing alternative, simpler methods that might have been used to kill Patrick than dropping him out of an aeroplane? One of them was 'mowing him down with a car'. A meaningless casual remark, or something more?"

"This is becoming grim."

"It gets grimmer," said Holmes. "In March of this year, Victor Anstruther's brother blew his own head off in a gun-cleaning accident."

"Good God."

"He was a keen shot, Harold Anstruther, by all accounts. Victor Anstruther owns a hunting lodge up in the Cairngorms, on the banks of Loch Morlich, not far from Aviemore. Victor is a huntsman too, but it was Harold who liked to stay there the most. In the summer he would stalk deer, sometimes in the company of a ghillie but often by himself. In the winter and spring he was apt to go rough shooting for pheasant and hare, usually alone. He was proficient with every kind of gun and is unlikely to have made so rudimentary an error as cleaning a rifle with a bullet loaded in the breech. Yet that is precisely what appears to have happened."

"You think otherwise."

My friend sounded pained. "What is so accursedly aggravating about all this, Watson, is that I am forced to piece together data from second-hand sources, none of them absolutely unimpeachable. I am out of the game – have been for some while – and no longer do I have the contacts and connections that I used to, and thus the general wherewithal to build cases through the direct, hands-on accumulation of evidence. Newspaper reports lack forensic detail. Journalists have been known to be sloppy. I wonder if I were not retired, if I had remained in touch with the workings of the world, would I find myself reduced to scrabbling around in libraries to scare up facts as I do now?"

"Holmes, you mustn't berate yourself. You have been attempting to draw together a sequence of events that occurred months ago, in various far-flung parts of the country. Thus far, you have been doing commendably well. Even in your heyday you might still have wound up resorting to just the same measures. Pray continue."

"Thank you, old friend. Your confidence in me is heartening. Suffice to say, there was nothing inherently odd about Harold Anstruther's death other than that it seemed a most uncharacteristic blunder. A fact that merited a mention in several of the articles about the incident, however, was that a small quantity of wine was discovered on the floor of the gunroom beside the body."

"Ah, he had been drinking. That might explain how he overlooked the presence of the fateful bullet."

"Yet nowhere did I find any reference to there being a bottle in the room, nor even a glass. It may be that nobody thought it needed saying, but I find it an intriguing lacuna, don't you? Wine spilled but no wine container on the premises."

"Sloppy journalism, as you say."

"The final piece of the puzzle – indeed, the key to it all – was the death of Lady Partlin-Gray. Lady Inga was Norwegian by birth. She and Sir Josiah met at the turn of the century, when he was buying out a steel company based in Stavanger. She died in June, and her demise was by some margin the grisliest episode I am here relating. You may recall the headlines."

"I'm not sure I do."

"You will when I describe the circumstances," said Holmes. "It caused quite a sensation. The Partlin-Grays' marriage was, shall we say, one where monogamy was not a prerequisite on either side. If the gossip columnists' insinuations are to be believed, Lady Inga was the type to conduct affairs on a regular basis with anyone from high-born nobles to lowly stable boys. Sir Josiah, meanwhile, has gained notoriety for his liaisons with a string of music-hall actresses and opera sopranos. That said, the two of them were often to be seen out and about in one another's company, he squiring her to charity balls and suchlike, and it was remarked that they always seemed close and affectionate in public."

"It can be that such an arrangement suits both parties," I said. "Not that I would condone it, but serial infidelity is not an uncommon practice in the upper echelons of society. It keeps the relationship fresh, so they say."

"Lady Inga was found dead in a forest near the Partlin-Grays' summer retreat, a log cabin overlooking a fjord outside Fredrikstad in her ladyship's native land. She appeared to have tripped and fallen headlong into a ravine. It happened at night, and hence the assumption was that she had been on her way to or back from a tryst with a lover in a nearby village when she met her end. And it was a miserable end."

I now began to remember something about this incident. "Yes, when they discovered her body it had been torn apart by wild animals. Isn't that the story? Wolves, I believe."

"Either she died instantly as a result of the fall or she was rendered insensible or otherwise unable to move, both scenarios leaving her vulnerable to predatory and scavenging beasts. Bite marks were clearly visible on her flesh. There is no question that the body was mauled, in all likelihood by wolves."

"I must say that, for her sake, I hope she broke her neck in the fall and knew nothing more. It would have been kinder that way. To lie there conscious, perhaps paralysed, as the wolves approached..." I shuddered.

"One intriguing if gruesome detail was that Lady Inga's lungs had been pulled out through the back of her ribcage. The assumption was that wolves were also responsible for this mutilation."

"You think they weren't?"

"I was, by this stage of my researches, beginning to perceive a pattern to these deaths."

"I'll take your word for it that there is one, but at present I cannot see it."

"What do you see then, Watson?" Holmes asked.

"I see a series of deaths which have befallen close relatives of three men who are friends with one another," I said. "The deaths are grouped close together in time, but statistically that is not extraordinary, in my view. Harington's elderly father dies of a senility-related illness. Anstruther's brother suffers a tragic, careless accident. Partlin-Gray's wife goes astray in a Norwegian forest, loses her way in the dark, falls into a ravine, and is partially eaten by wolves. All very unpleasant and unfortunate, but I daresay one could take any three men and find a similar distribution of tragedies in their lives."

"You're forgetting Craig Mallinson and Patrick."

"So let's add a fourth to the tally. It still doesn't seem to be wildly beyond the bounds of probability."

"And that," said Holmes, "could be exactly how it is meant

to seem: a concatenation of deaths by natural causes or innocent mishap. To the casual observer, nothing is amiss. But you and I are not casual observers, Watson. We are alert to the existence of schemes and sequences. We pierce the surface of things. We cross-reference and double check, and that is how we solve murders."

"They were murders?" I said. "All four? You're quite positive about that?"

"Firmly so. Let me tell you why."

CHAPTER THIRTY-FOUR

THE PANOPTICON PERISCOPE

"But first…" Holmes crossed over to the periscope which was attached to one wall of the safe room. "Our enemies have had ample time to regroup and prepare. We must keep a lookout for them."

He put his eye to the viewing slot and turned a handle mounted on the periscope shaft. I heard cogs mesh and chains clank.

"I call this my 'panopticon periscope," he said. "I have constructed it so that the reflecting mirror at the top can rotate through a full three hundred and sixty degrees. The shaft follows the chimney breast and its tip protrudes through the roof, camouflaged as a cowled chimneypot. I have a view round the entire perimeter of the cottage. Admittedly it is not a good one tonight, but I have left lights on in several rooms and the illumination cast from the windows is helping to penetrate the mist."

"An ingenious device," I said.

"When it comes to my own safety, I compromise on nothing, least of all inventiveness," said Holmes. "Now, to continue…"

While he kept watch on the outside world via the panopticon periscope, my friend outlined his reasons for thinking that the deaths he had been describing constituted a spate of connected murders.

"It is the dates that are so striking," he said. "Do you not detect a certain regularity in the frequency of the deaths?"

"Let me think. December, March, June, September... Why, they occur at three-month intervals."

"And furthermore, the precise dates align with a set of major calendrical events. Eustace Harington's father died on the twenty-second of December."

"That's customarily the shortest day of the year."

"Known as the winter solstice. Harold Anstruther's gun 'accident' took place on March the twentieth. The vernal equinox."

"Then Lady Inga Partlin-Gray presumably died on midsummer's day."

"June the twenty-first, also known as the summer solstice. And what was last Friday?"

"The autumnal equinox," I said. "My goodness me, a clear, unambiguous pattern."

"Too clear and unambiguous to be purely random," said Holmes. "The odds against it being happenstance are astronomical."

"Yet in another sense astronomical is precisely what it is."

"Well put. The deaths align, with terrible accuracy, to the celestial mechanics which govern the seasons and the earth's orbital relation to the sun. The equinoxes are, of course, when the sun takes exactly half a day to travel from horizon to horizon and the plane of the earth's equator tilts to the point where it passes the sun's centre. The solstices are when the sun appears at its highest and lowest in the sky. In summer, the solstice marks the beginning of the sun's declination – its gradual daily decrease in perceived altitude. In winter, the opposite."

"So each of the four men committed the murder of a relative on one of those days. What for? To what purpose?"

"That I do not know. One can only speculate that there is some profound significance in the dates, possibly of a mystical nature. But also, each of the four men *cannot* have committed the murders."

"How so?"

"Here we come to the nub of the matter," said Holmes, turning away from the periscope to give me a sardonic look. "On the face of it, each man has a reasonably solid motive for killing his respective victim. For Eustace Harington, there is the prospect of an inheritance."

"You told me there wasn't much money left in the family coffers."

"There was still a house and land for the claiming, and more than that, a title. Harington has money of his own already, plenty of it. All he would need to make his life complete is a 'lord' to go in front of his name. Men have murdered for less."

"But... his own father?"

"The fellow was old and ailing. Eustace could be said to have been merely hastening the inevitable. As for Anstruther, he and his brother were on the outs. Harold Anstruther was everything Victor is not: a wastrel, a sponger, a ne'er-do-well. He had never done a stroke of work in his life. Victor supported him financially and unstintingly, affording him a playboy lifestyle which he did nothing to deserve. There would have been a definite tension in their relationship."

"As there must have been between Sir Josiah and Lady Inga Partlin-Gray," I said. "For all the apparent 'freeness' of their marriage, I can imagine the existence of a constant undertow of jealousy and resentment. Can a husband and wife truly be happy with each other if both are seeking affection elsewhere?"

"As for Mallinson and Patrick, we know from Mallinson himself, and from Elizabeth Vandenbergh, that they had been at odds all summer."

"And yet Mallinson's sorrow over the loss of his son seems entirely genuine. You cannot dissimulate that level of grief. If he is Patrick's murderer, then he is either a sociopath or an incredibly gifted actor."

"He is neither," said Holmes. "Nor is he Patrick's murderer. This is what I am trying to convey to you. None of the four killed the person he is most likely to have killed. It is not possible. And it is not possible because all of them have cast-iron alibis. They were at the Colonial and Overseas at the time. Here, I have proof."

He fished out a scrap of paper from his pocket. It took me several moments to decipher the jottings on it, which were in Holmes's own hand, somewhat crabbed at the best of times and made worse by the evident haste with which he had been writing. The text consisted of columns of letters and numbers, as though it were some abstruse code.

In the event, it was simply a list of dates, beside each of which were sets of initials: CM for Mallinson, JPG for Sir Josiah Partlin-Gray, VA for Victor Anstruther, and EH for Lord Eustace Harington. These appeared in various permutations, sometimes all four, never fewer than three.

I checked the four specific dates when the murders had occurred:

22/12/12	VA EH CM
20/03/13	JPG VA EH
21/06/13	JPG CM EH
22/09/13	CM JPG VA

In each instance, the man whose relative had perished had been at the club, with two of the others also present.

"By a process of elimination," said Holmes, "you will be able to establish who was *not* there each time."

"Sir Josiah in December, Mallinson in March, Anstruther in June and Lord Harington in September." I was agog. "So you're saying that – that they colluded? They exchanged murders?"

"Yes, in a kind of sinister round-robin, cunningly devised so as to allay any suggestion of guilt or impropriety and allow each man perfect deniability. Sir Josiah was the only one not at the club on the day the previous Lord Harington died – but could he have been in north Devon? Might he have been staying as a guest at the family seat, a good friend of the heir to the estate, there to offer company and consolation to the father in his son's absence?"

"During which time he could have administered an overdose of the Peruvian Gold."

"Indubitably. Either forced an excess of the stuff down the enfeebled old man's throat in one go or somehow prevailed upon him to drink a series of dosages in quick succession, perhaps at hourly intervals, counting on Harington senior being too befuddled to realise he was receiving it at more than the prescribed frequency."

"Or else Eustace Harington could have provided a special mixture just for the occasion with extra-strength quantities of cocaine in it."

"Capital, Watson! I hadn't thought of that. Yes, that could well be how it was done. A phial of liquid looking exactly like the normal medicine only many times more concentrated – lethally so."

"Then, by that token, it was Craig Mallinson who did for Harold Anstruther, arranging things so that it looked like a gunroom accident."

"Mallinson is a strapping fellow," said Holmes. "I wouldn't put it past him to be able to overpower the dissolute Harold, then place the barrel of a loaded rifle under his chin and pull the trigger."

"And also pour the wine on the floor, so that everyone would leap to the conclusion that Harold had been inebriated."

"Hardly a leap, given Harold's habits."

"What about Lady Inga?"

"Victor Anstruther might have waylaid her in the forest, struck her on the head with a tree branch or the like, and then thrown her into the ravine, knowing it was likely that wolves would come and ravage the body to such an extent as to erase all traces of foul play. The only point that needs making here is that she could not have 'lost her way in the dark', as you opined just now."

"Why not? Because she knew the countryside well, being a native? Oh, wait. I see. Midsummer in Norway."

Holmes nodded. "Land of the Midnight Sun. Night never truly falls in extreme northern latitudes in the summer. The sun barely dips below the horizon before rising again. At its darkest, the sky is still twilit."

"In the gloom, Anstruther would have been able to see well enough to sneak up on her."

"And still have long shadows to lurk in."

"And Patrick Mallinson? Eustace Harington is the only one of the four left who has not been assigned a murder."

"He is the logical culprit. How he did it, though, is most fascinating and diabolical. In order to ascertain that he used the method I believe he did, I left London yesterday at noon and took the train from Waterloo to Weybridge in Surrey. From there, it is less than a mile to Brooklands."

"The motor racing circuit," I said.

"Not quite," said Holmes. "The aerodrome."

CHAPTER THIRTY-FIVE

FLYING LESSONS

"The aerodrome, in case you don't know, is situated within the ambit of the racing circuit," said Holmes. "There is a clubhouse and, next to that, an encampment known as the Brooklands Flying Village. I encountered several louche young men there, heirs to wealth and privilege, loitering by their tents swigging champagne. They're the worst kind of idle rich, braying and abrasive. Flying gives them a thrill otherwise missing from their sedate, feather-bedded lives. Many of them race cars around the track as well, for much the same reason.

"A number of aeroplane manufacturing companies have set up shop on the site – Vickers, Sopwith, Hewlett And Blondeau Limited – offering flying tuition. I made myself known to a fellow called Farnwell who works for Sopwith. He agreed to the hire of his services for an afternoon. I wanted him to show me just how quickly and easily one might acquire the basics of aviation. A crash course, you might say."

"With none of the crashing, one would hope," I said.

"Ha ha, Watson. Most droll. Farnwell led me out to a Sopwith

Tabloid, a two-seater biplane which is unusual in having those seats positioned side by side instead of fore and aft. It's a bit hugger-mugger in the cockpit, but the advantages for a learner are obvious. The instructor can give a practical demonstration, in flight, of how the controls work, and the learner can then take over, if the mood comes upon him. As it did with me."

"You actually piloted the thing?"

"Once we were airborne, I took the yoke for a while, yes," said Holmes. "Very exhilarating it was, too. Mallinson is right: there is an extraordinary freedom to be found in the skies. When you're up there, it is as if you are a breed apart, a strange hybrid of human and bird. Oh, it's noisy all right – the roar of the propeller, the buffeting of the wind. Malodorous, too, with the engine exhaust. You come down with a sooty face, reeking of oil and petrol, and numb from the cold. But it's worth it. The views I had over Surrey – they alone justified the entire enterprise. From Box Hill in the east to Hindhead in the west, I felt as though I could see the entire county. I thought this must be how God feels, surveying His creation, especially that most favoured part of it that we know as England."

"Steady there, Holmes. Hubris."

"Ah yes. What was it Mallinson said? 'The dreams of Icarus'. One must not fly too high in the heavens, lest one provoke divine displeasure and suffer for it. At any rate, under Farnwell's expert tutelage I established that a reasonably fit and intelligent individual could become an aviator with little difficulty. Back on the ground, he told me that at a rate of a lesson a day, I might be proficient enough within a fortnight to apply for my pilot's licence from the Royal Aero Club. All one needs to be able to do is ascend in a machine and follow a figure-of-eight course at a prescribed height, whereupon the certificate is granted.

"I asked him if he knew of Craig Mallinson, and he did. Mallinson had obtained his licence at Brooklands, he said. I had already inferred as much from the photo in *The Illustrated London News*, which had been taken at that aerodrome. Had Farnwell been the one who taught him? 'No,' he said. 'That was Serge.' By 'Serge' he meant Prince Serge Vincent de Bolotoff."

"Russian?" I said.

"Bulgarian, actually," said Holmes, "and he claims to have been the fifth ever man to fly, though there is some debate over the assertion. Nonetheless, he is a noted aviation pioneer who is currently constructing a large tandem triplane of his own design in a shed at Brooklands. Farnwell took me over to introduce us, but unfortunately his majesty had elected not to show up that day, so I was unable to interview him. Not that it mattered, in the event. Farnwell was more than useful enough. According to him, de Bolotoff gives lessons only to the most exclusive of pupils, those able to meet his extortionately high fees."

"Such as Mallinson."

"And also Lord Harington. Farnwell mentioned the two in the same breath, since Mallinson had brought Harington to Brooklands just this very summer, to receive instruction from de Bolotoff."

I shook my head incredulously. "That would seem to put it beyond dispute, then. Harington was at the controls of the Grahame-White on Friday night, with Patrick the passenger. But how was Patrick ejected from the aeroplane?"

"I discussed the matter hypothetically with Farnwell," said Holmes. "He was of the view that a passenger could be dropped from the front seat of a Type Seven simply by flying the aeroplane inverted."

"Wouldn't the safety harness prevent that from happening?"

"Not if it had been tampered with, the straps partially cut through so that they would snap if subjected to the full hanging weight of a body."

"But you inspected the entire plane, harnesses included. You quizzed Mallinson about them. Wouldn't the passenger one show signs of having been interfered with?"

"It had been replaced, of course. That's why Mallinson was quite confident about showing us the plane. He would never have let me near it if the harness had still been broken. That would have been a dead giveaway. Nonetheless I observed that the passenger harness looked newer and cleaner than the pilot's. The buckles were shinier, not tarnished by use; the leather likewise. Mallinson must have detached the old one and installed its replacement the day he returned to Settleholm, unless Harington did the job as soon as he came in to land on Friday night."

"Bold of Mallinson, nonetheless, to let you inspect the plane so closely."

"He is nothing if not bold, Watson. Consider the fact that we saw him out in his Grahame-White on Sunday morning, allegedly searching for Patrick when he knew perfectly well that the boy was dead."

"He did it so as to deflect suspicion."

"What better way to make it seem as though he could not possibly have been involved? An innocent man would have done precisely what he did, which is go looking for Patrick at first light. Yet it was just a ruse."

"This all makes a ghastly kind of sense," I said. "But –"

"Wait." Holmes held up a hand, squinting harder into the periscope's viewing slot. "I think I see movement."

I held my breath for several long seconds.

"No," said Holmes. "False alarm. Just an errant village cat. What were you going to say?"

"Merely that Mallinson engaged you to look into Patrick's death. Why would he do that when he knew a friend of his was the perpetrator and he himself was complicit in it?"

"You'll have to ask him that yourself. My theory would be that it was the lesser of two evils. Inspector Tasker had told him that Sherlock Holmes happened to be present when Patrick's body was discovered. What else could Mallinson do then but bring me in on the case? The great consulting detective on your doorstep, already tangentially involved in the affair of your son's death and likely to become embroiled deeper. How to make the best of it? Hire him and direct him to prove it was suicide. The only other option would have been to warn me off, and that would have been tantamount to a declaration of guilt. Mallinson is much too canny and crafty a player to have fallen into that trap."

"A tremendous risk, though, using you like that. Did he not think that it might backfire?"

"Probably, but we're dealing with ruthless, shameless people here, Watson. People who prepare for every contingency. We already know they don't tolerate loose ends. Think of poor Dr Wilcox, mown down in a London street so that he wouldn't be able to air his suspicions about Peruvian Gold, if he even had any. I wonder who drove that car. Was it a Mercury, by any chance? With Victor Anstruther behind the wheel? And what about the fire at Tripp's? That shows much the same approach: dispose of all witnesses or anyone who might stir up trouble."

"So poor Miss Vandenbergh was another loose end," I said, "as are you and I now. Jenks has already tried to 'tie us up' once. Twice, if you count him throwing me off the pier. He must be in on it, mustn't he?"

"Clearly. And there will be another attempt to 'tie us up', and soon. In the meantime, I shall round off my narrative. In point of fact, there isn't much more to tell. This morning I took it upon myself to inveigle my way into Settleholm Manor. Mallinson employs a workforce of nearly a dozen just to keep the building and grounds shipshape. He has twice that number of people below-stairs to ensure the smooth running of the household. With some thirty-odd underlings swarming around the property, who would notice one extra? So, having cobbled together a disguise, I showed up at Settleholm and set to work."

"How brazen of you."

"I have found, Watson, that the more audacious one is with such stratagems, the more likely one is to pull them off. The moment I was on the premises looking purposeful with a pitchfork in my hands, no one gave me a second glance, not even Jenks. To anyone who enquired, all I said was that I had joined the staff only that day, having lately left the employ of Eastbourne Borough Council and looking to supplement my meagre municipal pension with a little odd-job gardening work. I was Albert Tuppen, distantly related to a family of that name down East Dean way, born in Dorset but a Sussex resident since the early seventies. I could easily relate the details of Tuppen family life and history if need be. Mrs Tuppen has given me a solid qualification in that subject, whether I like it or not."

"After just a few hours in her company, I feel I could credibly pass myself off as a Tuppen too."

"The only person I was worried about convincing was Craig Mallinson himself. Not that I thought he would penetrate my disguise, but he would surely have some idea who was and was not on his payroll. As it happened, though, his path and mine never crossed. He stayed indoors, busy."

"With what?"

"Everyone at Settleholm assumed it was the preparations for Patrick's funeral this Saturday. He had guests, what's more. He has been entertaining all day. At lunchtime I caught a glimpse of them through the dining-room window as I was pruning back the wisteria. Can you guess who they might be?"

"A stab in the dark: Partlin-Gray, Anstruther, Harington."

"Watson, never let it be said that no brain lurks within that large round head of yours," said Holmes. "Our four plutocrats were together at the table feasting on fine victuals and toasting one another with vintage wine."

"Celebrating four murders achieved in such a way that none of the culprits appears anything but innocent." I grated my teeth. "Yet they have not counted on the deductive genius of Sherlock Holmes."

"I would agree, except that now, thanks to you, they know that we are wise to their scheme."

"Again, I'm sorry."

"It is of no great consequence. I would have had to get them to tip their hand eventually. You have accelerated the timescale, that is all. Jenks will have informed his master by now that he caught us but failed to kill us. I predict a second attempt fairly shortly. In fact, unless I'm much mistaken…"

Holmes's mouth set in a tight line. He spun the handle on the periscope rapidly, first clockwise then counterclockwise.

"Brace yourself, old friend. Here it comes."

CHAPTER THIRTY-SIX

UNDER SIEGE

"Four of them," said Holmes. "No, five. Two are closing in from the front. The other three have vaulted over the garden wall and… My bedding plants. Trampling them without a care in the world. Horticultural philistines." He clucked his tongue. "Very well. A two-pronged assault it is. Watson, take over from me. We shall co-ordinate our efforts. You be my eyes. I shall concentrate on repelling the siege."

"Repelling…?"

"Quick. No shilly-shallying."

I assumed Holmes's position at the periscope while he addressed himself to the rack of knife-switches beside it. Cotton-sheathed electrical cords led upward from them, each branching off in a different direction across the safe room ceiling and thence to some other part of the house.

My view, via the periscope, was of the section of village green immediately fronting the cottage. The upper mirror was angled so that it looked down the pitch of the roof all the way to the small porch over the front door.

Two men dressed head-to-toe in black were stealing towards the door. Both wore woollen balaclavas with holes for the eyes and mouth, which lent their heads a macabre appearance, like skulls in negative.

"Let me know when they look as though they are about to try the doorknob," said Holmes.

"One of them is reaching to grasp it even as we speak."

Holmes threw one of the knife-switches. "He is wearing leather gloves. That will provide some impedance to the shock."

"The shock?"

"A substantial electric current is now running through the brass doorknob. Enough to make the fellow think twice before touching it again."

We heard a muffled shout from above, and I caught sight of the intruder flying backwards, landing on the grass with an ungainly bump.

Holmes chuckled. "Well, I don't need you to tell me that it worked. How is he? Unconscious?"

The man rolled on the ground, clutching his arm. His colleague was bent over him in a posture of concern.

"Not quite," I said. "The glove definitely protected him, and he held the knob only briefly. I worry, though, that this deterrent of yours might cause ventricular fibrillation and death. That surely cannot be your wish."

"Of course not," said Holmes. "The current is set at two hundred volts, well below the danger level. All the defences I have built into the cottage are non-lethal. But that isn't to say they are not disagreeable. Now, turn the upper mirror round. Let's see what's happening at the back of the house."

The three other intruders were congregated in the garden. I could tell they were perturbed by the cry which had come from the other side of the cottage. One of them, the shortest of the trio, was carrying an all too familiar double-barrelled shotgun. He appeared to be exhorting the other two to ignore what was going on elsewhere and continue their approach to the back entrance.

"Are they by any chance near the beehives?" Holmes asked.

"Five or so yards away."

"Excellent."

He threw another knife-switch.

"I have just completed a circuit which sets a buzzer going beneath each hive," he said. "I adapted the buzzers from electric doorbells. They set up a vibration at approximately the same pitch and volume as the sound bees make when they are alarmed and angry. This will rouse the colonies from their slumbers and put them on the offensive. Already I imagine one or two of the workers have emerged, an advance guard."

I could just make out a few small dots circling outside the entrance to each hive.

"So you have decided to apply your knowledge of apiary to something other than the production of honey and wax," I said.

"I am nothing if not versatile."

"The same might be said for your bees."

The number of dots outside the hives was growing rapidly, and several of them were gravitating towards the three men, who had their heads cocked and were seemingly in a state of some consternation, unable to fathom what the low electrical buzzing they were listening to portended. I watched the one with the shotgun – Jenks, it goes without saying – start to swat at the air around him. The other two followed suit.

Soon they were flapping and flailing their arms as the bees swarmed around them in an aggressive cloud. One man flinched and slapped at his face. Evidently he had been stung through his balaclava. With a petulant gesture he made for the garden wall. Still trying to deflect the bees, he slithered clumsily over onto the green. Another of the three, the one who wasn't Jenks, did likewise. The gamekeeper braved the insects' assault a little longer, batting them away from him and stamping them underfoot when he could. He too, however, had to admit defeat eventually, and withdrew, retreating to the other side of the wall.

Holmes returned the knife-switch to the off position, at my suggestion. The bees stopped flying around so agitatedly and drifted back to their hives.

The five intruders gathered at the front of the house to confer. One of them jabbed a finger towards the ground-floor windows, and Jenks responded with an emphatic nod. I relayed this information to Holmes, who took hold of yet another knife-switch in readiness.

Jenks used the butt of the shotgun to knock out a windowpane. We heard the faint tinkle of breaking glass. Then he inserted his arm through the empty pane in order to release the catch.

Holmes threw the third knife-switch, there was a deep firework-like *bang*, and Jenks recoiled. Cursing, he extricated something from his hand.

"What did you do?" I asked.

"Merely triggered a gunpowder-propelled nail embedded in a tube within the window frame just next to the catch. It would have pierced his hand to a depth of at least an inch."

I gave an exaggerated wince, although I felt precious little sympathy for the odious Jenks. He, at that moment, was performing a dance of rage on the green. I could only imagine the obscenities that were spewing forth from his lips.

Once more the five men conferred. Then Jenks stormed up to the front door and subjected it to a series of hearty, powerful kicks. Holmes and I heard it slam open, the wood of the jamb splintering.

Now the five were inside the house. Their footfalls resounded overhead as they searched the property thoroughly from top to bottom.

"Any more of your deterrents available?" I asked.

Holmes shook his head. "They are all exterior to the house. But rest assured those five men will never find us, not down here."

I concurred, but several times they came close.

Finally they assembled in the sitting room, their voices filtering down to us through the false bookcase. I recognised the harsh tones of Craig Mallinson, barking out queries. "Where the devil are they? They must be around. Someone has been toying with us with those infernal booby-traps. They must be here and they must be able to see us. How else could they have managed it?"

Another of the five, in an effete, refined accent, said, "If they are concealed anywhere, Mallinson, there is a sure-fire way of getting them to reveal their whereabouts."

"Harington," Holmes whispered to me. "His lordship has a slight speech impediment, a tendency to lisp his 'r's."

"You mean replicate here the thing that happened to that frightful woman's costume shop?" said Mallinson.

"Quite," said Harington. "When I said 'sure-fire', I really meant just 'fire."

"Splendid idea. Wherever they are, let's smoke them out. Jenks! Have you matches on you? There's a heap of old newspapers here that looks tinder-dry and ready to burn."

"Right you are, sir," said Jenks.

"Burn," I said to Holmes. "They're going to set fire to the cottage. Just like they did to Tripp's Costumiers."

"Did they?" said Holmes.

"Didn't they? It must have been them, surely. Mallinson has just admitted to it, more or less."

Before my friend could reply, Mallinson said loudly, "Sherlock Holmes. I know you can hear me. You and your bumbling amanuensis – you have until the count of ten to give yourselves up. Otherwise your house goes up in flames, and you with it. Ten."

Holmes's expression was grim and glum. We were in a terrible quandary.

"Holmes," I said. "You can't really be thinking of doing as he asks?"

"Nine."

"We have done our best, Watson. But we have been outmanoeuvred. *Force majeure.*"

"Eight."

"They will kill us if we hand ourselves over to them."

"Seven."

"Not necessarily, old chap. From the sound of it, it seems they want us alive."

"Six."

"So the threat of burning the place down is merely a bluff?"

"Five."

"No, I'm sure they would go through with it, leaving us to die either by fire or by asphyxiation. But why warn us first unless the option of surrendering is genuine?"

"Four."

"So either we perish now, slowly and horribly, or submit to their tender mercies."

"That's the sum of it."

"Three," said Mallinson. "Last chance, Mr Holmes. Come out and show your faces. Two."

"Talk about the devil and the deep blue sea," I said.

"At least we will have a fighting chance," said Holmes. "Down here, trapped like rats, we have none."

"One," said Mallinson. "Right-ho, Jenks. Strike that match."

"No," Holmes called out. "Don't. You have won. We will come quietly."

He triggered the release mechanism and the false bookcase swung outward.

"Mr Holmes." Removing his balaclava, Mallinson peered down into the safe room. He was gloating. "And Dr Watson. So nice to see you again, gentlemen. Out you come, the pair of you. Careful now. No sudden movements. Up out of your little bolthole to face the music."

CHAPTER THIRTY-SEVEN

HUMAN SACRIFICES

They pushed us out of the house and across the village green to the roadside, where a pair of cars awaited. One was Mallinson's Humberette, the other a Mercury Thunderbolt double phaeton, considerably taller and longer, a powerful beast with something of the oceangoing yacht about its lines.

Holmes and I were bundled into the rear seat of the Thunderbolt. Our hands had been tied behind our backs with lengths of spare sash-window cord which Jenks had found in the cottage. The gamekeeper, despite his injured, bleeding hand, was good with knots. So tightly were my wrists fastened, in fact, that my fingers tingled with loss of circulation.

Jenks took the passenger seat, cradling his shotgun in his lap. The barrels were pointed backwards at us.

Into the driving seat climbed a lanky individual whose face, once he had divested himself of his balaclava, was pinched and pale. Childhood-acne scars stippled his sallow cheeks, and his eyes were hooded and deep-set, with a melancholic cast to them.

"Victor Anstruther I presume," said Holmes. "A pleasure to meet you."

"The pleasure is all yours, Mr Holmes," said Anstruther. He executed a series of operations to get the car going, priming the starter motor and switching on the ignition coil. The Thunderbolt coughed, then purred, the engine's thrum reverberating through the steel and wood coachwork and calfskin-upholstered seating. Anstruther threw the car into gear and we were off, with Mallinson and the other two intruders – who could only be Partlin-Gray and Harington – leading the way in the Humberette.

Headlamps cast dual cones of light into the mist as we travelled out of East Dean in convoy. Trees were skeletal shadows. It felt as though the world was in stasis, we the only things moving in it.

"This is a fine piece of automotive engineering, Anstruther," said Holmes. "Top of the Mercury line. You must be proud of it."

"Be quiet," said the car manufacturer. "I have no interest in making idle conversation."

"Can you not at least take a compliment? I have never ridden in anything so sleek and comfortable. Independent suspension on each wheel, am I right? And a sliding-mesh transmission. Very smooth. Although you may want to change up a gear, as we are about to hit thirty miles an hour."

Anstruther grumbled but did as Holmes suggested, tugging on the gear lever so that the car would not conk out.

"So, now that we have broken the ice," my friend continued, "perhaps you would be so good as to fill in a few gaps in my knowledge."

"You heard the gentleman," Jenks growled. "He doesn't care to talk to you, so button your lip."

"Forgive me, Jenks, but it is not you I'm addressing. After all, who are you? You're no one. Just the hired help. Craig Mallinson's attack dog. Whereas this is Victor Anstruther, one of our nation's premier industrialists, no less."

Jenks's finger curled round the shotgun trigger. "If I didn't have my orders that you're to be kept alive for now…"

"But you do have your orders, don't you? And like any good lackey you'll obey them." Leaving the gamekeeper to fume and harrumph, Holmes returned his attention to our driver. "So, Mr Anstruther, the four of you have conspired to murder one another's relatives. I can see superficial reasons why the deaths might have been desirable, and yet the motive in each instance appears somewhat tenuous, lacking in depth. You, for example, may not have liked your brother much or approved of his lifestyle. You may at times have resented and even despised him. But to have him slaughtered like one of the dumb beasts he liked to hunt? That seems rather drastic, if you don't mind my saying so."

"It had to be," was Anstruther's terse reply.

"That's it, is it? Your only excuse? 'It had to be.'"

"Yes. You don't understand. You couldn't understand. The reasons are beyond your comprehension."

"I think I do understand," said Holmes. "At any rate, I can just about follow the warped intent behind all of it."

"Oh, you can, can you?" said Anstruther. Briefly he took his eyes off the road to scrutinise Holmes in the rear-view mirror. "And what is our intent?"

"Sacrifice," my friend said simply.

Anstruther was silent for a while. Then he said, "I told Craig it would be a mistake involving you in this. I said there was a danger you might figure it out. But he was adamant. 'Holmes won't have a clue,' he said. 'I'll misdirect him. Bamboozle him. Distract him. And if he does still somehow get too close to the truth, well, we have become adept at handling potential troublemakers, haven't we?' I was unconvinced, knowing something of your career history, but Craig insisted that you are past your best…"

"How wrong can a man be?" said Holmes. "Yes, sacrifices.

That is what you have performed, you and your cronies. A series of human sacrifices, each more elaborate than the last, carried out over the course of a year on days that are traditionally held to be of cosmic importance. Who started it all off, I wonder. Who planted the seed? Was it Eustace Harington by any chance? Here is a man versed in the habits and lore of South America, intimate with that continent's indigenous people and their past. Human sacrifice was commonplace among the Aztecs and Incas, indeed almost routine. They appeased their gods with ritual killings. Lord Harington would have had that in mind, surely, when the four of you sat down together to hatch your scheme."

"Eustace… was certainly an enthusiastic advocate of the idea," said Anstruther.

"And the rest of you became swept up in it soon enough. Harington went first, using subterfuge and strong drugs to dispose of his father. Sir Josiah, of course, played his part. The success of that led you to make the second murder – that of your brother – a little bit more dramatic. You, sir, are a classical scholar. The wine tipped onto the floor beside your brother's corpse – that is what is known as a libation, isn't it?"

Anstruther nodded in such a way as to indicate that he was mildly impressed.

"Libations of wine, poured onto the earth," said Holmes, "were one of the ways the Ancient Greeks honoured both the gods and the dead. Odysseus does it in the *Odyssey*, and Electra in the *Oresteia*. Those are august exemplars to follow – the man whose cunning brought down the city of Troy and the woman who abetted her brother in the murders of their mother and stepfather. What a noble pair of precedents! Shall I go on?"

"Please do, Mr Holmes. You are clearly enjoying yourself, and there will not be much more opportunity for you to do that."

These words had a chilling ring to them, and I wondered

why Holmes and I were being kept alive now when earlier in the day Jenks had had no qualms about trying to kill us. What had brought about this change of heart among our enemies? Did some other, no less undesirable fate lie in store for us?

"Very well," said Holmes. "The third death, that of Lady Inga Partlin-Gray, bore overtones of medieval Norse practices. Specifically: the method of execution known as the blood eagle, which is referred to in the Nordic sagas, skaldic poetry, and the *Anglo-Saxon Chronicle*. By all accounts, Norsemen weren't averse to human sacrifice, usually by strangulation or immolation, but the blood eagle was a particularly gruesome form of lethal torture visited upon captive enemy warriors. It involved the back of the subject's ribcage being sliced open and the lungs being drawn out, with the broken ribs spread so as to form wings. I can think of few more hideous ways to die. You did it yourself, didn't you, Mr Anstruther? To Lady Inga?"

I saw Anstruther's hands tighten on the steering wheel until his knuckles had gone white. Then, relaxing his grip, he said with steely calmness, "It had to be."

"Again, 'It had to be.'"

"She didn't suffer. She was dead already after I struck her. I have carved up the carcasses of deer that I have shot in Scotland. It wasn't so much different."

"The scent of her blood attracted wolves, as you hoped. Their depredations were the perfect cover for the atrocities you committed on her body. I can think of only one person who was unkinder to his victims, and that was Jack the Ripper."

"You cannot rile me, Mr Holmes, if that is your goal. You cannot rouse me to anger or cripple me with guilt. I am far too sanguine and firm of purpose for that. What I did, what we have all four done, is for the greater good. The good of all."

"Oh really?" said Holmes. "Tell me more."

"All in good time. Everything will be revealed in due course."

"Well, until then, let me expound on the fourth and final death, Patrick Mallinson's. This one had an Ancient Egyptian theme, and we all know that Craig Mallinson used to live in Egypt until his wife died, and still has considerable mining interests there, which are currently overseen by the older of his two sons. Hence its very specific cultural relevance to him, just as Lord Harington's father's murder was culturally relevant to Lord Harington, and your brother's to you, and Lady Inga's to her husband. Patrick was sent off into Eastbourne to commission a costume for himself, one that would make him resemble the god Horus. Later, his skin was etched with temporary markings in the form of hieroglyphs. Whose idea was that? His father's, I suppose."

"Yes."

"So there was a ritual. Candlelit? With incense? Did you all four attend?"

"Yes."

"And was by any chance the sideboard in the hallway at Settleholm Manor pressed into service as an altar?"

"It was. How did you know?"

"I didn't, not until now when you confirmed it. However, it seemed a likely supposition. It would account for the scuff marks on the floor. The sideboard had been heaved out into the middle of the hallway. When Sir Josiah went over and stood by it the other night, I believe he was intending to try and cover up the marks, knowing they might be construed as suspicious. Instead, he achieved the opposite result of drawing attention to them."

"He's normally more canny than that."

"It was late at night, and he had had at least one glass of wine," said Holmes. "At this ceremony I am talking about, I imagine Craig Mallinson officiated, anointing himself high priest. Patrick, dressed as Horus, grudgingly submitted to the indignity of it.

Why? Because he was a good son, not perhaps as blindly loyal and dutiful as his brother, but still keen to please his father and his father's friends. He might not have known what the ritual was for but he went along with it regardless. Yet he was uncomfortable. It disturbed him. The whole business was causing friction between him and his father, manifesting in their arguments over his place at Cambridge. Am I still hewing close to the truth? I haven't diverged from it in any respect?"

"Not so far."

"Excellent. You four had developed a taste for this mumbo-jumbo stuff by then. You were really getting into your stride. All of the foregoing, however – the costume, the ceremony – was mere preamble. At last the autumnal equinox came round, the time Patrick was scheduled to be killed. Lord Harington cajoled him into joining him aboard the Grahame-White for a night flight. Did Patrick take much persuading? Some, I imagine. He must at least have suspected something was up. Yet this was Lord Eustace Harington, his father's bosom friend, a peer of the realm. How could he reasonably refuse?"

"He went meekly enough," Jenks piped up. "His lordship took the precaution of sitting down and having a drink with him beforehand. Several drinks, actually. Patrick never had much of a head for the hard stuff. He was in quite a gay mood as we walked out to the barn. Docile as a lamb."

"Ah yes, Jenks, you were there, weren't you? Someone laid out the firepots to serve as a runway. That would have been your task, too menial for Lord Harington. What you were in effect doing, as you were well aware, was marking out poor Patrick's path to the scaffold. How did that make you feel? He was just a young lad, his whole life before him. Possibly you had known him since he was a small boy. You would have watched him grow up. I daresay you were even fond of him, somewhere in that shrivelled black heart of yours."

Jenks, scowling, said, "My feelings are none of your business. I had a job to do. I did it. That is all."

"Yes, like the little soldier ant you are, scurrying around mindlessly at your master's beck and call."

"Really, do we have to put up with this?" the gamekeeper growled to Anstruther. "He is insufferable. I should have gagged him as well as bound him."

Anstruther made a placatory gesture. "He is trying to worm his way inside your head, Jenks. Sow seeds of discontentment. Unsettle you. Do not let him. Do not give him the satisfaction."

"Are you getting paid extra for all of this, Jenks?" Holmes asked. "You have gone above and beyond your duties as Settleholm gamekeeper. What has Mallinson promised you in reward? A small fortune? Or is it enough just to serve in this grand, psychopathic enterprise? Play a role in whatever absurd, fanciful dream it is that these men are chasing? I've often wondered about the mindset of the henchman. What does he get out of being the villain's strong right arm? Does he wish to bask in reflected glory? Is it just about the money? Is it the chance to indulge his bullyboy tendencies while passing the burden of blame onto someone else? Perhaps he derives a masochistic thrill from being pushed into heinous acts he would otherwise never have had the nerve to commit. It is something, I reckon, to do with the man who can barely think for himself, happily letting someone else do the thinking for him. Does that not describe you?"

Jenks's response to this taunting was to bellow out a roar like a wounded bull. "They are going to kill you, Sherlock Holmes! You and your friend. Slit your throats and let the blood pour out!"

Holmes sat back, obscurely satisfied. "Well, Watson, there we have it. We know what to expect now. We, too, are to be sacrificed."

"Yes," said Jenks. "Yes, you damned well are. Like goats. I may not have enjoyed sending Patrick to his doom, but you two – you who have hurt me, led me a merry dance, killed my dog – you I am going to watch die with pleasure. I will even wield the knife, if they let me."

"Oh, I doubt they shall, Jenks," said Holmes. "Eh, Watson?" He nudged me in the ribs with an elbow. "Why would the organ grinder relinquish control of the organ to the monkey?"

Jenks just shook his head in disgust. For my part, I could not see what Holmes hoped to gain by goading the man, unless it was simply for his own bizarre amusement. I myself could see nothing funny in any of this. Nothing at all.

CHAPTER THIRTY-EIGHT

THE LONG MAN

A breeze was stirring, the mist thinning, as the two cars crossed over a saddle in the ridge of the Downs and descended into a combe – a shallow valley. Shortly, the Humberette pulled over to the side of the road, and Anstruther drew up behind in the Thunderbolt. Mallinson climbed out and indicated that we were to do the same. Wherever our destination was, we had arrived.

Holmes and I stood side by side, under Jenks's baleful glare, as the four plutocrats gathered at the rear of the Humberette. This presented me with my first look at the only member of the quartet whose face I hadn't seen yet, Lord Harington. He had soft, jowly features, cherubic lips and a pendulous nose. His gestures were flamboyant, and his grin, which was of the quick, furtive kind, exposed shambolic, rickety teeth. On one of his cheeks a large red welt stood proud, which he scratched at several times. A bee sting, courtesy of Holmes's home defence system.

Mallinson produced a large wicker hamper from the boot and began unpacking it. Out came four sets of heavy purple velvet robes, which the millionaires duly slipped on over their clothing.

Leaning my head close to Holmes's, I muttered, "I trust you have some plan for getting us out of this."

"It is in hand," came the reply.

"Shut up," Jenks snapped.

The robes were all hooded, so that the four plutocrats now resembled monks. From the hamper Mallinson next produced a set of objects. One, an ornate Egyptian eye carved in onyx, he kept for himself. The others he handed out. To Partlin-Gray he gave a metal swastika, to Anstruther a Greek war helmet, and to Harington an Aztec-style stone carving of a small bird.

Finally he extracted a curved ceremonial dagger with a jewel-encrusted pommel. I couldn't help but gulp as I saw its blade glinting like a crescent moon in the headlamps' beams. Despite Holmes's assurances, this situation was not looking good for us.

Mallinson opened a five-bar gate and ushered everyone through. We crossed a field in single file, Jenks at the rear, his shotgun fixed unerringly on Holmes and me. The millionaires all carried their objects before them as though they were sacred relics. The hems of their robes swished through the long grass.

The ground began to rise, evolving into a series of natural stepped ridges. Ahead, steep hillside loomed, and on its near-vertical flank I discerned a glimmer of white which resolved itself into the crude outline of a giant foot, then a leg, then finally the torso and head of a vast two-dimensional figure carved out from the chalky soil, a couple of hundred feet tall.

"Windover Hill," said Holmes. "This is the Long Man of Wilmington."

The entirety of the chalk figure was just visible through the gradually dissipating mist. Viewed from below, the Long Man appeared to be in proportion, an artful piece of Stone Age *trompe l'oeil*. Yet he was still weirdly misshapen, his head more like an inverted flask than a human head. His arms, crooked at the elbows, stuck out like crude wings, leading to small, rather dainty hands, each of which held a quarterstaff that was fully as tall as the Man himself.

He had no face, but for all that I found him daunting, even forbidding. He appeared to be glowering down at us like some hulking chthonic deity, a being conjured to the earth's surface from a grim netherworld. I recalled Holmes telling me that this spot marked the last resting place of an actual giant, slain by a fellow giant. At that moment, in the depths of that long gruelling night, I could almost believe the legend was true and immense bones lay buried beneath our feet. It was a place steeped in mystery and misery, violence and death, the abode of a monstrous, unquiet spirit.

"Chin up," Holmes said. My feelings must have been etched all too palpably on my face. "Neither you nor I will be a sacrificial goat here tonight. I swear it."

Our little procession halted at the base of the Long Man. Mallinson directed his three co-conspirators to form a pattern around Holmes and me, with Jenks covering us from the side with his gun. Each of the four became the corner of a diamond, with Mallinson at the apex and us in the centre. Although they appeared to be equals in all respects, there was a clear hierarchy within this group. Mallinson was the ringleader, the dominant personality among them. The other three subtly deferred to him.

"Let us stand back-to-back," Holmes said to me. "Face out and show them we are no cowards."

With Holmes's shoulder blades pressed against mine, I did my best to put on a brave front.

"Gentlemen," Mallinson said. "We come to the fulfilment of our design, the culmination of great hard work and considerable personal loss. We have done so much, given so much. We four, who are in positions of unparalleled privilege and power, stand ready now to reap the rewards."

Some acoustical trick of the landscape lent his words a strange sonorousness, as though he were speaking in a cavern, his voice amplified and echoing.

"We are here tonight to call on gods," he continued. "Old gods. Neglected gods. Gods whose priests and worshippers are long since dead. Gods who were once appealed to in times of dire need to lend mortals strength and courage.

"Gods of war.

"In this place where a giant died in conflict, where the very earth is infused with his spilled blood, we call on the ancient deities who were once synonymous with the clash of arms and the inflicting of death."

Mallinson held up his onyx Egyptian eye.

"I myself call on Horus, falcon-headed god of the sky, who was charged by his mother Isis with defending the people of Egypt from evil and who was habitually invoked when the pharaoh's troops marched to war. I bear his symbol, the hieroglyphic eye, which represents wrath. To him I have given my one and only son, in tribute."

He turned to Partlin-Gray.

"Whom do you call on, Josiah? Name your chosen god."

"I call on Thor," said Partlin-Gray. "Thor the thunderer, god of storms and protection, slayer of frost giants and dragons. Thor who wielded the hammer Mjölnir and to whom all Viking warriors would pray before entering the fray. I bear his symbol, the swastika rune, which represents lightning. To him I have given my wife, in tribute."

"And you, Victor?" said Mallinson. "Whom do you call on?"

"I call on Ares," said Anstruther. "Ares the Olympian, the destroyer, the slaughterer, the bane of enemy troops. Ares who was beloved by the Spartans, the greatest warrior race that ever lived. I bear his symbol, the Corinthian war helmet, which represents martial prowess. To him I have given my brother, in tribute."

"And you, Eustace?"

"I call on Huitzilopochtli," said Harington. "Huitzilopochtli, Aztec sun god, hater of darkness, who shone so brightly in heaven that the souls of dead warriors had to use their shields to protect their eyes against his light. Huitzilopochtli, who was born from his mother Coatlicue's womb clad in full battle armour to defend her from her rebellious demon offspring. I bear his symbol, the hummingbird, which represents swiftness, vigour and penetrative power. To him I have given my father, in tribute."

As the four intoned these utterances, I found myself lapsing into a kind of appalled disbelief. Could they not hear themselves? Were they oblivious to how preposterous, how deranged they sounded?

Yet there was nothing but solemnity on their faces as each importuned his respective pagan god – that and a terrible firmness of purpose which some might take as sanity and some as sanity's opposite.

"O you four war gods," said Mallinson, "Horus, Thor, Ares, Huitzilopochtli, heed us now. We stand on the brink of a great conflict. Military forces are gathering overseas. England's foes conspire and arm themselves. All is as we desire. We beseech you to ensure that that which is looming on the horizon assuredly comes to pass. We call on you to guarantee the arrival of war, which you love and is your reason for being.

"This past year we have sacrificed to you, as few else have done in recent times. We have surrendered up the lives of family, our own flesh and blood. We have given you our near kin, and you have responded as we wish, by influencing the minds of men so that the drums of battle now beat louder and clearer than ever and the outbreak of hostilities is inevitable. You have answered our prayers by paving the way for a war that will be like no other war in history, a war of wars, a world war. For this we thank you with all our hearts.

"Tonight was intended merely to be a restatement of our desires, as we hold your totems in our hands and formally show gratitude for your kindness.

"But now, in one final act of sacrifice, we offer you a man whom many regard as our nation's greatest hero. With his intellect he has seen off countless plots to undermine England in the past, foiling the machinations of spies, traitors, seditionaries and saboteurs. He has been one of our country's most loyal and indefatigable servants, a stalwart soldier in the struggle against evil.

"We each have presented you with a loved one, as a token of our devotion and obeisance. Now, we all four together present you with this man, this prize, this trophy, Sherlock Holmes, to die in your names."

My anxiety deepened into terror, and I perceived that the usually unflappable Holmes was himself unnerved, for I could feel him shivering behind me.

My companion's voice, however, was even, and his tone phlegmatic, as he said, "How terribly flattering, Mallinson. I see I am to be thrown into the pot, along with your relatives, to add savour to this blasphemous stew you have cooked up. How awfully convenient, too. The man who has rumbled your plans now becomes a part of them, in order to silence him. What will your gods make of that? Do you think they'll be truly pleased that you're offering me to them only because it gets you out of an awkward spot? I imagine that sort of behaviour might annoy them, rather than commend you to them."

After the briefest of hesitations, Mallinson said, "They know we are sincere. They will sympathise. Gods of war understand the necessity of succeeding at all costs."

Holmes's shivering seemed to be intensifying. Yet he kept talking. "Anything is permissible in order to secure victory, is that what you're saying? The end always justifies the means?"

"Anything and everything. For what it's worth, I regret that things have come to this pass, Mr Holmes. You are an exemplary man. I admire you. At this moment, however, you are needed dead more than you are needed alive."

"How galling, though, to die in such an inconsequential manner, as some piece in an abstract, metaphysical jigsaw puzzle assembled by madmen."

"Oh for God's sake, Craig," Partlin-Gray snapped. "Must we take all night over this? Get on with the ritual, so that we don't have to listen to any more of the fellow's pestilential prattling."

"Hit a nerve, have I, Sir Josiah?" said Holmes. "You yourself have the sneaking suspicion that, beneath it all, this is mere tomfoolery. You don't believe that ancient gods have answered your prayers by fomenting war in Europe. It is quite absurd to think that the turmoil we are seeing on the continent is anything but the consequence of political posturing and the desire for territorial gain. Why should ancient gods be involved at all, when men are quite ready to start slaughtering one another regardless."

"We have remembered them," Mallinson butted in before Partlin-Gray could reply. "We have sacrificed to them, shown fealty to them, when no one else has in centuries. Our faith has stirred them from oblivion and brought them back to life, and they owe us for that. They are paying off their debt."

"So worshipping gods is like a business transaction?" said Holmes. "Quid pro quo? 'You scratch my back, I'll scratch yours'? I'm no churchgoer, but I don't think that is how religion works."

"Perhaps not modern Christianity, but the older faiths? That's *exactly* how they work. Bargaining. Propitiation. Gifts in exchange for favours. An admirably straightforward system, much like signing a contract."

"Craig…" said an impatient Partlin-Gray. "He doesn't need to be told all this. Just get to the point. The hour is late, and I'm cold and damp."

The other two muttered in agreement.

"Very well." Mallinson readjusted his grip on the dagger. "Jenks? I think Dr Watson should go first. Mr Holmes has delayed us enough. His reward for dragging the proceedings out is that he can wait a little longer for his own death. Dr Watson, anyway, is supernumerary. He needs to die only because we cannot allow him to live."

Jenks shouldered his shotgun and moved towards us purposefully.

"Delayed you?" said Holmes. All at once he ceased shivering. "Yes, I have. Just enough."

Jenks reached out to grab me. He, obviously, would hold me down while Mallinson applied the dagger.

I braced myself, tensing. I would not go quietly.

Then Jenks recoiled. Something protruded from his abdomen. It looked like the hilt of Holmes's jack-knife.

"Oh you…" he groaned, and crumpled to his knees, then keeled over onto his side.

Blood was seeping out around the knife, staining his shirtfront. Instinctively, in his pain and confusion, he moved his hands to the weapon in order to extricate it.

"No," said Holmes. "Don't do that." His arms were suddenly liberated from their bonds. Lengths of window cord slipped from his wrists to the ground, showing ends that had been roughly severed.

Jenks frowned up at him in befuddlement.

"I have stabbed you in the mesenteric cavity," Holmes said, "in such a way that I believe I have missed the vital organs. The knife is acting as a kind of plug, helping to staunch the blood flow. Pull it out and you risk bleeding to death. Is that not so, Watson?"

I nodded. "With immediate proper treatment, you may

survive. Be thankful that my friend has shown you more mercy than you would ever have shown us."

"I, on the other hand, will show you none," said Mallinson, and he lunged at us with the ornamental dagger raised.

Holmes kicked out, catching him with his toecap on the shin, just below the knee. Mallinson crumpled to the ground, grimacing in pain.

Next instant, my friend seized me by the elbow and we fled.

The three other plutocrats were too astonished by this sudden reversal of fortunes to act straight away. They could not fathom how Holmes had slipped his bonds and delivered Jenks a crippling injury, then felled Mallinson.

As for me, I scarcely cared at that moment *how* we were free, just that we *were* free. Later, I would piece the chain of events together, and Holmes would confirm my deductions.

Holmes, it transpired, had spotted the jack-knife in my jacket pocket. A telltale bulge had alerted him to its presence. When nudging me in the ribs during the car journey, he had taken the opportunity to pluck out the knife surreptitiously and palm it, right before the unsuspecting eyes of Jenks, whom he had been needling in order to fluster him and keep him distracted. While Holmes and I were standing back-to-back at the Long Man, he had opened the knife and used it to saw through the cord around his wrists. What I had taken for shivering was the action of cutting. Since the knife had lain between us, hidden from view, none of the others present had seen a thing. Holmes's debate with Mallinson had been merely patter, misdirection, while he performed the trick of liberating himself, which he had followed with the somewhat less subtle trick of plunging the knife into Jenks's belly. It seemed that the matter of our escape had been, as he had asserted, "in hand" – quite literally.

We charged downhill, pell-mell. It is no mean feat, running

with one's hands tied behind one's back. Without my arms swinging to serve as a counterbalance, I felt as though I could fall over at every step. Fortunately Holmes was there to support me with a steadying hand.

Just as we gained the five-bar gate, the shotgun boomed behind us. We both ducked instinctively. Pellets splintered the gatepost.

Anstruther, with his hood thrown back, took more careful aim. He owned a hunting lodge. He was a skilled gunman. He wouldn't miss a second time.

Holmes shoved me through the gate ahead of him, then dived after. The shotgun went off again, and I heard my friend gasp.

"Holmes!"

"I am hit," he said with a hiss. "Just winged. It is not too bad. Now go. Go!"

We sprinted to the cars. There was no time for Holmes to cut me loose, nor any sharp implement available to do it with. Holmes clambered into the driving seat of the Mercury Thunderbolt; I took the passenger seat.

"You know how to drive?" I asked.

"Not as such," he replied. "But I know the theory, and I watched Anstruther. I can replicate what he did."

After two failed attempts, he got the car started. He stamped on the clutch and shifted the gear lever. The Thunderbolt jerked forward, then shuddered to a halt.

Holmes tried again. I noticed blood dripping from his left hand. His coat sleeve was shredded at the cuff. Anstruther may only have "winged" him, but the injury looked severe nonetheless. He could barely use the arm, not without great discomfort.

The car vibrated into life again, and Holmes pulled away from the roadside. There were shouts and cries from the field. The four plutocrats were almost at the gate. I glanced back and saw that Anstruther had appropriated not only Jenks's shotgun but the pouch in which the spare shells were kept. This was not good news for us.

Mallinson, hobbling somewhat, got behind the controls of the Humberette. His colleagues leapt into the other seats. With much greater finesse and dexterity than Holmes, he started the car up. It roared down the road after us.

The chase was on.

CHAPTER THIRTY-NINE

FLIGHT IN A THUNDERBOLT

Anstruther's Mercury Thunderbolt was the faster and more powerful of the two vehicles, but Mallinson was the better driver. He had experience and expertise where Holmes had none. He also did not have shotgun pellets embedded in his flesh, hampering his movements.

Holmes drove like the wind, careering along the narrow road with an urgency that bordered on recklessness. The mist, not yet fully gone, was at its thickest where it lingered in dips and hollows in the landscape. At times we were plunging through a whiteness so dense we could scarcely see the road. More than once the Thunderbolt's wheels struck the verge on one side or the other and the car shimmied crazily. Holmes fought to maintain control, grappling with the steering wheel as though he had a bull by the horns and were trying to wrestle it into submission. The wheel's wooden rim was slick with blood from his hand.

Despite his best efforts, however, Mallinson was gaining on us in the Humberette. Worse, Anstruther was upright in the back of that car, with the shotgun raised.

"Holmes…" I said.

"I know. I had thought a gravely injured manservant might detain them for a moment or two and give us a decent head-start. I was wrong."

There was a blast, and the wing mirror on Holmes's side disintegrated.

"Hold on tight," he said, and threw the Thunderbolt into a slaloming manoeuvre so as to present a more difficult target.

I was hurled about from side to side in the passenger seat. It was all very well for Holmes to tell me to hold on tight, but how could I with my hands still tied behind me?

A second shot from Anstruther put a starred hole in the windshield.

"The man has little respect for his own automobile," Holmes commented.

"Why should he care?" I said. "He makes them. He can always manufacture himself another."

We reached an incline, and Holmes shifted down a gear in order to compensate. He mistimed the change slightly, and for a heart-stopping moment the Thunderbolt's engine spluttered and the car slowed. My friend hit the accelerator pedal hard. The car bucked, there was a ferocious roar, and all at once we were racing forwards again, at speed.

Back in the Humberette, Anstruther was on his feet once more, having reloaded the gun. He was braced against the car's rocking motion, while Partlin-Gray, who was in the back seat beside him, helped steady him by gripping his waist tightly.

Anstruther closed one eye and took aim. The gap between the cars now stood at a little over a dozen yards.

"Prepare yourself, Watson."

"For what?"

"This."

Holmes stamped on the brake, and the Thunderbolt came to a screeching, juddering halt. The Humberette rammed into us a split second later, Mallinson unable to stop in time. Anstruther lurched forwards, and the gun discharged. The flash lit up the interior of the Humberette like a camera bulb, and we heard a shrill scream.

It came from Lord Harington, who had taken the shotgun round at point-blank range in his back.

He continued to wail in abject agony even as Holmes re-engaged gear and pulled away.

Mallinson, with a furious growl, restarted the Humberette, which had stalled. In no time he was hot on our tail again. I saw Harington writhing in the seat beside him, making spastic efforts to clutch his back and somehow stem the bleeding. I could imagine the size and raggedness of the entry wound. Unless he was very lucky, it would prove a fatal one. Mallinson, however, appeared unbothered by his friend's injury. The same went for Anstruther and Partlin-Gray. They were hell-bent on ending this chase and eliminating Holmes and myself, to the exclusion of all other concerns.

The shotgun blew away a section of the Thunderbolt's coachwork. Shards of wood and metal sprayed over us.

The car itself was not co-operating as it had before. When the Humberette had shunted into it from behind, something in the chassis had either snapped or been twisted out of true. Holmes was having to struggle hard to keep us going in a straight line. We kept veering to the left. From below, a nasty grinding sound was growing louder and more insistent.

"I think we bent an axle," Holmes said. "The bearings are going. I don't know how much longer we can carry on."

"There must be somewhere where we can pull in and take cover. A farmhouse, a vicarage, an inn – *somewhere*."

"There is a place, perhaps a mile up the road."

"Where?"

"Settleholm."

"Mallinson's own house?"

"It is the only building I know of that's close enough. Unless you have a better idea..." He glanced in the rear-view mirror, then grabbed the back of my head and thrust it towards my knees with a cry of "Down!"

The next instant, the part of the windshield directly in front of me shattered to smithereens. Had Holmes not shoved me out of the way, it would have been my head.

We sped on, the Thunderbolt making increasingly distressed and recalcitrant mechanical noises.

A low flint-and-brick wall appeared at the side of the road, indicating the boundary of the manor. I braved a quick look back at the Humberette, to see that Lord Harington was now unconscious, having succumbed to shock. I doubted he would come round. His head lolled on his neck, jerking with every jounce of the car.

As for the other three, their faces, lit weirdly by the nimbus of light from the headlamps, were masks of pure righteous rage. There was no other thought in their minds but destroying us. Their eyes seemed to blaze.

The manor gates hove into view.

"One more time, Watson," said Holmes. "Hang on."

He wrenched the steering wheel hard over, and the Thunderbolt went into a slewing, right-angled skid. Its nose hurtled towards the gates, which were shut and latched.

The collision was tremendous. I think Holmes had been hoping that the impetus and weight of the huge car would be sufficient to bash the gates wide open.

The gates, however, were sturdier and solider than that. They withstood the impact well. One of them was knocked partly off its hinges but remained in place.

It was the Thunderbolt that came off worse. Its front end crumpled like an accordion. Its bonnet tented upwards.

Holmes came off relatively unscathed, whereas I was thrown headlong, helplessly, against the dashboard. I struck it with stunning force, and for a time saw nothing but bubbles of light bursting before my eyes.

Then Holmes seized me and shook me, returning me to my senses.

"Come, Watson. This is not the time for dozing."

He hauled me bodily from my seat. We scrambled out and squeezed ourselves through between the front end of the car and the gate. The radiator spat and steamed. The Thunderbolt looked like a toy that had been picked up and dashed to the ground several times by an irate toddler. One wheel had been jolted free from its fixture and had rolled several yards down the driveway, where it now lay on its side.

The Humberette had drawn to a halt in the road behind it, and Mallinson, Partlin-Gray and Anstruther were climbing out. Holmes yanked me along by the scruff of the neck as the three plutocrats slithered through the half-ruined gateway, abandoning Harington in their haste to catch us. Regardless of whether they could have done anything to help their critically hurt co-conspirator, it was still a callous, ruthless act. They had treated Jenks the same way, leaving him to fend for himself in a field with a knife stuck in his belly. Such was the measure of these men.

Down the linden-lined driveway Holmes and I staggered. He was bleeding. I was half dazed from the crash. By contrast, our three pursuers were still in fine fettle, and one of them was armed.

I am not the sort of man who puts any store by miracles, but at that moment I was certainly praying for one.

CHAPTER FORTY

Dea Ex Machina

We skirted round the side of the manor, Holmes eschewing the main door because we would be too exposed as we ascended the front steps, especially if the door turned out to be locked. By now the mist had been reduced to just a last few wispy shreds, and a bright crescent moon, waning from full, bathed everything in silvery light.

Next to the driveway turning circle there was an Italian garden, bordered by a high yew hedge. We hurried past a sunken pond where a cherub fountain spouted lazily onto the lily-pads.

Our pursuers were but yards behind us. They would have been closer if they had not paused to divest themselves of their robes, which were impeding their ability to run. A shot from Anstruther, more an aide memoire than a serious attempt to maim, punched through the thick foliage of yew by our heads with a rustling hiss.

We entered a narrow walk which led to a bower. Here there was a choice of turns. Left terminated in a grotto flanked by statues of Aphrodite and Dionysus. Right, which we took, saw us passing beneath a vine-wreathed pergola. Holmes knew exactly where he was going. During his stint as gardener Albert Tuppen he had had ample opportunity to acquaint himself with the layout of the grounds.

We emerged onto a lawn. The west wing of the house lay to our right, and Holmes guided me towards the servants' entrance, a half-glassed basement door at the foot of a stone stairwell. The door was locked, but my friend bashed out a pane with his elbow, reached through and turned the key on the inside.

A boot-room, then a scullery, then a laundry – we threaded our way through the manor's labyrinthine below-stairs realm. In the kitchen Holmes paused to snatch a meat cleaver hanging from a rack above a marble chopping slab.

"Not much defence against shotgun rounds," he said, "but any weapon is better than none. Also, it is high time you were freed."

He parted my bonds with a couple of quick, deft slices with the cleaver. Then onward we ran, until we reached the back stairs.

Up on the ground floor, we passed through a dining room and a library. Neither afforded a hiding place large enough to accommodate us.

We came out into the vast, capacious hallway, and Holmes's eye fell on the two suits of armour positioned at the foot of the main stairs.

"Ah, now that's more like it," he said. "A sword will present us with…"

His words trailed off. The swords which had accompanied the suits of armour when last we had been here, were now gone. Each pair of steel gauntlets cupped nothing but empty air.

"Singular. Why would Mallinson remove the swords? It makes no sense. There is no way he could have foreseen that you and I would find ourselves in his hallway, in need of weapons. I've heard of taking precautions but this is foresight that's almost clairvoyant. Unless…" The corners of his mouth turned up in a wry, enigmatic smile. "Very good. Yes. In the absence of *firangi* or *khanda*, why not?"

"Holmes," I said, neither understanding the import of his words nor caring, "shall we attend to the more pressing issue at hand?"

Our three pursuers were, to judge by their footfalls, currently in the library. It was only a matter of moments before they entered the hallway.

"We should try one of the bedrooms," I went on. "We could buy some time by barricading ourselves in. While our enemies are occupied breaking down the door, we could fashion a rope out of sheets and lower ourselves out of the window."

My plan seemed sound to me, and I started up the staircase. Holmes followed, but stopped after just half a dozen steps.

"I'm not sure if this is our best bet," he said. "Do you smell smoke?"

I sniffed the air. I detected the faintest whiff of burning. "Yes. What does it mean?"

"If I am correct in my surmise, then nemesis looms for our enemies."

Just then Mallinson came charging into view below, the ceremonial dagger tucked into his belt.

"There!" he cried. "Got you at last. Victor?"

Anstruther skidded to a halt beside him. Up came the shotgun.

Holmes raised the cleaver, ready to throw. But he seemed to be waiting for something.

A scream issuing from the library set all of us pivoting round in that direction.

"Josiah?" Mallinson called out. "Was that you?"

A second scream came, this one blood-curdling in its duration and intensity. It was hoarse and agonised, the sound of a man in dire torment. I have to say that it made every hair on my body stand on end.

A third scream was truncated, becoming a ghastly wet choking.

"What is this?" said Mallinson. "Is there someone else here?"

"There is, isn't there?" I whispered to Holmes. "And you know who. That's why you brought us here. Settleholm was your destination all along."

My friend's eyes gleamed. "Help is indeed at hand, my friend. One could call it a *deus ex machina*. Or, to use the correct gender, *dea*."

"Go and look," Mallinson told Anstruther.

The latter shook his head. "You go."

"I only have this knife. I don't have a gun."

Anstruther thrust the shotgun into his hands. "Now you do."

Mallinson was torn. Holmes and I were still on the stairs. On his very person he had a convenient means of disposing of us. Yet there was the baffling question of what misfortune had befallen Partlin-Gray.

This, in the event, was partly answered when Partlin-Gray himself staggered from the library. He was clutching his throat, blood gushing out over his hands like lava from a volcano. A pair of further wounds, one to his chest, the other to his stomach, were also bleeding, albeit not so profusely.

His mouth worked. His eyes rolled. He tried to speak, but all that came out were garbled syllables, liquid noises like the final gurgles of a man drowning.

He collapsed to his knees. His hands fell from his neck. A crescent-shaped gash fissured his throat from ear to ear, like some hideous grin. His partly severed windpipe was visible, as were blood-jetting arteries.

He toppled forwards, face-first onto the floor. In no time his prone, motionless body was the epicentre of a fast-spreading crimson puddle.

"My God..." Anstruther breathed.

Our gazes having been fixed on the dying Partlin-Gray, we

had failed to notice the figure standing behind him, until now, when she took a further step forward into the hallway and the moonlight shining in through the windows limned her.

It took me a moment to recognise her.

It was Elizabeth Vandenbergh.

But also, it was not.

She was dressed in a costume. She wore an ornate golden headdress, a plethora of gold necklaces, a yellow bodice, diaphanous blue pantaloons, and bracelets on her ankles and wrists. A long black wig hid her blonde hair. Huge fan-shaped earrings framed her face. Her arms were bare, her feet unshod.

The finishing touch for this ensemble was the most garish of all, and sinister too: a garland of miniature skulls hung around her neck, falling almost to her navel.

In either hand she brandished one of the swords from the suits of armour. The blades of both were bloodied.

In her eyes was the glow of pure, all-consuming hatred.

She advanced into the hallway, stepping over Partlin-Gray's body as though it was no more than a log which happened to be lying in her path. Her bare feet traipsed through his blood and left prints behind on the chessboard tiles as she closed in on Mallinson and Anstruther.

"You," Mallinson said. "Patrick's woman."

"I have a name," said Elizabeth.

"Yes. Miss Vandenbergh."

"I had that name once. Now I have another."

"What is the meaning of this? You have killed Josiah. Are you quite mad? Do you have any idea what you have done?"

"Look at me," Elizabeth replied. Her voice was low and even. "I am more than I ever was. I am reincarnated. Reborn in fire. I am Elizabeth Vandenbergh no longer. I am vengeance. I am destruction. I have a name... and it is Kali."

CHAPTER FORTY-ONE

A Fusion of the Noblest Instincts and the Basest

It made for an extraordinary, gruesome tableau.

On the one hand, Elizabeth Vandenbergh dressed as the Hindu goddess Kali, carrying a pair of bloodied swords.

On the other, Mallinson and Anstruther, their jaws slack with startlement.

By the library door, the body of their colleague Partlin-Gray, freshly slain.

A handsome baronial hallway transformed into a scene from *Le Théâtre du Grand-Guignol*.

The smell of burning was getting stronger. A haze had begun to fill the gallery that overlooked the hallway. Somebody had started a fire in one or more of the upstairs rooms, and I had no doubt that it was Elizabeth.

"Now really, my dear," said Anstruther. "Put those sharp things down. I have no idea what manner of hysteria has overcome you, but you had best snap out of it. To have murdered one of this country's pre-eminent citizens in cold blood – you are clearly not in your right mind. Your attire confirms it."

"Don't try and sweet-talk the bloody woman, Victor," said Mallinson. "Just go over there and disarm her."

Anstruther took a step forward. He must have reckoned that Elizabeth had sneaked up on Partlin-Gray in the library, taking him unawares. That was the only way she could have bested him. Anstruther could not imagine her to possess any degree of swordsmanship.

It was a fatal misreading of the situation.

Elizabeth moved with sinuous speed and grace. It was almost as though she was infused with the spirit of the warrior goddess she was impersonating.

I suppose Holmes and I could have warned Anstruther to be on his guard. But we did not.

She struck him in the shoulder and simultaneously the thigh. She withdrew both blades then stabbed again, now skewering him in the stomach. A third attack in as many seconds saw her sink the points of the swords between his ribs. Throughout, Anstruther merely stood there helplessly like some sort of practice dummy. The sword thrusts came too thick and fast for him even to recoil.

Once Elizabeth pulled the blades from his chest, however, he fell. Tremors ran through his supine body as though he were afflicted with St Vitus dance. I watched him gasp for breath, clinging to the last dregs of life. His hands formed strange, gnarled shapes in the air.

Then he was gone, his body stilled, his soul escaping to whatever hell awaited it.

That just left Mallinson. He belatedly swung the shotgun towards Elizabeth, uttering a curse which slandered her and all her gender.

With an almost preternatural turn of speed, Elizabeth was upon him. She batted the gun from his grasp with the flat of one blade. Then, with a sidelong sweep of her foot, she brought him crashing to his knees.

Taking up position behind him, she crossed the swords in front of his neck so that they formed an implacable steel X. Mallinson's head was bowed like that of a condemned man at the chopping block. All it would take was for Elizabeth to wrench both swords back with force and he would be decapitated.

"Wait," said Holmes.

He descended the staircase. Tendrils of smoke were creeping along the gallery, and the crackle of flames was now distinctly audible. Settleholm Manor was on its way to becoming an inferno, meeting the same fate as Elizabeth's shop.

"We had an understanding, Mr Holmes," Elizabeth said.

"That we did, madam. I am not going to halt you in your vengeance. I simply desire a word with Mr Mallinson first."

Mallinson growled something defiant and uncomplimentary.

"What was this about, Mallinson?" Holmes asked. "Was it all merely a bid for divine intercession in sparking conflict? I find it hard to accept that four hard-nosed businessmen would be so credulous."

"Why not?" said Mallinson. "Faith in any kind of god can reap rewards. Faith can move mountains, isn't that what they say? If one wishes for a war, is it not prudent to enlist the aid of gods who have one single reason for being, one attribute alone that is of relevance?"

"Martial gods. Yes indeed. But why would you and your colleagues want there to be war? Why would anyone?"

"I'm sure you have deduced why, Mr Holmes. If not, then you aren't half as clever as I thought."

"I have. You are a man who mines and imports minerals. One of those minerals is potassium nitrate, commonly called saltpetre. Saltpetre, as every schoolboy knows, is a principal ingredient of gunpowder. Another of those minerals is sulphur, also a principal ingredient of gunpowder. A pan-European war would see your product in greatly increased demand, would it not?"

"Very much so."

"And take the late Mr Anstruther here. I am certain he would have found his production lines turning out new vehicles for the military – staff cars, ambulances and the like. Artillery pieces too, perhaps. And Sir Josiah over there. His steel mills would be turning faster than ever to meet the demand for metal for arms and munitions. And as for Lord Harington, would he not be sending huge quantities of his medical supplies to the battlefront for the treatment of wounded men? All four of you stood to profit handsomely from fat government contracts and a wartime economy. In other words, this madness you concocted together – this *folie à quatre*, if you will – was born of the basest motives. It was all for the sake of profit margins and the augmentation of your already sizeable personal fortunes."

"We would have benefited materially, yes," said Mallinson. "Is that so wrong?"

"Setting aside for one moment the millions of strangers' lives that might be lost as a result of any conflict," said Holmes. "Would mere financial gain, however substantial, truly compensate for the family members you so coldly and brutally despatched? Therein lies the real tragedy in all of this. You were so bound up in your grand mystical project, you four, that people became as nothing in your estimation. Even the ones closest to you, the ones you should protect and cherish, were reduced to the status of pawns. Mere kindling to be thrown on the bonfire and stoke the flames."

"I gave up my own son. Can you not appreciate the strength of character that required?"

"The less favoured of your two sons," said Holmes. "Not Clive, your true heir, the older boy who has followed obligingly in your footsteps. Clive, who has even been prepared to live out amid the heat and dust of Egypt, minding your commercial interests there for the past four years. *He* still lives. He gets to carry on the Mallinson name for you, the Mallinson lineage. Patrick, on the other hand, you liked less and found troublesome. He was surplus to requirements. You could, in a sense, afford to lose him. Likewise Sir Josiah dispensed with a wife who had increasingly come to mean nothing to him, each of them growing more estranged from the other with every extramarital affair they engaged in. Victor Anstruther divested himself of a parasitic brother, Lord Harington a father already close to death. Your blood sacrifices were not quite as profound as you make out. They were less of a hardship, more a case of doing away with inconveniences. What you call strength of character, I see instead as a pitiful, selfish kind of weakness."

"Holmes," I said, "we are in a burning building. Perhaps now is not the time for a lengthy disquisition on morals."

The smoke was drifting down through the posts of the gallery's balustrade. My eyes were beginning to sting.

"Yes, yes," said my friend impatiently. "Mallinson, the duration of life remaining to you may be counted in seconds. Miss Vandenbergh has you at her mercy and will have no compunction about executing you. I cannot prevent her. The least you can do is admit the error of your ways."

"I was not wrong," Mallinson declared. "I am never wrong."

So saying, he reared up. The ceremonial dagger flashed in his hand. He plunged it backward, catching Elizabeth in the leg.

Then he was off at a run, even as Elizabeth sagged, the dagger protruding from her thigh.

"Curse me for a fool!" Holmes ejaculated, smacking his forehead. "I ought to have confiscated that thing from him. Watson, attend to Miss Vandenbergh. Raise the alarm, too. The domestic staff are all sequestered in the east wing. Get them out before the fire spreads. I, for my part, will see if I can salvage something from this."

With that, he hastened off in pursuit of Mallinson.

CHAPTER FORTY-TWO

The Heat of the Moment

Mallinson had left the house by the front door. Holmes disappeared after him.

I helped Elizabeth to her feet.

"We must go outside," I told her. "Can you walk?"

"I can try."

She hobbled along beside me, even as the smoke in the hallway grew eye-wateringly thick.

Once we were out on the front steps, I guided Elizabeth across the turning circle to a patch of lawn some distance from the house. I lay her down, making a pillow of my jacket for her head.

"Back in a moment," I told her, then hurried round to the east wing of the manor. Already a handful of servants were emerging from a side door in their nightclothes, awoken by the rumble of the fire and the odour of burning. I exhorted them to rouse the rest of the staff, and when I was confident that they appreciated the urgency of the matter, I returned to Elizabeth's side.

Examining her wound, I determined that it was unpleasant but not life-threatening. The rate of blood flow indicated that neither the femoral nor the genicular artery had been cut. Unlike with Jenks, the blade in this case could be safely removed, once precautions were taken. I fashioned a tourniquet from my belt, lacing it around her upper thigh. Then I tore off strips of my shirt to use as bandages and wadding. I warned her that I was about to extract the dagger.

She made not a sound as I pulled it out, nor as I applied pressure to the wound to stem the bleeding. Her fortitude was remarkable. I had seen battle-hardened soldiers sob like infants at such pain.

"Will I live?" she asked.

"With the appropriate treatment and care, I don't see why not."

"I don't know that I want to any more," she said wanly. "I thought that if I became Kali, if I pretended to be something other than myself, it would be easier to commit murder. But now that I have done so, now that the heat of the moment has passed, I am overwhelmed by remorse."

"I should not concern myself about that right now, if I were you."

"They deserved it, though," she said. "Mr Holmes explained to me what they'd done. How could they? How could they have been so callous, so heartless?"

"Please compose yourself, Miss Vandenbergh. I am attempting to apply a dressing."

"And my Patrick, what's more. My dear, sweet, innocent Patrick. When Mr Holmes came to me this morning, it was to tell me that my life was in peril. They were willing to kill anyone, he said, not just their sacrificial victims. There had been a Harley Street physician, apparently. Someone who might potentially have caused trouble. They eliminated him. Mr Holmes feared for me. He also begged my help. I fitted him out to look like an elderly gardener. Then I asked him what I should do. He advised me to lie low, hide until the whole affair was resolved. After he had left, I hit upon a way of doing so which would also free me to even the score with Patrick's murderers."

"The fire at the shop…"

"I set it," she confirmed. "If they assumed me dead, they would not be expecting retaliation from me. They would not even think to look for me. I escaped via the back yard once the blaze took hold. All I salvaged from the shop was the materials for a Kali costume. I wanted to teach those men a lesson. I wanted to show them that gods were not to be trifled with. Goddesses too. It seemed fitting."

"Holmes knew of your intentions, did he not?"

"Yes. I told him what I was going to do, in so many words."

"Did he condone it?"

"You would have to ask him that yourself. Possibly he felt that justice would be best served by someone who had a personal stake in the matter. All I know is that I was happy to destroy my shop – my life – if it meant that I might avenge Patrick. I do not know if I shall sleep easily from henceforth, though. You and Mr Holmes may feel obliged to turn me in to the police for my crime. If so, I shall not resist. I have done what I have done. Kali has destroyed. The defender of wronged women has left her mark. See?"

She was looking at the house. The entire upper storey of the manor's main section was aglow from within. Flames flickered in every window on that floor. A pane shattered from the heat with an explosive crack, and smoke billowed out between the empty mullions.

"But there were four of them," she said. "I accounted for two. A third has escaped. Where is the fourth?"

I did not have the heart to tell her that Lord Harington was already dead. It was ironic: the man who had been most guilty of the death of her lover, the actual murderer, had met his own end before she could get to him.

"You must rest," I told her. "You have lost a lot of blood."

She put her bloodstained hand on mine, also bloodstained. "You are a good man, Dr Watson. A good, good man. Your wife is lucky to have you."

The light from the burgeoning fire brightened. Deep within the manor, timbers groaned. Flames roared. The servants were huddled nearby, and I heard them gasp in horror and despair. They realised, as I did, that summoning the fire brigade was fruitless. The house was beyond rescue. It would burn to the ground long before help arrived.

I looked around, wondering what had become of Holmes and Mallinson.

Then, rising into the sky from somewhere in the grounds of the estate, I saw a point of incandescence. It gained height, growing larger and brighter, expanding.

All at once it burst like a firework, with a low boom.

It fell like a comet.

It plunged to earth and was extinguished.

The fire at the house raged on.

CHAPTER FORTY-THREE

BRANDS OF JUSTICE

Friday dawned cold and cheerless, grey and gloomy. A drizzle set in that would last the whole of the rest of the day.

Holmes and I sat facing each other in the sitting room of his cottage. Both of us were so exhausted, so utterly enervated, we could scarcely move, let alone speak.

At last my friend stirred himself to fill and light his pipe, whereupon I felt emboldened to broach a conversation.

"So that's it, is it?" I said. "Nothing happened?"

"Oh, it all happened," said Holmes. "But we were never there."

"And you think Inspector Tasker will find that acceptable when he interviews us, which he is doubtless going to at some point?"

"Tasker will believe as much as his limited imagination will allow him to."

"But the events of tonight will cause a furore. Four of the country's top businessmen dead, and in dramatic circumstances too. Great pressure will be put on the police to account for it all and make arrests."

"I confess there will be interest in the matter from many

quarters. The gentlemen of the press will have a field day, once they get wind of what's gone on. Our best recourse, you and I, is simply to play dumb. If asked, we shall tell Tasker that we gave up on the case, as he had been advising us to do, and yesterday went to Settleholm Manor in order to inform Craig Mallinson of our decision. What occurred there occurred without our involvement and is beyond our comprehension. We arrived in time to see the fire take hold, we assisted in making sure the domestic staff were safely out of the building, and that is all. We shall say the same to anyone else who may care to question us."

"You think Tasker will swallow it?"

"If we stick adamantly to the story, he will have no choice. No one can testify to the contrary, save for two individuals, neither of whom, for their own reasons, will aver otherwise."

"You're certain about Jenks?"

"Quite certain. We saved him, after all. Had we not driven back to Windover Hill in the Humberette and taken him thence to All Saints' Anglican infirmary, he would in all likelihood have died."

"It is remarkable that he did not. He lay there in that field with your jack-knife in his guts for over an hour. The man's constitution is formidable."

Holmes nodded. "His compliance is assured, in that as long as he remains silent about the truth of who stabbed him and why, you and I will remain equally silent about his role in the plans of Mallinson and friends. It is a kind of mutual blackmail, or, if you rather, an armistice. Each party could land the other in hot water, and therefore neither will."

"It seems somehow wrong, though," I said. "Jenks ought to stand trial. The number of times he tried to kill us…!"

"I have long come to regard death as an occupational hazard, Watson."

"And he was an accomplice in Patrick Mallinson's murder."

"He was, all said and done, a stooge. Besides, consider his situation. He is hardly in a position now to be able to claim the significant financial reward Mallinson promised him. He is out of a job. He has an injury which will continue to plague him for months to come, if not years. And perpetually hanging over him is the threat that his misdeeds might be exposed. He is not a man with a bright future. I would say he has received a satisfactory degree of punishment."

"And what of Mallinson himself?" I said. "You have not yet vouchsafed what transpired after you set off in pursuit of him."

"There is little to tell," said Holmes. "I knew where he was headed. The barn."

"His biplane."

"Exactly. All was lost. His only recourse was to fly the scene."

"Literally."

"When I caught up with him, the barn doors stood wide open and he was already in the cockpit with the engine running. I considered throwing myself aboard the aeroplane to subdue him, but that seemed an almost suicidally reckless course of action. So instead I picked up a canister of the naphtha gel that was used to fill the firepots. I hurled that at the Grahame-White even as Mallinson was taxiing out of the barn. It splashed its contents all over the machine. I thought this would be an incentive for him to stop and disembark, but he either felt otherwise or was too bent on escaping to perceive the hazard to himself."

"The plane caught fire."

"A spark from the engine exhaust ignited the naphtha. The fuselage was well ablaze as Mallinson took off. He was doomed the moment his wheels left the ground."

I remembered the fireball I had seen rising into the night sky, then falling to earth.

"It is poetic justice, I suppose," I said.

"Yes. As was the justice which Elizabeth Vandenbergh visited upon two of his cronies."

"You knew she would be at the manor that night. You knew what she had in mind to do. Is that not a case of taking the law into your own hands?"

Holmes exhaled a lungful of tobacco smoke in such a way that I could not see his face. It temporarily obscured his expression, making him inscrutable.

"Watson," he said, "do you honestly think that the likes of Craig Mallinson, Sir Josiah Partlin-Gray, Victor Anstruther and Lord Eustace Harington would ever have faced any other kind of justice? Men that powerful, that intimately and inextricably connected with the establishment? They are part of an elite, untouchable, above the law. Their money and status would have seen to it that, even if any team of Crown lawyers had been able to build a watertight case against them, it would have been thrown out of court. These are people who can do as they please, with impunity. However heinous the crimes they have committed, no judge in the land would convict them. Chances are they would never even be brought to stand in the dock."

"What a dim view you take of our legal system."

"Realistic only, my friend. They would have got away with it. You know that. They themselves knew that. Whatever bribery it took, whatever favours had to be called in, they would have got away with it. I made the decision to allow them to face another brand of justice, one they would be less able to cozen or cheat their way out of. Or rather, I let that brand of justice take its course and did nothing to hinder it."

"Miss Vandenbergh... Where is she now?"

We had left Elizabeth at Settleholm when we went to fetch Jenks and drop him off outside the infirmary. She had not been there when we returned. Holmes made a few careful, probing enquiries among the staff, but with the fire roaring away, their home going up in flames before their very eyes, none of them had even registered the presence of anyone else at the scene, let alone seen a woman sneaking away.

Holmes shrugged. "Who knows what has become of her?" said he. "One thing is for certain. If anybody happened to lay eyes on her this morning, they wouldn't recognise her. They would see only someone disguised as Kali the destroyer. Perhaps she will find her way back to southern India and the arms of her princeling lover. Wouldn't that be a happy ending for all concerned?"

Holmes puffed on his pipe.

"Of course, I do not foresee a happy ending for the rest of us," he said bleakly. "War beckons. It is unavoidable. I would say that in a year from now, maybe sooner, hostilities will have broken out. There will be some instigating incident, some spark to ignite the spreading oil slick. Who knows what or where it will be? When nations are spoiling for a fight, it doesn't take much to give them an excuse to take up arms. Perhaps just the death of some prominent individual is all that's needed, and then – conflagration."

I thought of Patrick Mallinson and the smouldering ruin that Settleholm Manor had become, and a despondency settled upon me.

"I wonder whether there is something to this gods business after all," I said. "Might the four blood sacrifices genuinely have had an effect? Could Horus and the others be influencing the political situation from their various otherworldly realms? Are they what is driving nations to this madness?"

"Tush, Watson! Don't blame the divine for something that is inherent in all of us: the bloodlust men so often fall prey to, the desire of one nation to prove its superiority over another through military might and massacre. It's our nature to wage war, and we seldom need prompting in that regard, least of all from deities."

"I am minded to go down on my knees and seek intervention from a higher power myself, if I could only bring myself to believe He might avert what's coming."

"Well put," said Holmes. "But let us try not to dwell on such sombre matters, when there is so much about them that is beyond our control. You have one more day and a night on the coast, Watson. I will endeavour to make it more enjoyable for you than the rest of this week has been. I hear that a good meal is to be had at the Grand Hotel. What do you say to a late luncheon there? My shout."

With effort I roused myself from my depression.

After all, none of us truly knows what the future holds. As long as there is today, and companionship, and fine food, we must be thankful for that and try not to be fearful of what tomorrow may bring.

Afterword

Inspector George Tasker did indeed quiz Sherlock Holmes about the events at Settleholm Manor not long after they occurred. He even journeyed up to London to interrogate me too. It was a bootless endeavour. For all his suspicions, he could not prove conclusively that my friend and I had any direct connection with the fire or the deaths of Craig Mallinson, Sir Josiah Partlin-Gray, Victor Anstruther and Lord Eustace Harington. It must have been terribly frustrating for him, the way we stonewalled him, yet it was necessary, if only so that Elizabeth Vandenbergh's role in the proceedings might remain undiscovered and she might stay, as it were, "dead". I remember Tasker railing at me quite vituperatively, insisting that I was a liar. I denied the accusation with vigour, which was of course a lie in itself.

The press, naturally, made hay. Some of the yellower papers were so enthralled by the story, with its intoxicating mixture of wealth, celebrity and unexplained, gruesome death, that for a whole week their front pages mentioned little else. Speculation was rife, and the theories which some journalists came up with to explain it all bordered on the harebrained. There was talk of a suicide pact, mass insanity, a drinking game gone badly awry, even the involvement of a German spy ring. In the absence of hard facts, the vacuum was filled by imagination.

In the end, however, interest waned, as it always does. Soon enough people forgot the name Settleholm Manor. There were other things to think about, and indeed worry about.

Less than a year later, Europe was hopelessly enmeshed in war.

Holmes, as my readers may know, played a part in foiling the machinations of various of the Kaiser's agents in the run-up to the conflict. Indeed, not long after I left him and returned to London, he became fully engaged in the matter of closing a security leak by which British military secrets were reaching the Germans through the auspices of the spy Von Bork and his ally Baron Von Herling, the diplomat. The case took him to America and Ireland, but I was unaware of any of this until August 1914 when Holmes drew me in to assist at the dénouement, which took place at the port of Harwich. By then I had become the owner and licensed driver of a car of my own – albeit not a Mercury, for that marque had gone into receivership following the death of its owner.

Thereafter, I signed up once more with my old regiment, the Army Medical Department, now known as the Royal Army Medical Corps, and served behind the lines in France and Flanders, as an ambulance driver among other things. Holmes, meanwhile, continued to do his bit for the war effort back home, fighting the good fight against our enemy's subtler, more insidious campaigns.

Whether or not the deities who were invoked by Craig Mallinson and his friends were in any way responsible for the war is moot. The only recorded instance of any kind of manifestation of the divine during the conflict is the legendary apparition known as the Angels of Mons, an omen which occurred in the self-same month that Holmes thwarted Von Bork. The forces of good prevailed nonetheless, through commitment and determination, not to mention colossal sacrifice of life, and perhaps also through the grace of the one true God.

In December of 1913, Holmes reported to me by letter that he had engineered a meeting with Clive Mallinson shortly after he arrived in England from Egypt. He wished to pay his respects and offer his commiserations. He said he found the young man to be in low spirits, which was hardly unexpected given that he had just suffered the loss of his father, his brother and his childhood home in one fell swoop. Nonetheless Clive, who was the spitting image of the elder Mallinson, right down to the shock of raven-black hair, seemed sanguine. He was, it would appear, made of the same stern stuff as his father. Holmes foresaw that he would not be destroyed by this tragedy.

In this, my friend was both correct and incorrect. The following year, Clive Mallinson signed up as a member of the British Expeditionary Force and marched across France to the Western Front. He was killed during the very first German assault at Ypres.

The gods of war got him too, in the end. Or perhaps it's the case that the young Mallinson felt he had nothing to risk by becoming a soldier. Death had flapped its dark wings over him already. It had gorged itself on Mallinson blood. Why would it need to take any more so soon?

As a footnote, in the spring of 1914 I received an anonymous letter by steam-packet mail, postmarked Mysore.

All it said was:

> Kali has sheathed her swords and retreated to her palace on
> the hill with the monkeys and mynah birds. She limps a little
> when she walks, but otherwise she is well and all is well.

Acknowledgements

As a prize at a charity auction, I offered the opportunity for someone to have their name appear in *Sherlock Holmes: Gods of War*. The winning bidder was Craig Mallinson, on behalf of his girlfriend Ellie, a.k.a. Elizabeth Vandenbergh. So generous was the donation Craig made to the Chestnut Tree House children's hospice in Arundel that I insisted he too lend his name to a major character in the book. After no consideration at all (his words) he agreed to adopt the role of chief villain.

I am indebted to William Maness, who serendipitously came along and helped me out with his expertise on aviation and particularly planes from the pioneering era such as the Grahame-White Type VII.

I am also deeply indebted to Miranda Jewess for her keen editorial insight and encyclopaedic knowledge of Sherlockiana.

J.M.H.L.

ABOUT THE AUTHOR

James Lovegrove is the *New York Times* best-selling author of *The Age of Odin,* the third novel in his critically-acclaimed *Pantheon* military SF series. He was short-listed for the Arthur C. Clarke Award in 1998 for his novel *Days* and for the John W. Campbell Memorial Award in 2004 for his novel *Untied Kingdom.* He also reviews fiction for the *Financial Times.* He has written *Sherlock Holmes: The Stuff of Nightmares, Sherlock Holmes: Gods of War, Sherlock Holmes: The Thinking Engine* and *Sherlock Holmes: The Labyrinth of Death* for Titan Books; his new series, *The Cthulhu Casebooks*, launched in 2016 with *Sherlock Holmes and the Shadwell Shadows.*

SHERLOCK HOLMES

THE STUFF OF NIGHTMARES
James Lovegrove

A spate of bombings has hit London, causing untold damage and loss of life. Meanwhile a strangely garbed figure has been spied haunting the rooftops and grimy back alleys of the capital. Sherlock Holmes believes this strange masked man may hold the key to the attacks. He moves with the extraordinary agility of a latter-day Spring-Heeled Jack. He possesses weaponry and armour of unprecedented sophistication. He is known only by the name Baron Cauchemar, and he appears to be a scourge of crime and villainy. But is he all that he seems? Holmes and his faithful companion Dr Watson are about to embark on one of their strangest and most exhilarating adventures yet.

SHERLOCK HOLMES

THE THINKING ENGINE

James Lovegrove

March 1895. Hilary Term at Oxford. Professor Quantock has put the finishing touches to a wondrous computational device which, he claims, is capable of analytical thought to rival that of the cleverest men alive. Indeed, his so-called Thinking Engine seems equal to Sherlock Holmes himself in its deductive powers. To prove his point, Quantock programmes his machine to solve a murder. Sherlock Holmes cannot ignore this challenge, so he and Watson travel to Oxford, where a battle of wits ensues between the great detective and his mechanical counterpart as they compete to see which of them can be first to unravel a series of crimes. But as man and machine vie for supremacy, it becomes clear that the Thinking Engine has its own agenda. Holmes's and Watson's lives are on the line as a ghost from the past catches up with them…

AVAILABLE AUGUST 2015

TITANBOOKS.COM

SHERLOCK HOLMES

THE WILL OF THE DEAD
George Mann

A rich elderly man has fallen to his death, and his will is nowhere
to be found. A tragic accident or something more sinister? The
dead man's nephew comes to Baker Street to beg for Sherlock
Holmes's help. Without the will he fears he will be left penniless,
the entire inheritance passing to his cousin. But just as Holmes
and Watson start their investigation, a mysterious new claimant
to the estate appears. Does this prove that the old man was
murdered? Meanwhile Inspector Charles Bainbridge is trying
to solve the case of the "iron men", mechanical steam-powered
giants carrying out daring jewellery robberies. But how do you
stop a machine that feels no pain and needs no rest? He too may
need to call on the expertise of Sherlock Holmes.

TITANBOOKS.COM

SHERLOCK HOLMES

THE SPIRIT BOX
George Mann

Summer, 1915. As Zeppelins rain death upon the rooftops of London, eminent members of society begin to behave erratically: a Member of Parliament throws himself naked into the Thames after giving a pro-German speech to the House; a senior military advisor suggests surrender before feeding himself to a tiger at London Zoo; a famed suffragette suddenly renounces the women's liberation movement and throws herself under a train.

TITANBOOKS.COM

SHERLOCK HOLMES

THE ARMY OF DR MOREAU
Guy Adams

Dead bodies are found on the streets of London with wounds that can only be explained as the work of ferocious creatures not native to the city. Sherlock Holmes is visited by his brother, Mycroft, who is only too aware that the bodies are the calling card of Dr Moreau, a vivisectionist who was working for the British Government, following in the footsteps of Charles Darwin, before his experiments attracted negative attention and the work was halted. Mycroft believes that Moreau's experiments continue and he charges his brother with tracking the rogue scientist down before matters escalate any further.

TITANBOOKS.COM